Prince of Rhodes

Prince of Rhodes

R A Usher

SigmaDelta Books

First published 2020 by SigmaDelta Books

ISBN 978-1-5272-5794-8

Copyright © by R A Usher 2020

First Printing, 2020

Please address all enquiries to
SigmaDelta Books
21 Malbank, Cheshire CW5 5LU
www.sigmadeltabooks.com

Ομώνυμος - Homonyms

The Prince of Rhodes has played out the scene,

This, his testimony to the events he has seen.

Not every mortal or guest sees,

The island named Rose that rose from the seas.

Rhodes, the island that grew out of the blue,

For millennia cooled, as the Aegean breeze blew.

An island whose spirit is in every vein,

Don't fight the sensation, it's always in vain.

Trekking through Rhodes historical sites,

Saving the island was in his sights.

All tourists that pass the Rhodian deer,

Will always revisit, and hold Rhodes dear.

~ R A Usher 2020

Contents

Preface

When I started this project, I intended it to be a piece of non-fiction. I wanted to write a textbook set in Rhodes. I aimed to illustrate *Greek Filoxenia*. I planned to use it with my learners in England; it would be a resource for the courses I deliver in customer service and hospitality. Then something happened.

My imagination took over, and my fingers ran with it. The book became a piece of fiction and took over my life. I must thank my wife for her patience, and for listening to me rabbit on about an idea that would elevate the story to another level. I thank her for being my greatest critic, and her honesty when something didn't seem right or needed editing. I would also like to thank her for accompanying me while carrying out research. A week in Rhodes sounds like a lovely holiday – though perhaps not when your husband drags you around the island to collect map references and descriptions. I must also thank Heather Cadwallader and Tracey Wood for volunteering to proofread for me. A special thank you goes out to five beta readers, who stepped forward when I put out a plea for volunteers. They have done a fantastic job and provided positive suggestions. In alphabetical order, they are

1

Lorraine Jones, Helen McVeigh, Lyn Rushton, Julie Ryan and Lyn Watson.

I owe a thank you to my editor, Paul Usher, without whose encouragement this book would still be handwritten scribblings.

I would like to save the most significant thank you for the characters of the book for popping into my head at appropriate times. Also, for releasing me between writing sessions so that I might go about my everyday life. I might add at this point: that all characters are entirely fictional, and any resemblance to persons living or dead is entirely accidental.

I hope you, the reader, enjoy this tale and perhaps even recognise elements of it when you visit Greece. I thoroughly recommend spending as much time as you can in Greece. At the end of the book, you will find a chapter on the locations of the island, particularly those used in the story (Appendix 1). There is also a chapter translating any Greek language I have used (Appendix 2).

I have added a special challenge to you, the reader. It would spoil the story for me to reveal this challenge at the beginning, but let's say it's something of a treasure hunt. The third appendix will tell you how to take part – and offer a special reward. So, pay attention – and enjoy.

EOS – Of the Dawn

What will my legacy be? What will people remember about me? Was this my destiny? These were just three of the many questions I'd been asking myself as the traffic moved at the pace of a handicapped snail. The windscreen wipers were unable to clear my thoughts or the gallons of water falling from the sky. As we approached a red light, a sudden flash of lightning and an immediate crack of thunder woke me from my inner thoughts. "Bloody hell. God's angry today," I announced to my wife and kids. The caravan hitch rattled, and the car juddered to a halt. The change in volume of the engine suggested it'd taken on a life of its own. The traffic light turned green. The rev counter rose to the maximum red mark and fell back to zero. It was less than a moment before it again climbed back to maximum, and there it stayed. The car filled with the acrid fumes of burnt rubber and stung my eyes. Teenage Alyss screamed, "Dad, what's happening?"

"Shit, everybody out!"

A clunking emanated from the engine like a hammer bouncing on an anvil. It made me imagine a smithy was shaping metal into some medieval weapon somewhere inside that ancient engine. The Volkswagen Eos spluttered her last polluting gasp, gave up the fight, died at the light. She'd grown weary and had dragged a heavy caravan around the south coast of England for the last time. Eos, goddess of the Dawn. Goddess my arse, her only connection with the dawn was her persistent failure to start in the mornings. I'd always dreamt she would be immortal, or last at least another few years. This was another in a long line of events that some people might say you look back on and laugh about. Perhaps you do if it's an isolated incident. I remember disasters from thirty years ago, and I still don't laugh about them.

I looked at the traffic queuing behind my dead Eos. Their horns playing a chorus of laughter. I just pointed at the smoke pouring out of the bonnet and shrugged at them. I muttered quietly to myself. "What the fuck do you expect me to do about it?"

What will people remember me for? The patron saint of fuck-ups, that's what. God no, spare me that.

≈≈≈

Back in the relative safety of our three bedroom semi, Kam said it was the worst trip we had ever taken the kids on. The twelve-hour journey home via the back of a recovery lorry, piss-wet through, sealed the decision: the time had come to sell the caravan, and there wasn't much discussion needed. What discussions we did have centred around what to spend the money on. Obviously, I voted for a replacement car, but not a Volkswagen. Kam disagreed.

Kam, my wife, my anchor, with a natural ability to point

out my features, which she called faults. If my ego inflated like a hot air balloon and headed skyward, she ensured it didn't float away completely. Being the level-headed one in the family, she balanced everything out.

She suggested, "Why would you waste the money on another bag of bolts, just to have another bad choice blow-up on us?" And then she raised her eyebrow. *Did she just question my judgment?* I started to recall my long list of mistakes. She announced, "Time to take our first foreign holiday."

Great. All I wanted was a new car, and she'd made her announcement in front of the kids. Alyss squealed, Lindon shouted, "Yessss".

"Dad loves the sun and beach holidays. He should be rewarded for everything he does for us. We'll use the caravan money to give him his reward."

What? Uh? A new car would be a better reward. I slumped back in my chair, and my shoulders dropped. I'd been done over, and the Eos wasn't going to be replaced.

"I want to go to America," chimed Alyss.

"Get stuffed. Just because you love Justin Bieber," teased Lindon, throwing his weight around because he was two years her senior.

"He's Canadian actually," she retorted.

"That doesn't make him a better singer. We should go to Paris, that's where Parkour started."

"Why does every conversation between you two have to be an argument?" I'd interrupted to block what was about to follow.

"No. Paris isn't anywhere near the sea, and it should be

5

your dad's choice. It's his reward," stated Kam.

But I want a car. Looks like I wasn't getting one, not now that everyone wanted a foreign holiday.

Soon after, we were *Googling* every possible destination. The Prometheus must have paid a fortune to Google for their ad campaign because it was the top hit on every search we did.

The Prometheus was an all-inclusive hotel on the island of Rhodes. In a place called Soroni. We booked a week at the end of May, which left us a few months to get passports – and get excited. The website announced 'Soroni: a village of few shops, a couple of taverns and a small beach, is totally unspoiled and an excellent place to relax and unwind.' It looked perfect.

The holiday was well-priced, so I got my car in the end. A second-hand Renault Clio. Another bloody goddess.

≈≈≈

"Nai is yes," said Alyss. We'd set about online Greek lessons. I found it more difficult than anticipated. They don't even have the same letters as us. She continued. "When we talk about water, it's an object. In Greek, everything can be one of three forms: Masculine, Feminine or Neuter."

"Neuter, isn't that what they do to cats?" queried Lindon.

The concept of using gender for anything other than hero and heroine, or god and goddess, lost me.

Kam and Lindon didn't want to learn Greek, and they dropped the lessons. She wasn't enthusiastic about learning a new language. "Rod, you do know that many Greeks can speak English don't you?"

"Yes, they probably do in big towns, but we're going to a

small village."

"You and Alyss learn Greek, and you can speak for me if I need you to."

I did learn some words:

Yiasas or *Yiasou* – Hello. It depends on whether you are addressing someone formally or informally.

Efharisto – Thankyou.

Like a naughty schoolboy with a new dictionary, I cut straight to the swear words. There's *skata*, which means shit. *Malaka* which doesn't translate, but generally means wanker. I had to clear my browser history when I found out what *Pippa* is. I thought it was the name of our future queens' sister. Something which I later discovered Greek people laugh about.

My favourite is *Gamysou*. It has a better ring to it than the English fuck you. This tickled me, my maiden aunt Sue had a gammy leg. Her legacy was the noise her left foot made as it scraped along the ground. It never lifted off the ground, and she swore like a trooper. She would be pleased if she could see she was helping me learn Greek. *She had a legacy. Why don't I? What will people remember about me? Rod Prince, the guy that could swear in Greek.*

GEORGE – The Taxi

May 23rd, 2013. The day arrived – one small step for mankind, a giant leap for Rod Prince. The plane touched down at Diagoras International Airport in Rhodes. The passengers erupted into a massive round of applause as if the pilot had succeeded in completing an impossible task. *What the fuck? Why don't I get a round of applause for just doing my job?*

I stood in the doorway of the plane, ready to descend the steps. I felt a punch in my face, a sudden rush of warm air akin to opening the oven to check on the Sunday roast. The clothes I travelled in accentuated the heat. I was dressed for the four degrees we'd left behind in Cheshire.

It was less than fifty metres to the airport buildings, but we still had to wait for a bus to take us there. I needed to take a couple of deep breaths of the warm air. I had trouble extracting enough oxygen from each breath. The bus filled up, no space between sweaty strangers. Everyone gasping for what little oxygen the air carried. On the plus side, so many people into such a small space meant nobody fell over when the bus lurched first to the left then to the right.

In the relative cool of passport control, we were at the back of a long slow-moving monster – with its 400 legs and 200 heads – straight from the Greek myths. The queue snaked towards its goal, and I became a voyeur of the behaviours of the beast's multiple heads. My gaze settled on Kam. As beautiful a princess as ever. Nothing like the other Camilla, the one who married Charles. The Royal marriage prompted Kam to drop the 'illa' from her name and stick a 'K' on it. She even changed her name by deed poll for her passport.

A guy ahead of us snapped at the nearest head. "You told me to give the passports to you!"

She glared at him. "And you didn't give them to me. You had them last."

I smiled inside, *that isn't going to happen to me. I'm Mr Organised.* And I dealt out the passports. "You will need these when you get to the front."

We managed to locate our luggage and identify our transfer. A driver called George and a battered taxi (well, 'Taxi-George' was the name on the car, at least). George's greying curly locks and beard reminded me of someone, like a mad scientist. *Einstein with a beard, that's it.* His other noticeable features were the sweat laden armpit-spots of his open-necked shirt and the stink of goat and wet earth. The only communication he offered was a tatty bit of white card: 'Princes' it announced in red board-marker. George gave a cursory nod, then loaded our cases and opened the cars doors without uttering a single word. This belied what a friend had told us. He'd said, "Greeks talk loud and passionately. Even a quiet chat sounds like an argument."

There was something odd about George. I just couldn't put my finger on it. I jumped into the front passenger seat and was embarrassed to see the steering wheel in front of me. The kids pissed themselves. George just smirked.

Moments later, George was behind the wheel. Gravel spattered the taxi rank as he launched us away, raising a chorus of "Malaka!" from a group of drivers. Without stopping for traffic, we accelerated through a red light onto the main road. I was first thrown hard to the left and then just as suddenly to the right. *Shit, the car has morphed into a roller coaster.* My stomach churned, akin to holding a fart in on a first date. The road was like a second-hand Scalextric set, all the straight pieces missing – and George didn't let the need to drive safely distract him from tapping away at his mobile. Most annoying was the constant *beep beep* from keying in his message. I glanced over my shoulder at Kam and the kids. The sight of her white knuckles clutching her shoulder bag tightly confirmed I didn't imagine the sensation of fear.

This is it. We'd spent all this money, to die on foreign soil. *What a legacy, the pinnacle of bad decisions.*

"At least the sun is shining," encouraged Kam, seemingly accepting our fate too. I dared to glance out of the window, expecting to see the face of death. Instead, I was met by a wave of calm: my first sight of the glittering blue Aegean. If this was heaven, I thought, I would gladly meet God here.

Without warning, the taxi lurched as George – texting all the while – swung the cab onto the forecourt of the Prometheus Hotel, barely stopping on the gravelled surface before skidding into the reception through the large glass doors. He jumped out of the car and, without a single word, hurriedly unloaded our cases. I offered him a five euro note as a tip – after all, we were all still alive. He gave me a puzzled look and reached out to accept the money, then got back to his mobile and his text conversation, while he sped off. The pea grit stung my legs.

Kam and I puffed nicotine plumes competing with the dust cloud left in George's wake. The kids marvelled at strange reptiles scurrying through flower beds. Lindon seized the opportunity for banter, and sniped, "Alyss, look, there's your twin." He was pointing to a green lizard sunning itself.

"Gamysou," she spat, knowing that he'd stopped learning Greek after session one. It seemed it wasn't just naughty boys that skip to the swear words. The confused expression on Lindon's face was a picture. He just grunted.

The expression on Kam's face suggested she was dazed, more than confused. "Bloody hell. No more taxis from now on," she groaned.

I wanted to agree. Instead, I let out a noncommittal grunt. I knew that in a week, we were booked to take the return taxi journey. Kam looked at me, and she recognised that grunt. I changed the subject. "Come on. Let's get this holiday started."

The reception area's walls were painted in a dark muddy brown. Like the living room of our elderly neighbour with a sixty-fags-a-day habit. The receptionist's face was lit mostly by the glow from her computer screen. It took a while for my eyes and reactolite lenses to adjust to the relative darkness.

"Hello... We... From... The UK... Here..." I handed over the printout from the travel company. I spoke slowly and emphasised my mouth shape for each word while gesturing with my hands. If I did that, then she would find it easier to understand what I was saying. I didn't know that the Greeks spoke English. George didn't speak anything, let alone English, and I thought he was Greek.

"OK, thank you and welcome to Soroni and the Prometheus Hotel. Let me check your reservation," said the receptionist. *Bugger*, now I appeared to be the one that couldn't speak English. She scanned her list of names, then she scanned it a little slower, and again for the third time. I tilted my head to examine the names while she had it in view, hoping I could show her where we were on the list.

"One moment, please, I will get the manager."

"Oh shit," I thought out loud.

"Skata," echoed Alyss.

"Rod?" Kam was giving me a look. "You told me you'd checked the reservation," highlighting another poor decision on my part.

I could barely hear her because my head was buzzing. This might have been the heat or too much nicotine. I was struggling to think of anything other than our predicament. We were two thousand miles from home and a week away from our booked flight.

A pale-faced, haggard-looking manager came back with the receptionist. He tapped keys on the computer and looked at me with a sigh. "I am very sorry, Mister Prince, but we have no record of your booking to stay at Prometheus."

'Oh shit' was no longer a powerful enough expletive to reflect my helplessness, but all I could mutter was an upgrade to "Oh fuck."

Kam and Alyss's eyes teared up as the panic in my voice signalled that all was not well. Of course, our predicament didn't appear to influence Lindon. "Dad, what does gammy sue mean?" The manager momentarily glanced up at Lindon.

I ushered him behind me. "Not now."

"Don't worry," was the reassurance offered by the manager. "It is our fault. We didn't confirm the booking. Let me make a call, and I will organise something for you. Take a seat across from the desk, and I will sort it out." The youngsters took the invitation to sit. Kam and I went out for even more nicotine. *At last, something that isn't my fault.*

"What a fucking nightmare. We should have gone to Blackpool – at least we'd have driven home." I ought to have been more reassuring to Kam. But to be honest, I needed my own reassurance that we weren't going to be sleeping in the airport for a week. The image of Tom Hanks in the film *The Terminal* flooded the void that once contained my brain.

Kam, usually full of good advice, chipped in. "You need to make a complaint when we get back home."

If we get home, I mused to myself. Flying home seemed as realistic as Icarus flying to the sun. I could only give another grunt. I just needed everyone to shut up so I could think – the manager came outside and volleyed seven sentences at me with the rapidity of a firecracker. "Everything is fine. I have told your children to join you. A taxi will be here shortly. It will take you to another hotel. They are expecting you. Sorry for our error. Goodbye." At which, he disappeared into the hotel. I'd have been more hopeful if he'd stayed until the taxi arrived. I supposed we were no longer his concern.

Lindon came running from reception. "We can get a tent and camp."

Alyss, in tears, followed in the turbulence he'd created. She looked pitiful as she struggled to manage three cases.

"They've sent for a taxi to take us to another hotel. So no, we won't be buying a tent," I snapped, irritated that Lindon wasn't as upset as the rest of us.

Alyss joined us. She looked at Lindon and hissed. "Gamysou."

Kam looked at me. "What's she saying?"

"I don't know. I'll look it up later." I'd lied. So far as that word was concerned, ignorance was bliss.

A speeding taxi swung onto the forecourt. *Thank god, this nightmare is finally over.*

"Oh fuck," I sighed, as a taxi skidded to a halt on the gravel. It stopped an inch away from our luggage.

"Look who it is," sighed Kam.

I can't recall every detail of the second taxi ride. One near-death experience is pretty much the same as another. George was seemingly still addicted to texting, and the roads to the next hotel got narrower with sharper bends. The climax: a narrow lane, shrouded on either side by a ten-foot-high bamboo forest. It reminded me of a film, where the good guys went into a field of maize to hide from the bad guys between the tall stems. Ahead of us, I could see more bamboo forest blocking the road. George glanced up but didn't slow. I squinted my eyes and gritted my teeth. My foot hit the floor hard as I pressed an imaginary brake. This made George look up again, and he swung the steering wheel hard to the left. The taxi entered a ninety-degree corner. My eyes now completely closed; I had a sensation of sliding or turning over in the taxi. Like we were the bathwater spiralling down the plughole.

Everything was suddenly still, and I sensed we'd stopped. When I opened my eyes, I could only gasp at the sight before me. It appeared to be a small village of colourful Greek buildings, none of which were more than two stories high. They were flat-topped, not a single ridge tile in view. Every surface was either vertical or horizontal. If I were to paint a picture of heaven, this is the image I would paint. I pinched myself and bit down hard on my tongue to remind myself I could feel pain. At least I wasn't dead.

George spoke for the first time in our presence. "Welcome to the beautiful Helios Hotel."

He wasn't wrong. It looked way better than the Prometheus. Who on earth would want a room on the tenth floor? He exited the taxi and unloaded our cases. Even though he'd almost killed us for a second time, I still felt compelled to offer him a tip. I pulled out another five euro note.

"No Mister Prince, no need to pay again, you have already given enough." He let out a thunderous laugh. Jumped in his taxi and disappeared into the bamboo forest and a cloud of dust. The bloody gravel stinging my legs again.

Alyss rubbed her legs and echoed my own thoughts. "Gamysou."

"This is more like it." We approached reception, and my heart was pounding in my chest. It felt as if someone was doing a clog dance and stomping all over my torso to some strange rhythm. *What if they haven't heard of us?*

"Oh, bugger."

"What now?" Sighed Kam, emphasising the 'now'. And she tutted for good measure.

"They didn't give me the printout back."

We entered the hotel and were hit by the coolness of it. A high ceiling and marble everywhere probably helped. A complete contrast to the Prometheus. So much light and cleanliness. There were images everywhere of what I assumed were different Greek gods. The walls, floor and ceiling, were all made of white marble. There were pictures, objects and antiquities that added colour to the white canvas. The dominant colours were the blue of the sea and the gold of the sun. A very well-dressed man interrupted my surveillance. "You must be the Prince family, we are expecting you. My name is Mikalis, and I am the manager of Helios Hotel. Welcome to Kamiros City, Rhodes."

Mikalis was a slender man, and he carried an air of authority. Slightly balding with a fashionable five o'clock shadow. He presented himself as a man that seemed professional in all he did. He spoke reasonable English. But his sentences also came in short bursts. It gave the impression of a man in a hurry.

He enquired about our needs. "A party of four? You will need a two-bedroomed apartment. Yes?"

I nodded in response, and then he uttered the words I didn't want to hear.

"Unfortunately, at the moment we don't have anything for you."

Oh no, here we go again.

Mikalis continued. "No, we do have something for you. But not right this second. Leave your luggage here while you explore the hotel and relax. Give me an hour, and your room will be ready."

Well, to say the hotel was beautiful was like saying Mount Everest is big. We explored the grounds, and we couldn't miss the fact that many of the buildings had their own private pool.

"Can we have one of those rooms?" pleaded Alyss.

"No, we'll take whatever they give us."

Alyss pouted the way teenage girls do. It was a good selfie pose. She must have thought so too because she started to play with her phone.

The blocks of suites were set up like a small village. The walkways between the buildings had famous Greek names like Socrates Street and Pythagoras Street.

Lindon climbed the steps to one of the two-storey buildings. "Look at this. I want room 208. Come and see," he shouted.

"Lindon get down, that's someone's apartment," admonished Kam, as she climbed the stairs.

"Rod. Come and look at this."

I tutted under my breath, not wanting to trespass on someone else's holiday. I'm sure I'd heard voices from inside the room. I was reluctant to become an uninvited guest. *I'm going to be immortalised for being deported for trespass.*

I was rendered speechless. Even the top floor apartments had their own pools. *A pool in the sky would be heaven.* As a lifelong sun worshipper, I imagined an opportunity to sunbathe naked when the kids weren't about.

Alyss had been playing on her phone. Out of the blue, she announced, "I can't find it."

"You can't find what?" queried Kam.

"Helios Hotel, it's not on Google, Snapchat, Trip Adviser, Helios Hotel doesn't exist."

I threw in an observation. "Kids today believe everything they read on the Internet. Of course it exists, look around you. You've spelt the name wrong."

Showing his impatience. Lindon asked, "What time is it? Is it an hour yet?"

"Almost," I replied. "We'll make our way back but don't build up your hopes for a pool. They'll be reserved for posh people."

Mikalis appeared before we reached reception. "Mister Prince, here is your key. Your luggage is in the room. I hope you will be comfortable. Please relax and enjoy your holiday. Everything is free." He handed me the key, and hope returned. As he walked back to reception, I glanced down at the brass key fob. The happy hormone surged through my body. Is it Endorphins or Adrenalin? Consciousness returned to my brain, and I managed to stay silent until Mikalis was out of earshot.

My excitement caused my voice to raise by an octave. "My good god, they've only given us 208."

THE FAMILY – *Holiday Survival*

Next morning, I woke first, shivering and disorientated. I sat up in bed and blew into my hands to warm them. It was like waking up in the middle of January. "Who put the bloody air-con on max during the night?"

"I did, I had a hot flush," responded Kam, at which point I didn't continue griping about it.

One by one, the family came to life, recovered from the adventure of our arrival. Lindon yawned. "What time's breakfast?" *That'd be right, thinking about his stomach as soon as he'd opened his eyes.*

Alyss's feet thudded towards the bathroom, closely followed by the hiss of the shower turning on.

"Don't be all day," I shouted as a token objection. Now only the girls could get ready for breakfast, given that it was an open-plan bathroom, and my teenage daughter would be naked. Lindon stayed in his prone position. *He'll wonder why he's dizzy when he stands up.* I went to the veranda to have some nicotine.

Oh yes, I forgot about that, my eyes squinting as I adjusted to the sunlight reflecting and dappling on the ripples of the water. *We've got a pool.* Having spent the previous six hours trying to get warm, I was once again checking the Sunday roast. It was reminiscent of the moment the plane door opened. I was gasping for electronically cooled oxygen. It was only seven in the morning, and the ultraviolet was stinging my skin. My body was crying out for caffeine. There was no way I was going to the restaurant without making myself presentable first. I didn't have a legacy, and I refused to let it be that I was unkempt.

Kam appeared. A towel wrapped around her modesty. "Oh God, I forgot we had a pool."

"Me too," was all my dry mouth could utter.

"You can't have a brew. There isn't a kettle or tea making stuff in the room."

"What? Even the guest houses in Blackpool have tea making facilities in the rooms," she observed.

Three cigarettes added some stimulation and compensated for the lack of caffeine. Fags helped make the long wait for Alyss to get out of the shower more bearable. I heard the flip-flop of her still wet feet exit the bathroom. I jumped up and took my chance to be next. As I passed her, she slipped on the slick tiled floor and fell square on her arse. "Skata!" she screamed.

My concern for her welfare distracted me enough for the suddenly hyperactive Lindon to beat me to the bathroom. The lock of the door clicked, and I banged on the door. "Lindon, it's my turn." All he did was let out a fart. *Great, now it's going to stink in there too.*

Time for another cigarette. "How much do you reckon fags cost here, sweetheart? I asked Kam.

"Dunno, you're the one that learnt to speak Greek."

I walked out of the fridge, the prickling sting of goosebumps once more replaced by the searing burn of the sun.

I gazed out across the lawns towards the sea. Two men with bin bags were ambling along in deep conversation. They were picking up every tenth item of litter they walked past. I did have a better vantage point than they did, but they might as well not try to collect any junk at all.

"Hey Kam, look at them lazy buggers, they're leaving more litter than they're picking up." No response, she was too busy sticking pictures of the pool on Facebook.

Mental note to self. *Get a job in Greece, do ten per cent of the work for…* "How much do you think they get paid out here?" I queried aloud to anyone that might be listening. *Maybe that was my destiny, emigrate to Greece and pick up litter.*

"I want to go home, there's no Wi-Fi," moaned Alyss.

"Don't worry. We'll see the manager guy, Stavros, and sort all the things that are missing."

"His names Mikalis," corrected Kam.

Lindon surfaced from the bathroom, laughing. "The water's run out," he mocked. I wasn't even sure of who he was mocking. I suspect it was me.

"That'll be right. It's alright for you lot, but I'm not going anywhere in public. Not until I've sorted my hair out."

Kam as resourceful as ever, whispered, "Wet your hair in the pool."

"I'm not bloody getting in there. It'll be freezing." Kam won. I knelt by the pool and scooped chlorinated water onto my head. I was surprised by how pleasant it was. I had to be quick. "Let me know if either of the kids spots me. I don't want to end up headfirst in the water. I momentarily plunged my head into the water to get it wet all over.

Oh shit. I felt contact on my back, and the water was swirling around me. The weightlessness made me lose all sense of up and down. The cold water made me catch my breath, and I was inhaling water. *Shit, I'm drowning.* I blacked out, and I don't know how long I was unconscious. I surfaced coughing and spluttering, gasping for breath and choking up water.

"Little bitch, you could have killed me," I screamed between coughing up mouthfuls of water. I was surprised she hadn't drowned me. I was shaking, Kam was pallid, Alyss looked scared, and Lindon just pissed himself.

At least one of us is enjoying the holiday of a lifetime.

≈≈≈

We entered the restaurant, not even sure of what the procedure was. I scanned the space. It was massive. It was big enough to house a couple of Olympic-size swimming pools. There was a rather imposing piece of artwork that looked down on diners. The image was that of Helios, the sun god, with his crown of flames riding a chariot of fire. It dominated the space. There was a sudden rush of cold air as I walked beneath it, and the hair on the back of my neck stood on end.

The most noticeable aspect of the people in the restaurant was the miserable look on their faces. I guessed they'd all been almost drowned by their kids. *Obviously not morning people.* Breakfast was buffet-style. We had to locate plates, load up with whatever took our fancy, and find a seat. Simple, but there were several problems. First, we had to wait until clean plates appeared from the kitchen. Once in possession of said plate, which was too hot to hold, we had to walk up and down the buffet guessing what the food was. I noticed a guy load up his plate with eight boiled eggs and a single slice of ham. The eggs were easy to identify; the meat was a guess. *If he eats that many eggs, he won't be able to shit for a fortnight.*

Another guest stuffed a baker's dozen of bread rolls into her tote bag. I headed for the bright lights, hoping that is where the hot food would be. Yep, hotdog sausages, fried eggs, baked beans and something that looked like bacon.

I queued for my turn. After five people had pushed in front of me. The guy behind me had been waiting for me to move. "You new here?"

I turned and nodded.

"OK. I'm going to push in and grab a serving spoon. You stand close and be my wingman. We'll keep the Russians away from the spoon. I'll pass it to you, and you pass it back, and so on. I've been here four days, and the Brits are calling it the Eastern bloc." And he laughed. I didn't get the joke, but I grunted to show my acknowledgement.

Finally, I had my plate loaded up, one rasher of bacon, half a hotdog sausage, three beans and a fried egg with no yolk. I scanned the room looking for my tribe, and I thanked God that they'd managed to find a table for four. I plonked myself down, exhausted from the fight to get what little food I'd got.

Kam had found us a table near the beverages. As she only had yoghurt and honey, she volunteered to get the coffee. This allowed me to start on my *full* English breakfast.

The problem with the blocking strategy raised its forkless head. I didn't have any cutlery.

"You should have picked that up when you got the plate," advised Lindon.

"Oh, I never thought of that, aren't you clever," I stated. I scowled my irritation at Lindon, and he decided no to pursue it any further.

I went in search of a four-pronged trident I could eat with. *Wouldn't that make it a quad-dent?* My eastern blocking mate was wandering around, in search of his missus.

"Excuse me. Where are the knives and forks?" I enquired from my new-found ally.

"Over by the plates, you should have got them when you got your plate."

"Yeah, I never thought of that," I said without any sarcasm at all.

One knife, one damn knife, and nothing else in the cutlery tray. I approached a nearby waitress, I presumed she was a waitress, she had an apron on, and a tee-shirt labelled Helios.

"Excuse me, could I have a fork please?" I asked, making a point of not using the sign language and slow speech I'd used yesterday. She squinted at me as if examining my very soul. Then she shrugged her shoulders and walked off. I was staggered and still forkless. *How rude, you just failed your NVQ in everything, missus.*

I went back to the table and commandeered Lindon's cake

fork. I used a bit of grubby tissue from my pocket, to wipe his germs off it. Cold, bloody cold, cold yolkless egg, three cold beans, cold bacon, cold half sausage and cold coffee.

As I shook my head in frustration, I caught a glimpse of a guy that had uncovered the fake barrel that housed the red wine. He proceeded to fill a two-litre pop bottle with it. I guessed he'd said to his wife, "You get the rolls, and I'll get the drinks. Then we'll head to the beach." I'm partial to a drink but not at eight-thirty in the morning.

My new pal came over and introduced himself and his family. I reciprocated. Then he bade us farewell as he headed off into Rhodes Town. "By the way, Rod, it's worse in the evening. It opens at six-thirty. And the Russians start gathering at six." I thought to myself, *Eastern Blocking. Now I get it.*

≈≈≈

We skipped the chance to play eastern blocking at lunchtime. Instead, we opted for the snack bar. It was set out like a bistro, except we weren't in France. I guessed it was designed to be a taverna. Not that I had ever seen a taverna. There were groups of tables and chairs scattered around a courtyard. Part of the table area was protected from the sun by a pergola. The pergola had what I guessed were grapevines growing over it. At least it provided some level of shade from the midday sun, which was high in the sky and scorching.

We picked a table in the welcome shade, and the kids wandered off the way they always did. I was expecting some kind of waitress service. A matronly woman, dressed all in black, came running as fast as her chubby-stockinged legs would carry her. All I could think of was my spinsterly headmistress from primary school. That's probably unfair on the headmistress, though she was like a hospital matron. This mistress had a long nose, round face and brown curly hair. She looked like a woman scorned, with masculine features including a hairy chin.

"Oxi, Oxi, Oxi!" she shouted, waving her arms furiously as if she was shooing away a wasp. It was here that we met our first Greek person that couldn't speak English. This event caught me off guard. I'd tamed my hands and broken English in the light of the previous day's events. As she approached, she grabbed my arm and pulled it up, as if she was trying to lift me. She was broad and sturdily built to the point where she looked immovable. She would have made a good rugby player.

"Is everything alright?" I enquired, to which she replied in a shrill voice "Oxi, Oxi, Oxi," and dragged me to another table. She made a cleaning motion with her hands a bit like *wax on, wax off,* from the scene in the Karate Kid movie.

"God, Kam she's going to karate chop us."

"No, she isn't. She wants us to have a clean table. Fool." The miserable matron smiled as best as her sour face would let her. As she left, I'm sure she muttered something like "Malaka."

The kids demonstrated it was self-service by cramming mountains of cakes on tiny tea-plates. They were slopping cola all over the marble tiled floor. *Nice one kids, now matron's got something else to moan about, watch you don't get rugby tackled,* I thought to myself.

"You kids are going to have to start eating properly. And

26

why take so many cakes? There won't be any left for anyone else."

"It's OK, we're on holiday," they chorused.

While Kam and I were choosing our snacks, I spotted beer taps and a fake wine barrel. *Well, it is the afternoon, and we are Brits, and the booze is all free.*

"Fancy a beer sweetheart?" I offered.

"That sounds like a plan," she responded as quick as a flash. Never one to miss a free drink, our Kam. That's why we'd gone all-inclusive, we didn't have to budget for our enthusiastic drinking habits.

"They haven't got any pint glasses. It'll have to be a coffee cup or one of these plastic tumblers." I demonstrated what a plastic tumbler looked like by holding the beaker in the air.

"Which holds the most?"

"Tumbler, just about."

"I'll have a tumbler," she replied.

To call them tumblers sounds a bit exotic. To give you a better idea, any supermarket in the UK will sell you a hundred of these for a quid. I poured four drinks. Not for the kids to share, but two each for Kam and me. It was something to drink while we ate our snacks. Cakes finished, Alyss announced "I'm going to the reception area. It's got a good Wi-Fi signal. You coming, Lind?"

"Nope, I'm going looking for fun."

"This is the life, and what a beautiful place," opened Kam, as we enjoyed our post-food nicotine.

"We definitely got lucky in the end, didn't we?" I suggested.

"At one point I didn't think we were going to get a holiday," she said. Then she went back to posting beautiful pictures of the place on Facebook.

I continued the conversation on my own. "I'd love to own a place like this. If it was mine, I'd make some changes. There are quite a few niggles that let it down. The guests and staff stop this beautiful place from being perfect." I thought to myself. *It'd be nice to pick my own legacy.*

"Talking of niggles, did you go and talk to Mikalis, about the water running out. And the Wi-Fi not reaching our room," *Oh, she was listening after all. How does she do that?*

"I went but didn't get a chance to speak to him. There was a crowd of foreigners at the reception desk shouting at him and kicking up a stink. I didn't want to impose. It looked like he had enough on his plate. I'll catch him later." In reality, I didn't want to appear like I was complaining. They had taken us in when we were in real need. You don't really complain about your saviours.

We spent the rest of the day relaxing by our pool, and the lazy afternoon included regular visits to the snack bar to get more beer. I made a mental note to try and get hold of a bigger container. I finally understood why the guy at breakfast was filling up his cola bottle with wine.

"Are we going to go to the restaurant early, as that Brit bloke told us to?" asked Kam.

"I don't think so. I'd rather wait until the rush has died down. It's open till nine. I must get his name again. We can't keep calling him Brit bloke." At which point we both drifted off into different dream states. Me, I imagined what I would do if this place was mine. I sensed I was destined to be at Helios.

≈≈≈

Later, the kids returned. "Right. Tomorrow I have the first shower, In case we run out of water again." I was staking my claim before the event.

Kam suggested, "We could save water and shower together."

"Who?"

"Me and you stupid. Not the flipping kids."

I felt the need to re-stake my claim. "OK. That sounds good. But we still go first."

"Lindon don't forget the hotel want men to wear long trousers for dinner."

We were all relieved to see there was no queue at the doorway to the restaurant. Even more relieved when we saw the place was almost empty. It was worth waiting until later to avoid the fight to get to the food. I'd grabbed a plate and remembered the cutlery. I managed to get a full set. It was too easy. I proceeded to select what I was going to put on my plate. Salad, feta, tomato? No. I wanted meat and lots of it.

At the hot food counter, I scanned the labels which were at eye-level. Rabbit, Pork, Beef, Fish, Chicken. I decided beef and chicken sounded good until I looked down. It was clear that waiting until eight o'clock wasn't such a good idea. All that remained of the hot meats were five empty trays. Well, I say empty, but they did have greasy and congealed meat juices in them. *Shit, another fuck-up.* I looked hopefully at the waitress stood by the display. "Is there any more meat?" I almost pleaded. She squinted her eyes, shrugged her shoulders and wandered off. I wasn't at all upset by this, because I kind of expected it.

I caught up with Kam at the salad bar. "The kids have saved us a table," and she nodded to where they were sitting, with their mountains of cakes.

"Oh, you mean in case anyone else fancies a light salad?" *I must stop being sarcastic with family members.* In my defence, I was embarrassed that it was my suggestion to go to dinner late. I had no one to blame but myself, and that was hard to take. *Another poor decision. Well done, Rod,* I thought to myself. The salad was not nice. It consisted of wilted lettuce and stale feta, which had turned yellow. The freshest part was the tomato and cucumber.

"Yuck. I'm not eating that. It's too green," shuddered Alyss.

"I wanted meat," moaned Lindon.

"What's the matter? Are you getting fed up with cake already?"

For me, it filled the hole, and I washed it down with three plastic tumblers of beer, which was about half a pint in total. At least it was still early, and we could spend time in the bar. Kam suggested, "We should investigate the local tavernas for evening meals. It would be nice to be served our food from a menu, rather than having to fight for scraps with other guests."

≈≈≈

The bar was the complete antidote to the emptiness of the restaurant. It seemed like the 200-headed monster had arrived for a drink. There was nowhere to stand, let alone sit. Somehow, I didn't think eastern blocking would work in the bar. Lyndon and Alyss said they were going to explore. Kam and I started back towards the restaurant. She fancied a pint, and I wanted six tumblers. At the door of the empty eatery a poster declared: *'Entertainment every night in the amphitheatre 9 till 11.'* I scanned the list of days written below the headline 'Fakir Show'. That night was, indeed, Fakir night. "Well, let's hope everyone wants to watch a fire-eater," I sighed.

Sure enough at nine o'clock, the animation team encouraged people to go to the amphitheatre. Within minutes the bar had become as empty as the restaurant. I hoped that didn't mean they'd run out of booze.

A couple of teenage lads approached and spoke to the kids, then Lindon relayed to us. "Your friend from the hotel's inside the bar, and he's got a table. This is Thomas and Andrew – he's their dad. Me and Alyss are going to watch the show."

I looked at Kam. "Shall we join them in the bar?" I queried, not wanting to decide based upon my last attempt to decide something.

"Yeah, they seemed nice."

≈≈≈

"Hi, we didn't introduce ourselves properly earlier. We're Rod and Kam. We're from Cheshire, the first-timers. How was the visit to Rhodes town?"

He reached out and shook my hand. "It was great, but a little warm and crowded. It's our first time at this hotel too. We've been to Greece before. So we had some idea of what to expect. Tony and Tracey. How was your first day?"

"Yes. It's been good."

"My round," said Tony, "what would you like?"

"About ten tumblers of beer each," I joked.

I whispered to Kam. "I thought it was all-inclusive."

"It is. Tony's making a joke." And she tutted.

Tracey didn't say much, but Kam involved her in conversation. I took the opportunity to scan the room. The bar seemed OK. It was a good-size but barely big enough to hold a mythical beast with 200 heads. The walls were adorned with all manner of peculiar objects. A bent and rusty trident had pride of place on the main wall. Below this was a tailor's mannequin, with a black wig placed crookedly on its head. It reminded me of the woman sat opposite me. I looked at her and smiled, masking my guilt about what I was thinking. The mannequin had a stage-prop beard and an eye-patch over its nose. Tracey had neither. I guessed Tracey was a bottle brunette hiding silver hair, given the size of her crow's feet.

Tony returned with a large tray and eight beers, and every one of them in a separate pint mug. Real pint mugs. Tony was the complete opposite of Tracey. Shaved head, loud, and he did have a beard. It didn't take long to discover his political views were opposed to mine. "Unemployed people have only got themselves to blame," he opined. Given my job was helping unemployed people back into work in customer service, in one sentence, he'd managed to make my life's work irrelevant. He'd trampled all over the one realistic chance I had to leave a legacy.

I think the only thing we had in common was our taste for

beer.

"Got us all two each. You go up in a bit and get eight more. We need to make sure we have a good supply before the crowds get back at eleven. They stop serving at eleven-thirty on the dot," advised Tony.

"How did you manage to get beer mugs?"

"The barman looks after polite people. He'll always serve you first and give it to you in a glass. Get in here early and get your first beer in a glass. Don't let them clear it away, then every time you go for a refill take the glass with you. I've even got one in the room, for when I get a drink at the self-service taverna."

Tracey finally piped in – this must have been her specialist subject. "We even have four full sets of cutlery hidden in the room. We don't get caught forkless like you were this morning," she laughed. I grunted. *No wonder the hotel hasn't got enough glasses and cutlery.* I don't think they saw the irony in it. "In our defence, it was one of the waitresses that suggested we do it," she added.

As the evening wore on, we learnt lots about how to survive at the hotel. All the hacks necessary to make sure we fit in with their political philosophy of 'every man for himself'. By eleven o'clock, Kam and the kids had given up and gone back to the room. Tony and Tracey buggered off, taking their beer and tankards with them. I remained and sat at the bar, chatting to the bar staff. I followed Tony's advice to make sure they knew I was English and polite.

The fire-eater must have just extinguished his fire for the night because the number of guests momentarily increased, though nothing near the level of earlier in the evening. The lighting dimmed as another of the lights over the bar blew. I took that as a sign. My local dips the lights to signal closing time. With that, I staggered back to 208.

≈≈≈

The rest of the holiday followed a similar pattern to the first day. By day three, we were a bit more independent. In fact, we were passing on our skills and knowledge to other Brits as they arrived. I couldn't explain why, but there was something irresistible about the hotel. After our seven days there we'd fallen in love with Helios and its features. On the surface, it was a terrible holiday full of alien experiences. Inside, I sensed my destiny could be there.

Returning to the UK, we all felt at a loss. Kam sighed. "I think I have the holiday blues."

"Me too. Why don't we try and go back to Rhodes later this year?"

After a short discussion, we decided to return in August. This, in turn, led to another visit in October. We were inexplicably drawn to our Greek faulty towers. We were told that three visits in a debut season was a record. We envied those that lived there, and over the long British winter, dreams of emigrating turned into discussions of selling up.

I assumed Kam and kids shared the same magnetism towards Rhodes. They appeared to like the place as much as I did. Was I making another poor decision on their behalf? Like the time I insisted that a quarter of a tank of petrol would reach the next motorway service station? It didn't.

My emotions waved back and forth, like the Greek tide I

yearned for, unsure where I should be. Unable to settle. Was it possible to live in Rhodes and live a life most of us only dream about? Or when the reality of 'the everyday' took over, would life be as dull in Rhodes after a few weeks as it was in Cheshire? We all understood that living there couldn't be an eternal holiday. Visiting the beach or some tourist attraction every day would be tedious. Kam told everyone I was having a mid-life crisis, and I would grow out of it. In the end, she said it was my decision. I think she was abdicating any blame for when it might all go pear-shaped.

By Christmas, we'd decided to book another visit to Rhodes. This time in April, right at the start of the season. It was our Christmas present to each other and a chance to see everyday Rhodes. My new year's resolution was to give up the fags and save money for our trip. I gave up smoking and took up vaping. I was still addicted to nicotine.

ZEUS – *King of the Gods*

April 2014. The long cold winter in Cheshire had come and gone. April finally came, and we arrived for our fourth visit to what we'd started to consider our second home, though I hadn't gained the confidence to take the plunge permanently, at least not yet. Given the road crash that was our first visit, we'd started to hire a car and collect it at the airport. We just needed to grab our bags and go. This was to be a dry run, self-catering, an experiment to see if everyday living in Rhodes was a step we could take.

We'd barely checked in, and Kam and the kids were already arguing about wardrobe space. They were always tetchy from the four-hour flight, and I was no different. It was going to be a good few hours until I'd built up my nicotine levels to the point where I'd be half-human.

That moment was a perfect example of family banter. Lindon started it. "Alyss, Why did you bother bringing a bikini? Your fried eggs won't fill the cups."

Here we bloody go, I thought to myself.

"Dad, tell him," pleaded Alyss. She was an unusual teenage

girl because she didn't act years beyond her age.

I sighed but didn't rise to the impending banter session.

Lindon saw an opportunity. "I can't get into trouble for telling the truth. Isn't that right, Dad? You said that without honesty, we have nothing."

"Yes, but I also said be mindful of other people's feelings." *Damn. They did it again. They'd bloody dragged me into it.* I turned towards the door. "I'm going to give you guys some space to unpack and get the banter out of the way." I headed out, grabbing my e-cig. My new year's resolution had been to give up the more-expensive fags, to save money for our trip, and I needed some solitude with my new favourite toy after four hours in an airborne tube with a 200-headed beast.

My dad was gone when I was fifteen. I didn't have the chance to be the young pup challenging the alpha male for supremacy. I'd missed the apprenticeship of how to be a good father. I labelled myself as a family man. I loved my family but didn't have a clue if I was a good father. I had modelled myself on my dad, and he was a great man. But my legacy couldn't be that I was Bert Prince's son. I needed my own destiny.

When Lindon hit fifteen, I was in uncharted and choppy waters. Lindon seized the opportunity to banter often. It's not that I didn't love him, I did. He was my pride and joy. But wasn't he supposed to wait until he went to university to flex his muscles? I just wanted a quiet life. No upsets and confrontations and no bloody drama.

It was Alyss that provided most of the drama. More than enough to fill an entire episode of *Coronation Street*. God, another five years until she fledged the nest. Maybe I'm not a family man. I believed I was, but it comes to something when you look forward to work to escape the drama. I headed for the beach, my sanctuary from the arguments.

≈≈≈

Sat in the warm April sunshine. My confusion was akin to trying to play a word game with a plate of alphabet spaghetti. I listened to the waves break on the soft pebble beach. Each wave reminiscent of the sound made by a bag of marbles being tipped on the floor. The waves forming a slow, steady cardiac rhythm, while the pebbles were playing their own tune, a more sinister, erratic tune of confusion. I still had doubts. Were we doing the right thing? I pensively surveyed the panorama. I was searching for my answer in the infinite depths of blue. The artist's palette of azure started just a few feet from where I sat. I took a deep breath of salty air – not the fishy seaweed stink of a British beach. Pure and clean, this was unmistakably the scent of the Aegean.

I gazed out across the sea. Turkey was clearly visible. The orchestra of the waves and marbles was interrupted by the noise of another tube of tourists. The tube throttling back as it made its final approach to the airport.

The tube had landed, and the Aegean beach took centre stage once more. The sun felt warmer suddenly as the reflection from the water made me squint. I could hear the bugs in the trees fifteen feet behind where I was sat. Cicadas, that's what they're called. They provided the lyrics to the music of the beach. God had created a creature with such a hypnotic mating call.

It wasn't the mating call that keeps drawing us to the

island. It was something much more powerful, an imperceptible sense. *What was so special about this place? And why do we keep returning? How did we get here? Will the kids make friends? Will I make new friends?* Questions I'd been asking myself for the previous five months. Each question providing fuel for the fire of doubt that was burning the contents of my mind. *Am I overthinking again? Another bloody question I couldn't answer.*

The change of rhythm from the tumbling marbles and the warmth of the sun distracted me from possible answers. The relaxing sound of the waves, a sedative, broken by a different rhythm from the marbles. I tried to lay back and adjust to the different beat. *Bugger, I was enjoying the solitude.* Footsteps, that was the new beat. They got closer, and they stopped well inside my personal space.

"*Malaka.* Of course, you know how you got here," a man's voice laughed. It was the same laugh Lindon used when he mocked Alyss.

I tried to shield my eyes from the glare of the sun to make out the source of the voice. *What? Who? You don't know me,* was all that filled my mind. I knew I'd got here on an Airbus 320, a tube full of holidaymakers.

I sat up, squinting through the glare, to get a look at him. Then the cheeky bugger stood even closer, my neck almost hurt from looking up, he was that close. I could smell earth and goat. I looked up, and he was a formidable-looking man. A stern face with its fair share of crow's feet. Both the greying hair on his head and his beard were curly and unkempt. His olive skin suggested that he worked outdoors. Probably came straight to the beach after tending his goats.

I couldn't speak. *Who was this fucker?* Confusion stampeded through my mind. Was this a fight or flight moment? All I could do was frown. When the adrenalin kicked in, and the stampede subsided, I stammered the only Greek word I could summon. "*G…y…gamisou.*" This was about to go fight or flight.

"Hey, Englishman that's no way to talk to a friend."

"Friend?" I emphasised the word to illustrate I was asking a question. "I don't know you. You're a stranger," I said as if answering my own question.

He made me flinch as he quickly dropped down and plonked himself on the pebbles, too close for comfort. "Many years ago, a philosopher once told me that a stranger is just a friend you haven't met yet. We became great friends. Socrates was his name." I shuffled my backside away from him to recover some personal space. He reached out to shake hands. His hand felt rough and hard; the type of skin you could sandpaper wood with. A firm grip but not enough to crush my hand. I've always looked for that in a person. It shows mutual respect and trust. As we sat there showing respect to each other, he stared into my eyes. He was still shaking my hand. He was what I call a *lingerer* – someone that doesn't want to let go. *This man is desperate,* I told myself. *But desperate for what?* He maintained the lingering handshake and stare. I continued to squint, the sun shining in my eyes. *Was he playing the blinking game as I did with the kids?* He was obviously into this greeting for the long haul, and he placed his left hand on our shaking hands. It made me jump because the skin of his left hand felt noticeably softer as it settled onto the back of my thumb. I surrendered the staring game to look down and confirm what my thumb was telling me. The smoothness of his left hand contrasted the carpenter's tool that was his right hand.

When I broke eye contact, it triggered the end to the painful silence. Still with our hands firmly embraced. "*Yiasou*, people call me Zeus."

"Rod," my only response. *Oh my God not another one*, I mused to myself. I remembered a guy that used to run our darts league back home. He reinvented himself as Moses. Kam always told me I attracted weird people.

Finally, he let go of my hand. "*Oxi*, I am not an oddball. Zeus is the name I was born with."

Holy *skata*, I thought, had he read my mind? He let out another thunderous roar of laughter. "Oxi, I can't read your mind, but I know you. I know your destiny, and I know how you think."

I must be dreaming, I've only been on the island for an hour, and already the sun has addled my brain. I pulled out my e-cig and puffed a massive amount of nicotine-laden steam to block out my hallucination. But as the vapour dissipated, I could see he was still there.

 He bellowed out another loud round of laughter. "Of course, I'm still here! God, you are so easy to read. And I wager you are rubbish at betting. And I bet you are shit at chess." That laugh was starting to scare the life out of me. But he would have spotted that, wouldn't he? "*Nai*, but there's nothing to fear, Rod Prince. You're at a crossroads, trying to find your destiny, nai?"

I puffed on that e-cig like my world was about to end.

"I am here to help you."

I just grunted. How can this nut job help me find my destiny?

"Do you recall your first visit to Rhodes?"

"Of course. The trip started out as a nightmare. The manager at Helios saved our holiday." I gestured back towards the hotel.

And then it hit me. "You… you're George."

He totally ignored my realisation and continued with the earlier conversation. "No Rod, It was me who saved your holiday."

"You? You're the Malaka that nearly killed us!."

"I got you Room 208."

"Mikalis got us 208."

"Alright if you want to be pedantic, I got Mikalis to give you 208… Checkmate."

Finally, his response to my revelation came. "*Oxi*, I am Zeus. The taxi I was driving had the name George on it. But yes, that is where we first met."

Zeus selected a lower volume and spoke with a serious look on his face. The frown lines deepened. "I must apologise for what I put you through that day. It was necessary to ensure you could build a rapport with the island."

I looked at him. "Oh right, so you had to scare us all to death with a roller coaster of a ride. You almost killed us so that I could experience a rapport with the island? It would have been easy enough to have the same effect, without the terror ride."

I thought to myself, *control the sarcasm. If he is a nutcase, he*

42

might get violent.

He continued. "It's not the taxi ride I am apologising for. On the ride from the Airport, what did you think I was doing with my phone?" Then he answered his own question. "I was hiding your reservation at the Prometheus Hotel." *I bloody hate that, someone asking a question then answering it themselves.* Why didn't he just state the answer? The question was redundant.

Wait, what did he just say? I didn't believe what I thought I had heard. "You texted the hotel to hide our reservation, why would anyone do that?"

"*Signomi* and forgive me, but if you had stayed at Prometheus, you wouldn't be sitting on the beach with me now." His seriousness was highlighted by the lack of that irritating laugh. "I needed you to experience real filoxenia. Where a Greek host welcomes a stranger in need into their home and caters to their every want. It's as if they were already lifelong friends. This is something you wouldn't have experienced, at the soulless Prometheus. I needed you to meet Mikalis. To experience his version of filoxenia. I also had to put you into a position of need. Do you understand?" He paused and looked at me. "I really am sorry for that first day. But I did engineer the entire experience. Look on the bright side. You had a fantastic holiday. You also got a suite with your own private pool. You fell in love with Rhodes, with Helios Hotel, and you will have a lifelong friendship with Mikalis. Has that answered your question?" And he let out that stupid laugh again as he got up and started walking away, his footsteps echoing loudly on the pebbles.

I had to shout. "Wait, where are you going?" He spun

around mid-stride and almost lost his balance. Before he could answer me, I continued to shout. "No. It hasn't answered my bloody question. I know *what*, but I don't know *why*. Yes, we are drawn to the island, and now we are thinking about living here. But we don't know *why*? And to be honest, the filoxenia, as you put it, was only skin-deep. The veneer of hospitality was so thin. I'm surprised it wasn't eaten away by all the ants living at the hotel." He looked at me, the way only a Greek could when you disagree with them. I went in for the kill while he was still silent. "I could write a damn book about all the things that were wrong with the Helios Hotel. While you sped off in your taxi, you didn't hang around long enough to see what we had to put up with."

He took a few unsteady strides closer to where I was sat. "*Malaka*, you would have had it a thousand times worse at the Prometheus…"

I didn't give him a chance to elaborate. I retorted, "Yes, I have become very good friends with Mikalis. Yes, he went out of his way to meet our needs. Yes, we tasted his brand of hospitality. But there was so much wrong with the rude staff and the guests."

"Stupid Englishman, that's the point, that's why you're here. Helios needs you. The island needs you." His voice echoed out. He stared at me, letting it sink in. OK, now he had my interest. He returned and sat next to me again.

Thinking I'd managed to land a job opportunity, I continued my critique of the hotel.

≈≈≈

"So that's it. That's why you insult the Hotel?" He roared,

banging his rough hand down hard on the pebbles. "You lived like millionaires. At the hotel's expense and now you moan about plastic tumblers."

"*Oxi, Oxi, Oxi,*" I retorted, mimicking the matronly rugby woman. "I was doing what I've always done. I put myself in the position of someone that has paid a lot more than I had. Imagine a tourist. He has worked for fifty weeks of the year to have the holiday of a lifetime. He will have paid 5000 euro to come and stay at Helios for two weeks. I'm certain he'd expect a bit more cutlery than a knife at breakfast. He'd want to eat more than half a hotdog, three beans and an egg without a yolk. I'm not insulting Helios. I'm drawn to the place. If I wasn't, I wouldn't have visited three times in a season, and I wouldn't be here now."

"Ahah, got you, so you do know how you got here," scoffed Zeus, like a teenage kid.

"No, I don't. How does being drawn to Helios explain *why* I'm here? The place is falling apart, and I suspect it'll be the last visit. It'll be closed down before much longer."

"I am sure you will continue to stay there," he reassured.

"Hardly, have you seen it lately? It's opened for paying guests, and half of it is cordoned off. It's a building site, yellow barrier tape and mounds of dirt everywhere. It looks like a bomb site."

"*Nai,* I've seen it. Your description is a bit exaggerated. It's just a winter refurbishment. I promise it will come back better and stronger than ever, of that I'm sure. I am confident it will be fully open in the next two weeks." He paused and stared upwards as if he was looking for some divine support.

I reached for my hat as the sun was at its highest, and I didn't want to start my holiday with a sunburned nose.

He continued. "Did you know Helios is the god of the sun, and the sun goes through cycles? It rises in the east and reaches its peak at noon, then starts its journey back to the horizon in the west. It's a cycle, and the hotel is copying the sun. Helios will be back to its glory days. Gone are the days when the Phoenix would perish after five hundred years before rising again from the ashes."

He looked at me. "Modern times have seen to that. Today's *mortals* live for the here and now and want instant results. Today the cycle of the Phoenix is five hundred weeks, ten years, at most. We now live in a throwaway society. You see, Helios is reaching its time." I could see a twinkle in his eyes as he spoke, not sure if he was emotional or blinded by the sun. But it was a definite twinkle.

"You still haven't explained why I'm here," I remind him.

"And I will. These niggles you described, are the efforts of bad people. Their aim is to sabotage the hotel. The matronly lady that works in the taverna. Her name is Hestia, she is my sister, and she oversees food and cooking. She is one of the bad people that is trying to destroy the hotel."

"Well, you need to have a word with her. She's doing a bloody good job of destroying the hospitality. I take it she is responsible for the plastic cups too?" Humouring him in such a way that I didn't sound overly sarcastic. "Oh, and the Russians as well?"

"I have a word with her? I bet you didn't have a word with her either, did you?"

"No, I don't generally complain, and she looked like she could flatten me. I usually let things ride."

"That figures, that's why the hotel is on its knees." He looked at me accusingly as if it was all my fault.

"Don't blame it on me."

He glanced up at the sun. "I have to go, and you must catch up with your family. I will come to Helios this evening." The loudness of the pebbles resumed as he strode off towards George the taxi, leaving me totally flummoxed.

What the hell just happened?

He started to drive off, and he shouted back at me. "I forgot to say. Your water ran out because of my other sister. Demeter."

I waved, humouring him again. "Whatever you say!" *You're a fucking nutcase.*

I could feel the heat of the sun burning my skin. The temperature was getting to my head, and I was feeling dizzy. It was time to get some sunscreen on, and I needed a beer. I strolled back to the hotel, steaming my e-cig all the way.

Wait until I tell them I'd met another weirdo. He knows my destiny... my arse.

But he'd really got under my skin. He might be a bit eccentric, but I still got the feeling there was a job opportunity here – a chance to turn my dreams into reality. But is it what I really wanted?

Am I ready?

I thought hard to myself about our previous visits. I needed to know why we were so drawn to Helios.

HELIOS – *God of the Sun*

Kam and the kids had unpacked everything and left me with no coat-hangers. My case was under the dressing table in the bedroom. I just left it there. I could get clothes out as I needed them.

"Hey, you'll never guess who I saw down the beach… Do you guys remember George, the crazy taxi driver? He isn't called George. He's called Zeus."

"That's nice dear. Is he friends with Moses, and does he play darts?"

"No, he told me his name is Zeus, and he's coming to the hotel tonight."

"Maybe he'll bring Athena with him. Did you take your hat to the beach with you? You know how the sun gets to you."

"Now you're taking the piss."

To which she laughed and dived for the shower. Alyss came out of the bathroom in a cloud of steam and deodorant.

"Alyss. You remember George, the taxi driver, don't you? He's called Zeus, and he's..."

" ...Coming tonight with Athena. I know, I heard. Tell

someone that cares," she scowled. She was still upset that we were thinking about selling up and moving to Rhodes.

≈≈≈

We were dressed for dinner in our brand-new holiday clothes, bought from Primarni. My shirt and trousers were creased like the bark of a tree. This wasn't surprising given they had only just been removed from my suitcase under the dressing table. I was topping up my e-cig with an oregano flavoured e-liquid when I heard voices at the door. *Ding-Dong.* The doorbell chimed, and Kam responded, "Avon calling." *Why change the habit of a lifetime?* She was already walking towards the door to open it when it was opened from the other side. Kam jumped back with the shock of the door swinging towards her.

"George?! I mean, Zeus. I assumed you meant later this evening." He evidently hadn't showered because I could still smell the goat and wet earth. He immediately handed Kam a bottle filled with some strange coloured liquid – and a man who was stood with him handed her a set of shot glasses.

"We don't have time, and I wanted to speak to all four of you together." At which he strode into the lounge and plonked himself down on the sideboard. "Let me introduce my cousin. He is glad to have finally met you." And he gestured towards the other man. "Rod, this is one of my oldest friends, he shares his name with the hotel. This is Helios. Helios, this is Rod, Kam, Lindon and Alyss. They are here to help us save the hotel. Kam, pour six shots for us." Kam gave a concerned frown. "Shall I call the police?"

All six eyes of the rest of the Princes looked straight at me.

I eyed Helios. He was a handsome young man with mid-length golden blond hair and a cheeky grin. He had well-honed facial features, not at all like craggy Zeus. He appeared to be in his late teens. His skin was white as ivory, like Lindon's. I got the feeling he spent most of his time in his bedroom playing on a computer. *Harmless*, I thought. And I was intrigued. They were an odd pair, but I still felt there might be a job offer in the air.

"Take a seat."

"Rod, Helios oversees everything at the hotel that has to do with light—"

"Enough of this," I asserted, stopping him in his tracks. Kam and the kids looked at me, a little surprised at my confidence. I have to admit. I was a little taken aback myself. "Listen, Zeus, if that is your real name… What did you mean we are here to help you save the hotel?"

"Oh, you still haven't figured that out yet?" he questioned.

"Are you offering me a job?" I persisted.

Pallid Helios interrupted. "*Yiasas* family."

"Helios, you're the electrician? You want me to help fix up the hotel?" I queried. They both laughed at me.

"*Oxi,* his job is a little more complex than that. If it includes light, Helios manages it. Daylight entertainment, electric light, spotlights, enlightenment, flight information, customer delight…"

"Whoa, before you say sunlight, can we rewind a little please, did you say enlightenment?"

"*Nai,*" they chorused together.

They're bloody Tweedledum and Tweedledee now.

Helios approached me and entered my personal space. He

stood so close, I could smell his sunny disposition. His skin was as white as alabaster. It was almost blinding. He spoke softly, but quite seriously, with wisdom that belied his youthful appearance. Almost whispering, he confided. "I understand from Zeus you are searching for enlightenment. That is why he summoned me." He hastily corrected himself. "I mean, er, asked me to come over." And he flashed a cheeky grin.

Kam and the kids all looked at me again. I guessed what they were thinking. Lindon confirmed it by silently mouthing the word "weirdos".

Surely, my legacy can't be that I attract weirdos.

All I could think of was the Johnny Nash hit. *There Are More Questions Than Answers*. I wished I could hear another of his hits, *I can see clearly now*. All these pair were doing was convincing me that they were raving bonkers.

Kam, repeating my question, asked, "What do you mean we are here to help you save the hotel?"

Zeus looked at Helios and laughed. "Well, that is two of them."

I was flummoxed. "Eh? You what?"

"You're a worrier aren't you, Rod? What about you, Lindon? Or Alyss? Do you know what we mean?" asked Zeus.

"Nope," replied Lindon.

"Don't care," shrugged Alyss.

Helios spoke sternly. "Zeus, that's enough. Let's stop with the cryptic clues and mind games. We should enlighten them."

Zeus tutted like a kid that had been put on the naughty step. "Family, please join us in a toast to enlightenment."

Kam pointed out, "But Alyss and Lindon aren't old

enough to drink alcohol."

"It isn't alcohol. It is a sweet beverage we drink. We call it nectar."

The family looked at me to take the lead. *Dare we trust them?* I sniffed at it. It smelt like syrup. I let it touch my lips and then licked the sweetness from them.

Zeus smiled as I caught his eye. He looked into me like he could see right through me. "We can offer you more than just a job, Rob. We can offer you a legacy."

The confusion that'd been swirling in my head fell into place, and the nectar tantalised my nostrils.

Well, the nectar is free, and you only live once.

I necked the shot. The others took this as a signal to follow suit.

Alyss voiced her approval. "Mmmm nice."

"Too sweet for me, I'm afraid," was my judgment. It didn't taste nearly as nice as it smelled. I have a sweet tooth, but this was too much. My mouth felt like someone had given me a *jar* of golden syrup. It filled with spittle as if I was about to vomit the sweetness back up. I felt the heat and humidity rise in the suite. A bead of sweat trickled down my temple, and I started to feel irritated and confused again. "What is this? What in God's name are you two on about? You guys are crazy, and I must be crazy to be listening to you," I snapped.

"Take a seat," invited Zeus, pulling out his phone. "Helios turn on the TV." I took him up on his invitation because the heat was overpowering and had left me lightheaded.

As the smart TV burst into life, a video started to play. It was a video of our entry into a hotel suite. I recognised it as

208. We looked exactly the way we did last year, same clothes and all. *Cheeky fuckers had a camera in the room, and there must be a law against that. They're psychos.* I looked at Kam; she too had beads of sweat accumulating on her forehead. She must have been thinking the same as me. *Was the camera still running two hours later when the kids left us alone for an hour?* My cheeks burned as the blood rushed to them and formed an embarrassed blush. The sudden rush of blood compounded the effects of the heat I was experiencing. I experienced the same sensations that panicked me when we'd entered 208 a year earlier. My chest started to tighten and distracted me momentarily from the events on the TV:

> Two men stood in front of the full-length patio windows. The sun behind them was bright, and they were silhouetted against the whiteness of the sunlight. The camera angle didn't reveal their faces.
>
> The man to the right congratulated the other. "Well done George, you have almost completed your labour."
>
> "Helios, stop fucking calling me George, my name is Zeus," he bellowed.
>
> "I will start calling you Zeus when you stop swearing. I am Helios, the first King of Rhodes. I will not be sworn at. We aren't in Olympus now. This is my realm."
>
> The Zeus on the screen grunted.

As did the Zeus in the room. My chest tightened, and I struggled to concentrate. My entire upper body was sodden, and my clothes looked like they had been in the shower with me. *Shit. I'm having a fucking heart attack.* On the screen. Helios continued his script.

> "You must return my descendants to their resting
> places. Take them to the four royal and ancient
> cities of the island. I want it done before the sun
> sets, is that CLEAR?"
> "Set to 200, CLEAR."

"Shit my chest is on fire – help me," was all I could groan to my family. I glanced across at Kam, and she too was pallid, her clothes dripping moisture onto the floor by her feet.

> "Set to 400, CLEAR."

Another burning sensation.

Lindon shouted, "Why aren't you guys helping us? Get a fucking ambulance."

Alyss appeared to have passed out. I barely heard Zeus as he lowered his voice to a whisper. "Not long now. Just keep watching, and the pain will be over for you all.

The sound and visuals from the video seemed to fill the room, enveloping us … and the scene cut to a hospital.

> Crowds of nurses and doctors gathered in
> huddles.
> "We have lost them. We have lost the whole
> family."

All we could hear in the room was the sound of a quartet of heart monitors as they all flatlined in perfect harmony. It was like a scene from Casualty.

The video then cut to 208 again. Suddenly the suite felt ice-cold like a chilled wine cellar. The pain was gone, and my clothes were dry. I looked around at my family, and they were all sat bolt upright, like the trip to the emergency room hadn't just happened. *What the fuck? Had we been drugged? That was some daydream.*

Zeus and Helios were still in the room, and while we tried to gather our thoughts – and hold on to reality – they were just calmly watching the video of themselves that continued to play:

> "Zeus, you should make your way to the hospital in Ixia, pick up their Highnesses spirits for interment. Take Rod to Rhodes, bring Kam back here to Kamiros, Alyss will go to Ialyssos and Lindon will rest in Lindos."

We all sat in stunned silence. *Had the bastards secretly videoed our arrival to make some kind of medical drama?* The video cut to a scene in a mortuary.

> Following the convention of surname first, a nurse on the video used the victims' passports to write their toe tags.
> Prince, Rod
> Prince, Kam
> Prince, Lindon
> Prince, Alyss

The video ended, and the screen went black. Beyond bewildered, tired of the confusion, I just needed an answer. I turned to Zeus and demanded information. "What. The. Fuck. Was that?"

"That is the edited video of what happened as your bodies entered 208. After you were all killed. You didn't survive when the taxi crashed and overturned on that final bend into Helios," lamented Helios.

"B-B-B-But…" I stammered, unable to believe. "But we are still here… so that video can't be—?"

"I'm afraid it is real. As genuine as Zeus and me."

And that's supposed to make me believe it actually happened?

I pinched myself and bit down hard on my tongue to remind myself I could feel pain. And confirm I wasn't dead.

Lindon looked as confused as I was feeling. "What a fucking sick joke to play on someone!" he shouted.

The girls were in tears. I was as stunned. "What the hell do you mean, we were killed? I knew you were fucking nutcases! Get out!"

Zeus handed me a package. "Here are the contracts for you all to sign. It is the job offer you were seeking. There is some background. A job description and person specifications. Take care to read them all thoroughly, and they will answer all your questions. If you need to shed light on anything else, Helios will be on hand to enlighten you." And he went. Gone. I mean, *he vanished*, leaving Helios to face the consequences of our confusion. No goodbye, no irritating laugh, nothing – he disappeared, leaving just silence, and the sinking realisation: *this was fucking happening.*

I held Kam's hand tightly, closed my eyes, trying to cling to reality and deny it was happening. "Helios, please help us understand. There must be some kind of misunder—."

"Open the package. There are lots of answers to your questions." Without skipping a beat, I opened the packaging. Just as Zeus had said, there it was. A golden glowing contract of employment slid from the package and settled in my hands.

Contract of Employment

Background: Hotel Helios is under attack, as it has been for several years. The hotel is the very heart of Rhodes and if it were to stop beating, then Rhodes as you know it will perish. The ground that Helios is built upon is sacred and holds the spirits of the gods of Olympus. If this hallowed ground is disturbed, tourism on Rhodes will die. All life on the island will cease to exist. The roles you are filling have arisen due to a shortage of suitable applicants. Training will be available, and you will have ample opportunity to upskill. The company are looking for staff to seek out, and neutralise, those that are causing the hotel harm.

Company Structure: Olympian Dreams (Hereafter called Olympian) is jointly owned by four gods/goddesses (Hereafter called Deities). Together they will be referred to as the board or the company. The deities are **Zeus** (CEO, King of the gods), **Helios** (god of the Sun and Director of Light), **Hera** (Mrs Zeus, Director of Guest Services and goddess of Families), **Hades** (Director of Staffing and god of the Underworld and the Dead).

The Helios Hotel (Hereafter called Helios) is owned by **Mister Vangelis Filipos** and is the subject of much concern to the Olympian Board. The long-term goal of the Olympian board is to ensure that Helios continues to thrive, thereby ensuring the continued survival of Rhodes as a major tourist destination. Short-term goals include but are not limited to ensuring the ~~Phoenix~~ Helios completes its ~~rising from the ashes~~/refurbishment in line with the 500-week cycle discussed during your interview.

The Princes: Rod Prince, **Kam** Prince, **Lindon** Prince and **Alyss** Prince. (Hereafter referred to as the family or the Princes). The family has been bestowed with resurrective immortality.

The company have managed to inter your spirits, in the four holy cities of the island. Rhodes, Kamiros, Lindos and Ialyssos. Hades is the protector of said tombs. So long as the tombs remain undisturbed, you will retain your immortality. You have been given this status because you are all descendants of Helios.

Remuneration: You will each be paid a monthly retainer fee of four thousand euros. You will have the opportunity to define your destiny and leave an enduring legacy.

Roles and Responsibilities: The family will be expected to use all means and powers at their disposal. The family will ensure that our competitors are not able to threaten the key aims of the board. Over the last few seasons, we have seen an increase in the number of incursions and sabotage attempts.

Key competitors include but are not limited to **Prometheus** – God of Mischief. He is a trickster, and he hates Zeus. **Poseidon** – god of Seas, Rivers and Earthquakes. He is jealous that Zeus gave the island of Rhodes to Helios, believing Rhodes should belong to him as it rose from one of his seas. **Hestia** – Goddess of the Home, Food and Cooking. **Demeter** – goddess of Harvest and Agriculture. Both Hestia and Demeter want to remove tourism from the island and make agriculture its key industry and income stream.

You will be expected to piece together your experiences, identify each deity and the mortal forms they have taken. It will be your goal to destroy, thwart or undermine all attempts at sabotage. Your focus should also include mortals that may be in the employ of said deities (hereafter called cronies).

You are under no obligation to sign this contract. If you accept the role, you will retain your immortality. The cost will be that you may only leave the island with the express permission of the CEO. The contract has a fixed term until the 17th Day of April in the year 2018 (using the Julian calendar).

Should you decline the offer, your immortality will be revoked, and you will be free to leave the island. You will return to an unknown destiny, leaving your spirits at the four holy sites of the island. Remember that mortality brings the risk of death.

Please find attached non-disclosure agreements, for you to sign.

In 2018 the hotel will be closed for ~~rising from the ashes~~/refurbishment. Your task is to ensure it remains open and prosperous until the end of the 2017 season and subsequently reopens for business Easter 2019.

Signed

Zeus

Zeus for and on Behalf of Olympian Dreams - 17th April 2014

Please sign alongside your name

Rod Prince... 17th April 2014

Kam Prince... 17th April 2014

Lindon Prince... 17th April 2014

Alyss Prince... 17th April 2014

Your employment will begin when you sign this document.

Witness .... 17th April 2014

I looked up from the contract at Kam, the kids, and then at Helios. "You've killed my whole family!"

"Well, that's not strictly true Rod, on several points. One, I didn't kill you, Zeus did. Two, you are technically still alive, you're all immortal. Three, I am part of your family, and I have never died."

I buried my head in my hands, and, well, nothing – I could come up with nothing. I am generally an optimistic kind of guy, but I struggled to see any light at the end of this particular tunnel. The silence hung in the air like a dense fog.

Lindon was first to speak. "I want to be Kratos."

"What?" I snapped.

"I want to be Kratos, God of War."

Helios pointed out that "Kratos isn't real. He is a fictional character from a computer game. Besides, there is already a god of war. He is Ares, and we don't want to pick a battle with him right now. I might add, you are not a god yet, you are merely immortal. It's my guess that if you meet your KPI, Zeus may offer you a godship."

"What's KPI?" asked Alyss

"Key Performance Indicator," Helios and I answered together.

Helios added "Meet your KPI, and you get promoted. Fall short of your KPI, and you get sacked."

"You mean killed," I corrected. "I knew there was a catch."

"You are under no obligation to sign the contract. You can rip it up, pack your bags and go back to England. You will be free to carry on your life as it was… I mean *is*. You will return to your old life, no immortality, no legacy, no spirit. You must ask yourselves if you want a chance to fulfil your destiny? Or do you want to return to a life of mediocrity? You need to face your truth that you've always lacked confidence in yourself. I believe you need to take this risk to find your peace. Rod, you and your family, are the last of my line, and potentially you can be the greatest of all my descendants. Do you want to leave a legacy that will have a true impact? I will leave you alone to discuss it. Then I will come back before midnight and witness your signatures."

I grunted because it was all I could muster. His reply. "See you later."

BAD GODS – *Mischief*

For the next few hours, we spent a lot of time discussing our predicament. Discussing the paradox and drinking a lot of alcohol. We'd been killed, but we weren't dead. If we took the risk, we would live forever. If we didn't, we would eventually be gone and forgotten. But to the outside world, we were already dead. In short, dead, not dead, but might end up dead.

The last time I consulted with Lindon about anything was probably to ask him if he wanted an ice-lolly or an ice cream when he was about five. The consequences of this decision would have an eternal effect on him and Alyss, so I felt compelled to involve them in the search for an answer. "What do you think, Son?"

"I think it is worth the risk. Everything will be the same, but we will have money and lots of time. But I still want to be called Kratos."

"Helios told you he isn't real."

"Oh, right. And Helios, the god of the sun is real, is he?"

I sort of got his point. Before that day, I would have argued that Zeus, Helios and immortality were mythical.

"What about you, Sweetheart?" I asked, turning to Alyss.

"I'll miss my friends," she stammered between sobs.

This struck a chord with me too. I'd been searching for my destiny, my legacy. But I had always wondered how it would be to walk away from everything familiar. Would the price be too high? Could I dare to risk everything? "But what was Helios saying about being killed?"

"He never said that. You said it, Dad," corrected Lindon

"Yes, but he didn't deny it."

"We can't expect to fight the gods without getting a few scratches. Besides we're immortal."

I was still unsure of the risk we were taking. "I don't know. I'm not convinced they won't kill us if we fail to meet our KPI."

Then Kam put her tuppence worth in. "Well, maybe we could take a few more risks. Add a little bit of spice to life. Let's look at the consequences as if they were a set of balance scales. What have we got to lose by accepting the challenge? What have we got to lose by walking away? Then we can look at what we have to gain."

"You mean we carry out some kind of risk assessment." Finally, something I understood. *Unit Two of Health and Safety in Customer Service. NVQ Level One.*

We carried out the risk assessment, and it was no surprise that it confused me even more. In the end, Kam and Lindon wanted to sign the contract and take the risk. Alyss said she wished to return to her old life. But more importantly, she wanted us all to be together. Her decision was to sign if everyone else was going to sign. All eyes were on me.

"Come on, Dad, it'll be fun." *Didn't I just know he would say that?*

Kam pointed out, "You've been saying you wanted a bit more excitement in our marriage."

But this isn't the kind of excitement I had in mind.

All the while, I'd been fidgeting with the change in my pocket. Then I did something I couldn't have imagined possible at any other moment in my life. I pulled out a coin and spun it into the air. "Heads we sign," I shouted. The coin span with the speed of a child's spinning top. It hung in the air, as it reached its highest point flickering as it reflected the light it was catching from the downlighters in the ceiling. Then it started its slow and laboured descent as if gravity had deserted it. If I didn't know better, I would have said time stood still. Being the most agile of the four of us, Lindon reached out and caught it with his right hand. In a split second, he'd slapped it onto the back of his left hand.

Everyone adjusted their position and held their breath. And the decision was made. All that was needed was for Lindon to move his hand to reveal what the decision was.

"Are you sure you want to do it this way, Dad, on the toss of a coin?"

I took a deep breath. "In for a penny, in for a pound."

He lifted his hand to reveal the coin. And he said, "No, it is in for a fifty pence piece."

I rubbed my eyes to make sure I was actually seeing the head of Queen Elizabeth.

Finally, it was decided. We would take the risk, and if we didn't like it, we could walk. All that would be different is walk away now or walk away later. At least if we had immortality, we had time to change our minds. *If we sign then walk away later, doesn't that mean we haven't met our KPI? What was it Helios said?*

We enjoyed staying at the hotel, and we had stayed there often enough. Being paid for something you enjoy has to be a dream, doesn't it? Besides, we'd already been planning to sell up and move to Rhodes for a season. Kam had always wanted to see a Greek Christmas. Nothing in our plans had changed, with the exception that we couldn't leave the island.

In the end, it wasn't a difficult decision to make; it came down to live forever or die at some unknown time. And who knows, that time could be within weeks. Lindon and Alyss complicated it a little because he still didn't see why he couldn't be Kratos. And she still wanted to be in Cheshire. We'd also got a little side-tracked a few times. Especially the realisation that as descendants of Helios, Kam and I were related to each other. We hoped we were just very distant cousins.

Laughing. Lindon pointed out, "That makes Alyss an inbred. That explains a lot."

Alyss retorted, "And you too, dickhead." Lindon stopped laughing.

Helios returned, and he had a bottle of ouzo with him. "Have you made your decision?"

"Yes, we're going to sign. But we aren't happy about not being able to leave the island."

"Read the contract. You can leave the island you just need permission from Zeus. And it's only until April 2018, when your contract is up."

"What happens then?"

"You will be free of the contract. Depending on how successful you are, you will retain your immortality or not. Come on, Rod, it isn't a difficult contract to understand." He signalled his irritation by snatching the contract to show me. "Here…"

"Well, excuse me if I'm a bit confused, it's not every day you find out you are dead, not dead."

He handed the contract back to me. I tried to iron out the wrinkles with the side of my hand. *My legacy wasn't going to be a tatty piece of paper.*

"To celebrate, we should all have a shot of ouzo. It will seal the deal."

I was wary. "It's not that nectar shit again is it?"

"No, of course not. I prefer ouzo. Nectar is Zeus's tipple." Helios reassured me that we weren't going to be drugged.

He passed me a pen and a shot glass. I necked the ouzo and signed the contract.

The next moment we found ourselves in the reception at Olympian Dreams. Zeus was there. The reception area was massive with acres of cream and white marble. It looked classy, and there were statues all along one wall. The figures seemed to be positioned so that they could watch the reception desk. They appeared to be made of marble. Parts of each of the statues were decorated with coloured paint. They all had gold coloured decorations. This was a proper five-star place. The words 'Olympian Dreams' were written in two-foot-high gold letters along the same wall and above the reception desk. The brightness of the gold was highlighted by the spotlights used to illuminate the words. I glanced at the calendar on the wall, and it shouted out 17th April 2014. *Fuck me. We've teleported.*

"Ok we've signed your contract, what now?" I questioned Zeus.

"Simple. Book yourselves into Helios for the season."

I voiced my concern at his plan. "Won't that seem suspicious given that we've always done it a week at a time?"

I could tell he was getting irritated because his voice went up a few decibels. He was irritated. "OK then, go and have your week. Then keep extending it."

I tried to negotiate without pleading. "How about, we have our week. Then you let us go back to the UK. We have a lot of loose ends to tie up."

He obviously didn't trust us to come back. He resorted to threats. "You do know I can revoke your immortality anywhere in the world."

I tried to reassure him we weren't going to abscond. "I'm sure you can. We'll be back. We signed the flaming contract, didn't we? And while we're at it, I'd like the kids to finish their schooling. I want them to stay with their Nanna Mags during term-time. Can you give us permission to do that please?"

"OK, but always remember the non-disclosure agreement."

And that was it. We were loaded into George and taken back to Helios. It would have been more fun to teleport back there. Finally, we were able to start our fourth holiday at Helios Hotel.

≈≈≈

We didn't quite know how we'd handle our first holiday after finding out we'd been dead for a year. The ink wasn't dry on the contracts, and we were to carry on as usual. We just had a new normal. Our lives became one long dream, the sort you wake from, and you aren't sure if it was a dream or an experience that really happened.

I did take the opportunity to spend some one-to-one time with Mikalis. The sealed off part of the hotel was due to be opened in two weeks. By all accounts, it is normal for winter refits to run into the start of the season. The hotel was only half full, and he was having quite a tough time of it. The hotel had only been open for a week, and already reception was receiving complaints. Things such as no hot water, no water at all, the smell of sewerage, seaweed in the bay, ants in the rooms, cold food. But we didn't experience any of these issues. Could these events be the bad gods at play? *Not a damn clue,* was my internal conclusion.

Mikalis had his own theories. "Staff from a nearby hotel are coming in and complaining. I've caught someone that wasn't a guest at the hotel, complaining at the reception desk." His greatest concern was that his job was on the line. The owner, Mister Filipos, wasn't happy with the level of complaints, and there was only one person to blame. Poor Mikalis.

We didn't get introduced to Mister Filipos on that holiday. We guessed the important-looking guy, was him. Also, the fact that he was always shouting at staff confirmed it. He seemed a formidable man. I'm surprised to this day that the gods had decided to pick a fight with him. He was a stout man whose black hair was swept back. Greying temples bestowed him with a look of wisdom and experience. His thick eyebrows accentuated a stern look while he was shouting at staff. He never had to state he was angry. His face gave it away. He had the look of Edward G Robinson. No wonder Mikalis feared him.

We had developed a friendship with Mikalis, and it was sad to see him struggling to find solutions to the issues that were being raised by 'guests'.

"You should try being in my shoes," he said. "Only then you will understand."

I think he meant it as a figure of speech, but I took him up on his offer. I only had shorts and t-shirts in my luggage. A mythos logo on a white vest top didn't really present a professional image. He managed to rustle up a shirt and tie and some black trousers for me. *I'm sure he said to be in his shoes.* The outfit he provided didn't really go with my white trainers. I just had to hide my legs behind the reception counter.

I'd barely had time to orientate myself in reception, and my first complaint came along. I knew instantly that the approaching guest was going to complain. The body language, clenched fist, glaring eyes accentuated by the light bouncing off the marble walls. After years of working in customer service, you recognise the posture. It is like a champion boxer at a weigh-in. They come prepared for a fight. I pictured him standing toe to toe with me staring into my eyes with zero centimetres between our noses.

Disarm him, Rod. I put on my most charming customer focussed smile. "Good morning sir, how may I help you?"

He continued to glare, slammed his fist down on the counter and then started his tirade. "I have no water, and this hotel is a dump." Before I could even enquire about the room number, his volume increased. "I want a full refund, I have paid a lot of money to stay in this hovel. I want a pool upgrade, and I want water in my taps." All the while, he was thumping the table and waving his finger at me. *Keep talking like that, and you'll get fuck all mate*, I thought to myself. I let him continue his rant until he ran out of steam. Finally, I managed to get his name and room number.

I needed to get him out of reception. Other guests were starting to listen in and next thing the bandwagon would have been overloaded with passengers. "Come, Mister Ransom, let us go to your room," I invited. As I stepped from behind the counter, he glanced down at my feet. *Bugger*.

As we neared his room, I spotted the front door to the adjacent room was ajar. I could hear voices, and this prompted me to stop and knock on the door. "Hello?" I called. A woman came to the door. "Good morning madam, I am working with the manager of the hotel. Can I ask if you have had any problems with the water today?"

"No, it has been fine, we did lose it for ten minutes yesterday, but it wasn't inconvenient."

I had come out my corner fighting and taken the first round. I had another a guest illustrating that it wasn't something to get wound up about.

"Thank you and sorry to have troubled you."

Ransom grunted his displeasure. "That proves nothing. She probably used all of her water and mine." We went to Ransom's room, and as expected, the water was working. This irritated him, and he continued to grumble. "Don't try and make me out to be a liar. You call this a five-star hotel. More like two bloody stars. Whoever heard of a hotel where the water packs in?"

I was in danger of losing round two on points. I had to respond. I didn't want an obnoxious guest to think I was calling him a liar. I had to come up with some bullshit. "I am sorry for the inconvenience it has caused you. Unfortunately, sometimes on Rhodes, the water pressure drops under heavy usage. It is an island problem." And then I threw an uppercut. "Would you allow me to buy you a bottle of wine or a spirit by way of compensation?"

I'd boxed him into a corner. I'd left him with nowhere to go with his complaint. And then I threw the knockout punch. "Would I be able to tempt you with a bottle of the hotels finest champagne?" He had no choice but to accept my offer of restitution. If he continued to pursue his complaint, even his tour operator would think he was unreasonable. And I saved the hotel an expensive upgrade. *Was Ransom a bad god or the victim of a bad god? This job is going to be more difficult than I thought.*

I'd just got back to reception, and the poor receptionist was in the middle of her own heavyweight bout. She was losing the round and receiving her own verbal battering from another guest.

This one wanted his money back so he could go and stay at another hotel.

"I paid a lot of money for a room with a pool, and I expected it to be heated. My wife has caught a cold from swimming in it."

Surely, I didn't hear that right. Are you fucking kidding me? Put your smile on, Rod.

"I'm sorry to hear that, Mister…?" I enquired.

"Riley," he snapped.

"I am sorry for the way you are feeling. I would like to help you, but I am unable to authorise a refund of that amount. I don't have the authority. Would you like to start from the beginning and permit me to take notes so that I can fully understand what has upset you?"

"We booked a room with its own private pool."

"I see. And who told you it would be a heated pool?"

Gotcha!

I continued, "I am as concerned about your wife's health as you are. Would you allow us to call the local doctor out in case it is more than a cold? The hotel will pay the medical fees, of course."

He squinted and looked at me. I just stared at him, waiting for him to accept my offer. He didn't answer. His only response was to turn and walk away. *Now that's a mischief-maker.*

Mikalis appeared as Riley was leaving. I don't know how much Mikalis saw or heard.

"I am impressed, Rod. You aren't Greek, are you?"

I chuckled inside. "I think I might have Greek ancestors, from many generations ago."

Mikalis showed me a pile of papers on his desk. They were all written complaints, and there were around twenty of these. We were only in the second week of the season. He told me that they'd only had a hundred rooms filled to that point. Twenty written complaints from a hundred rooms. No wonder he feared for his job.

He passed me one from the top of the pile. A lady was complaining that on Sunday morning the gardeners were mowing the lawns and she couldn't read her book. He passed me a second printed email. From the similarity of the email addresses, it appeared to be from her husband. He was complaining the grass was too long. I didn't know when the hotel should tend to the gardens. But Mikalis certainly shouldn't have to get involved in the couple's marital disharmony.

In another complaint, the glass door to the shower had shattered. Despite the whole hotel hearing the argument that the couple had with each other. They tried to maintain that they weren't in the room when it shattered. I thought I'd seen it all. Every complaint I saw was trying to reclaim all or part of the cost of their holiday. Some tried to claim more than the price of their holiday.

Mikalis lamented, "What can I do? If I accuse them of lying, they complain about my service. If I meet their demands, Mister Filipos sees me as weak. I cannot afford to lose my job. I cannot win."

I felt so much empathy for him. "You can only do what you think is right. What is right for you? Be true to yourself. If it all goes wrong, at least you know you have done the right thing."

"I have a reputation…" He was interrupted by the ringtone on his mobile. "I am needed in reception. Another complaint."

"Please Mikalis. Let me see if I can deal with it."

"OK. If you need to refund, let me know, and I will authorise it."

"You can't. Some customers will always make unreasonable demands."

He countered with the old maxim, "The customer is always right."

"No, they're not. The customer always thinks they're right. It's our job to educate them. Let them see that what they are asking is not reasonable. Tell them what you can do for them. Sometimes that is enough. The two complaints I dealt with went away, and it only cost me a bottle of champagne."

As I left the back office, I could hear a booming voice. I turned the corner into reception and then I saw the face."

I put on my best customer service smile. "Good morning sir, how can I help you?"

"I want my money back. I am not getting what I paid for. You have robbed me. You are thieves."

"Sir. Could we go to your room where it is a little more private, and I can resolve your issues."

I started to walk towards the apartment blocks, and he followed, continuing his tirade. Once we were clear of the main building and alone. I turned and challenged the complainant. "What the hell are you doing?"

"Rod. You signed my contract. You were told to just be a holidaymaker."

"No, Zeus. You told me to identify, challenge and use all the powers at my disposal. I was presented with an opportunity to see people complaining at first hand."

"You are reckless and foolhardy. You are putting yourself and your family at risk."

"But we are immortal."

"Not if this escapade ends up with disclosure. Then where will you be?" *Did he just fucking threaten me?* "Your immortality is a gift from me, and I am your employer. You would do well to remember that." And he stormed off.

I returned to Mikalis' office. "That's resolved. He admitted it was a misunderstanding and withdrew his complaint. And it didn't cost the hotel a cent."

≈≈≈

Throughout the holiday I must have spent two hours a day with Mikalis. Either at the reception desk, which was light and airy. Or in his office, which was a dark smoke-filled cupboard. The conversations always followed a similar pattern.

Deep down, I knew that if the bad gods were doing much of the complaining, we could do nothing. I became Mikalis protector and the bond I developed with him during that week became an enduring one.

I spent a similar amount of time with Zeus, but I had trouble developing any kind of bond with him. He was a control freak, as you would expect from the king of the gods.

His manner, his tone and his volume generated fear. To be honest, we had no idea if what Zeus was telling us was correct. What if he was a schizophrenic with delusions of godliness? We had no evidence that he wasn't. The fear he generated gave us no choice but to believe him.

The end of the stay came around all too quickly. We couldn't really call it a holiday. I'd spent most of the time away from the rest of the family.

"Mikalis, thank you for making our holiday so special. We will be back to your beautiful hotel very soon, not sure about the dates, but we will be back in a few weeks."

"We wait for you, and thank you for listening to me," he replied. Then followed hugs and double cheek kisses all round.

As we walked out of the hotel, I saw a taxi pull onto the

forecourt. It was George. Zeus got out and loaded our bags into the boot. Then he looked at me. "Thank you all for everything. You will never know how much your sacrifice means to the island." He had obviously forgotten about the veiled threat he made when we last spoke.

Still irked that he dared to make threats. My resentment was still visible. "I don't think you know how much the success of your plan means to us. What with your personal lack of death experiences."

Given that we were about to have another hair-raising ride, I was surprised none of us showed any fear. What's the worst that could happen? He couldn't kill us.

Lindon must have been having similar thoughts because he made a comment. "It's kind of cool being a zombie."

I gave him a look that relayed my thoughts; *please shut the fuck up*. Zeus just roared with laughter.

≈≈≈

I've been a people watcher, a private person for most of my life. So, on returning home, my lack of holiday anecdotes for my work colleagues wasn't seen as unusual. Though I did share some holiday pictures to show how beautiful the hotel was.

The anecdotes did flow with my learners on the courses I delivered. *'Shrugging shoulders'* got an honourable mention. As did taxi drivers that have a duty of care to their passengers. It was during this time that I realised what a tedious and faceless existence my work had been up to this point. I'd convinced myself that I was making a difference. I was changing lives, and I was making people employable by helping them find work. Or I was teaching customer service and hospitality courses. I don't recall any learner ever saying that they needed my help. Or that my contribution would be remembered for all eternity. *Perhaps Zeus had done me a favour.*

≈≈≈

"I had a moment at work today. I found myself thinking that I'm glad we're where we are," I opened to Kam.

"That's weird, so did I," she agreed.

As the weeks passed, the whole family adapted to immortality. We were all much more confident, knowing nothing could harm us. We did have to tell Lindon to tone down his free-running activities. Reminding him that the non-disclosure agreement included negligence. Such as crossing the road without looking. If anyone saw him survive a fall from a tall building, he would have disclosed. He listened because he didn't want his immortality revoked. He was enjoying the whole fiasco.

Kam managed to find Mister Filipos on Facebook and sent a friend request. We had several conversations with him. Because he was mortal, we weren't sure how much he knew about our status. It soon became apparent that he was oblivious. To him, we were paying guests that enjoyed staying at his hotel and wanted to return. Oblivious or non-disclosing. I made a mental note to ask Zeus or Helios if they used social networking.

We raved about the hotel to family. When Kam's mum, Mags, said she envied us we invited her on our next visit. We decided the last week in May was when we would go. We borrowed money from Mags because we hadn't received our first salary payment yet. We booked online and made sure we printed the receipt for an expenses claim.

≈≈≈

The remainder of any time we spent together, was like a mythical game of *whodunnit*. We would look at pictures of the April holiday and try to guess who the bad gods and cronies were.

"I reckon the head housekeeper is one of them," calculated Kam, using her feminine intuition. "She seemed a bit shifty. Especially after she chased a guest with a carving knife. But if she is head of housekeeping, that would make her Hestia. And Hestia was the matronly karate lady."

"Can they take on more than one form?" I asked before answering my own question. "Hestia could be karate lady and the carving knife nutter."

"OK smartypants, that means it's pointless trying to figure anything out before we go back there," she responded. The same way children would if they had a kick about and one of them punctured the ball.

Lindon had become quite astute. He'd raised the question of disclosure. "We can't disclose, but that doesn't tell us who knows." We had signed up for the job, but we didn't have any idea who knew we had. Did Mikalis know? What about other gods? We still weren't sure if Filipos knew or not. Even though he was mentioned in the contract.

I assumed Helios' enlightenment would answer all the questions. But no, I still had Johnny Nash singing away inside my head. For a song with a chorus and just two verses, it soon gets mind-numbing *…And the more I find out, the less I know….*

78

Although I had more questions than answers, and that line started Johnny worming in my ears every day.

We all had an overwhelming sense that our minds had altered, almost like we'd gone insane and lost touch with reality. Maybe we had. But real or not, we'd started to think about things differently. Is it possible for four people to lose touch with reality at the same time? Even more, four people sharing the same *new* reality. I noticed we'd all become more analytical and tended to question everything.

At one-point, Alyss suggested, "Greeks had lots of famous philosophers."

Maybe she was right, and maybe she wasn't. I do know that Wikipedia listed 356 of them, almost one for every day of the year. Is that relevant? Maybe it is, maybe it isn't. More than once, I asked myself: *could I put up with an eternity of thinking like this?* The answer to that, of course, is yes. Because an eternity of philosophising might be better than having our immortality revoked.

HESTIA – Of the Hearth

We exited arrivals, unaware of what we were expecting. My concern was we could be bringing Mags into a den of wolves, and the wolves were all in sheep's clothing. How do you recognise a god when they don't want to be identified? I spotted George in the taxi rank, and Zeus looked like a weirdo.

I gave a smile and a nod to acknowledge that I'd seen him. He came scuttling across the traffic, stopping taxis and transfer coaches in his wake. Like Moses parting the Red Sea.

"Mags, this is Zeus, a friend we met in April. Zeus this is Kam's mother, Mags."

Zeus as smarmy as ever bent and kissed her hand. I had a sudden thought. If Kam was a descendant of Helios, then Mags could've been too. Unless it was Kams dad's side of the family.

"Rod, it's the latter," muttered Zeus, almost in a whisper. He grinned then spoke a little louder. "It is good to see you all again, where are you staying?"

"The usual, we have booked a hire car to drive ourselves there."

He looked sheepishly at me. "Umm, about the hire car…"

And I shot him a look that translated to "*don't you dare,*" before voicing my thoughts. "You've bloody cancelled it haven't you. Don't forget we have Mags in the car, and at seventy-five she won't adapt to your style of driving. No phone this time, please."

It was a bit of a squeeze, not to mention illegal, with me in the front and the other four in the back.

As we unloaded our cases from the back of George, I could feel the sun starting to burn my scalp through my thinning hair. Mags, in her naivety of our situation, pulled out a ten euro note and handed it to Zeus. Zeus looked at me, and I frowned at him. He appeared to understand my warning, and he politely refused to accept the tip. "No, you are family, I don't charge family."

Mags looked puzzled for a moment, and Kam reassured her. "He means we are close friends and the taxi journey was free."

"Mates rates," said Lindon.

Mags looked more confused than ever. "Oh, you are a very nice man. Thank you."

I was keen to get out of the gaze of Helios because he was now high in the sky. I lead the way into the reception area. "Let's get into the cool."

I shouted farewell to Zeus, to which he replied, "I will come and see you in an hour." And he jumped into George.

Alyss squealed "owwwww." Zeus had spun the wheels of George, peppering her legs with pea grit.

Lyndon gave her some sound advice. "When you see Zeus

get into George, you should move away from the back of the car. Stupid." *He sounded like he cared until he called her stupid.*

As soon as we were in the cool of the reception area, I saw Mikalis, he glanced up, and a broad grin appeared on his face. Apparently, he had been waiting to greet us. "Ah Rod and Kam, welcome back. Mister Filipos, look we have returning guests. They visited us last year, and this is already their second visit this year."

"Ah, Rod and Kam from Facebook," smiled Filipos.

"It's good to see you in real life," I responded. He didn't kiss me, but he kissed Kam's hand.

By this time, Mikalis had grabbed me and gone for the double cheek kiss. I could feel his stubble prickle the soft skin on my face knowing that by the end of the week, I would have a stubble rash. It reminded me why Kam made me shave whenever we had a date night.

"Let me introduce, Mags. She's Kam's mum."

Mags reached out to shake hands with Mikalis. Filipos demonstrating his dominance, grabbed it, dipped his head and kissed the time-worn hand.

Mikalis, knowing his place in the pecking order, waited before giving Mags a double cheek kiss.

The accommodation had already been arranged. We had been given 208 again, and room 209 was allocated to Mags. Alyss decided to share with her. This worked out well because it gave the rest of us time to catch up with Zeus.

"You have got to give us the means to contact you while we aren't here, we have so many questions," I stated.

"You could've called me on my mobile."

"You didn't give it to us."

"It's written on George. Look for yourself," and he gestured towards the car park. "Are you up for the job? I thought you were observant."

"Yes, but I'm not a bloody detective."

Zeus cleared up a few points. "No mortal on the island knows who you are and your situation."

"What about the gods?"

"That is a different matter. We have no way of knowing if they are aware of you."

"Can the deities take on more than one human form?" asked Lindon.

"Yes, of course, we are all shapeshifters."

"And us?"

"Oxi, Oxi, I'm afraid not. The powers you have at present are limited to your human abilities."

Lindon was left disappointed.

Zeus dangled some bait. "That's not to say I can't endow you with certain skills and powers in the future." He paused long enough to see a reaction. "Besides. I have already increased the power of some of your human qualities. Things like reasoning, analysing and logic."

"I noticed that one. I thought we were going mad, questioning everything."

"Now, you will understand why I can't empower you any further. Not until you are ready. For now, your role is to notice and report things that are going wrong."

"If you spot anything at all. If you think it is sabotage, you can intervene."

I likened it to a vaccine against Faulty Towers. I didn't have the faintest idea what intervene might entail.

"Your first task is to gain the trust of Filipos. To him, you are returning guests that like his hotel. An English family he has connected with on Facebook."

≈≈≈

Lindon and Alyss had become friends with the animation team on our last visit. They were keen to see if the same people were still working at the hotel. Alyss had fallen for one of them during a stay in the previous year. I had to remind her she was too young to have a boyfriend in his twenties. "You don't know who the bad gods are. We can't trust anyone at the moment not until we know for sure."

Alessandro called himself Sandro, and he was a dark-skinned Italian with mid-length black hair. His Latin origins were accentuated by a well-defined jawline and piercing dark eyes. My impression of him was that he was a calculating guy. He seemed to have a well-honed ability to read people. The way Zeus had read me. He seemed to enchant the whole family, myself included, but not in the same way that he had Alyss. I was impressed by his skill with guests. Kam, because a young Italian had showered her with attention and compliments. All features that would look at home on a godly CV.

I texted Zeus: "Can the opposition be Italian?"

The reply came back: "Of course, there are many Roman gods."

Kam and I agreed that Sandro might be one to keep our eye on.

Sure enough, he still worked at the hotel. Alyss brought him up to our suite to see us. More double kissing. He hadn't lost any of his Latin charms. He still knew how to make all guests feel special. I suspected that he wasn't an infiltrator. If he had been, he was making a bad job of it because all the guests loved him.

While thinking about the probability of Sandro being a saboteur, I started to understand how our task could be made a bit easier.

Later that evening, I had an opportunity to talk with Kam and Lindon. "We have to identify anyone that is spoiling the hotel's reputation. If they are adding to the service offer, we can ignore them."

"What about guests? Can they be infiltrators?" questioned Lindon.

Kam looked up from Facebook. "I've messaged Zeus."

Ping. "Yes, they can," said Kam without moving a muscle. "Anyone can, and he's using text speak now." She smiled. "*n-e-1*. How sweet, three thousand years old and he is using text speak."

More text exchanges ensued that enlightened us a little more. A deity can switch genders when they shapeshift. *Fuck me. The whole hotel could be full of deities, trying to piss in the ouzo.* The fact they might all be transgender didn't bother me. It was holidaying in "Hotel Zombie, that was the problem," I finished my thought out loud.

Lindon stood as if Man United had scored a goal. "Yes, zombies."

I sat down as if to counter his excitement. "You're flaming

enjoying this, aren't you?" He just grinned.

Always half an hour behind a conversation, I glanced at Kam. "That's not sweet. Little old ladies are sweet. Doddery old men are sweet. He's a zombie, like the rest of them." I corrected myself. "Us."

Lindon came up with an idea. "If we suspect we have found a deity we need a code word so that Nan doesn't know what we are on about."

Kam suggested, "What about saying *if this hotel was mine*?"

≈≈≈

That evening, we entered the restaurant, and the air was filled with a strange atmosphere. The hairs on the back of my neck rose like the quills of a hedgehog. I didn't have the luxury of curling up into a ball. The air was cold, the faces of the people in the room looked sullen, more like prisoners than tourists. Something was missing, yet I couldn't put my finger on it. It soon became clear that things might be seriously wrong. We saw several events that could be sabotage. There was a disruption to the supply of food at the hotel. Eastern bloc guests overfilling plates, loading up with more food than they could consume in a week. I spotted a couple with ten plates on their table; each of them was overflowing with food. "What a waste," I said to Kam. "They'll never eat all that food."

Without even querying my comment Mags joined in the game, not realising the importance of what she was doing. She nodded towards a lady at a table on her own. "Rod, look at her. She's put all of the apples in her pockets." I glanced at the large woman, and the bumpy outline under her clothes hinted that her extra bulk was caused by a tree full of apples. I was surprised the seams on her clothing could hold out. She really looked like the proverbial sack of potatoes.

I looked down at my own foodless plate and glanced at Kam. We simultaneously raised one eyebrow each. I muttered, "They're spoiling it for everyone. If this was my hotel, I'd put a stop to that." Silently suggesting that we needed Mikalis to address guests removing food from the restaurant.

Several times throughout the meal, we had cause to suspect a deity was present. Bless her; even Mags started to say: *if this was my hotel.* At least we could get on with our jobs, without risking disclosure.

Without any warning, Alyss jumped out of her seat, the chair legs screeching on the marbled tiles before it fell back onto the hard floor. Only when I heard the loudness of the clatter of steel on marble did I realise what had been missing. All eyes turned towards our table as if we'd farted in a library. Alyss didn't help as she shrieked, "Dad, look at her." And she pointed to a woman holding a camera. The woman was walking along the opposite side of the self-serve hot buffet station. As she drew level with us, she raised the camera. "She's going to take a picture of us."

Without a thought for what I was about to do, I took centre stage for the 600 silent voyeurs. I jumped to my feet and raised my right arm with my palm facing her. I screamed: "In the name of Zeus, STOP." I think King Canute had more chance of stopping the tide. I prayed inside that my bulging eyes, volume and red face might have some effect.

It had an effect alright, Mags and Kam both dropped their

cutlery. The silence in the restaurant was broken only by the clatter of the cutlery as it hit the floor. We all blushed as our audience gasped as one. The woman fumbled as her camera, in slow-motion launched into the air spiralling in the air before descending beyond her snatching finger into a bain-marie of hot gravy. She went pallid, countering our blushes. Her colouring had transferred to us by osmosis. She squinted her eyes. I stared straight back at her. My bulging eyes hurt from the length of time I held the angered stare. The woman turned and stormed out of the restaurant. She was closely followed by two other women, flanking her left and right. The woman on the right slipped in the trail of greasy gravy. *Bloody Witches of Eastwick*, I thought to myself. I expected a round of applause from the witnesses to the event, but there was nothing, not a whisper. The only sound that filled the room was from chair legs scraping on the floor as guests rose and left the dining room.

I bent to recover my chair and turn it to its upright position. My whole body was trembling, and I could feel my legs starting to collapse under me. I dropped onto the seat and lay my head on the table. I took some big breaths of air. I needed to get some life-giving oxygen into my system. I finally sat up and slumped back into the chair, taking more deep breaths.

Mags sounded as unnerved as I felt. "What was that all about Rod?"

I could barely answer, my mouth had donated all its saliva to the rest of my body. "That woman was about to take a picture of us, and I'm not having that. I don't want to be plastered all over Facebook or some review site." I looked at Kam and uttered the now-familiar phrase. "God if this was my place," and I attempted to down the jug of water from the table. Drinking it straight from the lip of the container. Most of it spilt down my face and onto my shirt.

"Too bloody right," reinforced Lindon as he looked towards the door.

Mags managed to pick up her cutlery without falling off her seat. She looked at Lindon. "Oh, don't swear love. It doesn't suit you."

I needed nicotine. And lots of it. As we left the restaurant, all remaining eyes were on the Prince family. Kam pre-warned me, "If that woman is out there, keep walking." I intended to. I only needed nicotine and alcohol.

Alyss sidled up to me so that only I could hear what she said. "She was a deity, wasn't she?"

I nodded and pulled out my e-cig, fired it up and inhaled a good amount of nicotine filled steam. My erratic heartbeat finally started to find its pace.

≈≈≈

As we approached the bar, I could hear the regular beat of the *sirtaki*. Its steady beat was giving my body a cardiac rhythm that calmed it and dissipated the overdose of adrenaline. As the music's tempo rose, I processed it as some kind of battle cry, like a bugler playing the battle charge. It was preparing me for confrontations to come.

We entered the bar, and my phone buzzed in my pocket. "Nice 1 M8 Ze." I made a mental note: *Inform Zeus, I don't like text-speech. And I'm not keen that my employer called me his mate.*

I swear the mannequin was smiling at me and the eye patch had been removed. It was reassuring to see the same staff, serving behind the bar. More double kisses. Greek men always seemed to have a five o'clock shadow within minutes of shaving. I wasn't sure if he'd guessed or remembered, but he anticipated correctly what we drank and asked Mags for her order. He clearly wasn't a bad god.

He gestured to a table in the corner of the room. "Go sit, and I bring drinks."

Lindon and Alyss stayed long enough to guzzle their colas. They wanted to go off to see Sandro. Kam stopped them long enough to suggest, "Take Nan with you. She hasn't met him yet. And I bet she'll fall in love with him."

Mags laughed. "I'm too old for young men. Your taxi driver friend is nearer to my age."

Alyss teased. "You haven't met Sandro yet."

I refrained from asking Mags how old she thought Zeus was.

Before they'd even left the bar, Kam moved closer to me. "Don't do that again."

I looked up from my pint. "What?"

"Shout like that. Everyone turned to look at us."

"I'm sorry. What was I to do? She was taking pictures, and they would be all over the Internet by now. We would be one step nearer to being revoked. Anyway, they were already looking at us because Alyss knocked her chair over."

"I don't think she was taking pictures of us. It's more likely she was taking pictures of the lack of food. To her, we would just be guests sitting in the background."

I was more concerned about where the hell 'in the name of Zeus' came from and had I disclosed our status.

As the sun dropped to the horizon, Helios came into the bar. "Well done, Rod. The gossip in Olympia is that she thought you were Zeus."

He paused to let that sink in before continuing. "Did she look at you like this?" And he did the squinting thing the woman had done.

"Yeah. I stared right back at her, like this." I gave him the stare and hurt my bloody eyes again.

Helios supplied all the missing bits of information filling in the gaps that we were dying or had died to find out. "When a god looks at you like that we are trying to identify you. When you stared back, you opened the channel allowing her to do just that. I guess when she couldn't see your spirit, she had no way to identify you as a mortal. She had no way to know who you were. When you mentioned Zeus, she must have put two and two together and assumed you were a god."

I panicked at that comment. "Have we disclosed?"

"No, don't worry, you did the right thing. They will be wary of you from now on, but they won't want to risk an all-out war with Zeus. If they can't identify you, then they can't be sure you aren't Zeus himself."

"Why don't they want to battle with Zeus?"

Helios looked at me as if I was stupid. "Are you kidding? Zeus can do anything to them except kill them."

Kam asked him, "Who was she?".

"That was Hestia, and she had two of her cronies with her. One last thing. That opened palm thing you did. It only worked because it was Hestia. If it had been a Greek mortal, you would have needed a new set of teeth. It is an insult to a Greek. It is called *mountza*." And he looked at us both and issued a friendly warning. "Use your new skills wisely, unless you want to pay for a lot of treatment from your dentist."

Let me get this right. "Screaming at a strange woman while facepalming her is a valuable new skill. I bet that would look good on a customer service CV."

He smiled. "I have a meeting with Zeus. I will catch up with you later."

The attentive barman must have spotted we'd finished our drinks. He brought the second round over.

Standing up. I introduced myself. "Hi, I'm Rod. And this is my wife, Kam."

"Yes, I remember you." He looked at me and frowned slightly as if I should have realised he would remember.

"I know. What I meant was, we never asked your name. We can't keep calling you barman," I questioned without asking him.

"Tsambikos, I am Tsambikos."

Mags returned, and her non-alcoholic cocktails had increased to three. "I can understand why you fell in love with the place. The sunset was beautiful. And you're right Sandro is a cutie."

As time progressed and the evening air became more refreshing, the bloody mosquitos came out to eat. The family returned to the relative safety of their bedrooms. Protected by mozzie nets and repellent plugins. I stayed to catch up with Tsambikos and risked being mosquito dinner. The beer had taken its revenge on me once again. The empty barstool next to me groaned as it became occupied. I looked up and saw it was Filipos.

He looked back at me. "Good evening Rod," before commanding, "tell me how you are finding the hotel?"

The open-ended question made it clear he wanted a conversation. My tongue loosened by alcohol, I thought to myself *you've picked the right time to ask.*

"It's beautiful," I started. Then I went straight into a monologue. I told him everything that had gone wrong on our previous visits and again today. Unfortunately, the poor sod didn't get a word in. I don't know if he was just polite, but he listened and didn't interrupt.

"Well, first there was the Prometheus, that had never heard of us…"

≈≈≈

"… and to top it all, I only managed to get a limp lettuce salad with stale yellow feta. And then I get in here, and there appears to be no order. It's like a rugby scrum. Have you heard of rugby?" And before he could answer, I signalled to Tsambikos for another pint.

Tsambikos glanced nervously at Filipos, then apologised. "I'm sorry Rod, but we stopped serving at half-eleven. Thirty minutes ago."

I was about to bid farewell and leave. Filipos spoke in Greek he uttered words I hadn't learnt yet. But Tsambikos soon produced a pint of beer for me.

"Thank you, Mister Filipos," and I took a sip. The feeling

in my throat started to tell me I'd drank too much already.

"*Parakalo synechise*, I mean please carry on," Filipos encouraged.

I relayed the events of our evening at Helios, taking care to not include my impersonation of Zeus. "There isn't much more, at the moment, but I'm sure something else will reveal itself tomorrow." I let out a sigh. "God, I wish this place was mine, it has got so much potential. It needs a bit of organisation. I'd suggest that you don't give the guests so much freedom and sort the staff out."

He latched on to the last bit. "What do you mean to sort my staff out?"

"Simple, train them not to shrug their shoulders. If a guest speaks to them and they don't understand, they should explain that they don't understand. Teach them enough English to be able to say, '*sorry I don't understand. I will find someone that does.*' To shrug your shoulders and walk off is downright rude in any language."

I was now on my soapbox. Two thousand miles from home and someone was asking me about my specialism.

"Even better, issue the staff with name badges. Under their name have one or more small flags to represent the languages they speak. Problem solved."

He nodded at my suggestion.

"And what about the guests having too much freedom?"

Now I know queuing is a peculiarly British tradition. But everyone will join a queue if it's the only route to the front.

"Guests aren't organised, from the moment they wake up, to the time they go to bed, they can all do as they please. Yes, there are posters that state there's a dress code in the restaurant. How many guests wore trousers at mealtimes today? Two, me and my son. I was discouraged from trying the boiled eggs for breakfast. The similarity between men in speedos and boiled eggs was way too close for my early morning appetite. There's no point in having a rule if it's not policed. Like I told you, if this were my place, I'd have a solution to all the problems I've met so far." Of course, I couldn't tell him of the one problem I had no solution to, not without disclosure.

I joked. "I need to win the lottery and buy the hotel from you." At which point, I could feel the bile starting to burn my throat. A timely reminder that I'd drunk way too much on a relatively empty stomach. Stirred up by an unhealthy overdose of adrenaline.

"It's late, and I'm afraid I should be making a move. I need to be up early tomorrow because I'd like to get a shower before the water runs out." And I smiled at him. He gave me a friendly smile back, offering his hand. I responded and shook it.

I slurred. "Thank you for listening to me. I do go on a bit when I've had a drink." At which point I hiccupped and giggled. Another mental note to self: *I'm going to have to stop getting drunk.* I giggled again.

"Listen, I have been very interested in what you have been saying. I like your ideas, and maybe we can talk some more tomorrow?"

"Of course, we will be in the bar about nine because that's when everyone goes to the entertainment."

"Not here in the bar. I would like you to come to my office at around ten in the morning. We will have coffee and carry on our conversation."

A terrifying thought crossed my mind as I prepared to stagger back to the suite. This chap barely knew me except for a couple of Facebook comments. He had no idea why I was there, and I'd spent the last hour slagging off his pride and joy. I guess my body language signalled my panic.

"I like your honesty, and I like the way you are thinking of solutions. I won't say anymore tonight. We will talk more tomorrow. *Kalinychta.*"

"Yes. I will come to your office at ten o'clock. Goodnight." And I began my drunken meander back to the room. I thought the lighting would be to my advantage until I spotted a snake with a frog in its mouth blocking my way. I turned to take another route as if seeing a snake was an everyday thing. My beer-sodden grey matter did try to process it. *Can gods transform into animal form? Better ask Zeus tomorrow. What if Zeus was the snake? What if he was the frog? Then who was the snake?* I quickened my pace but staggered each time I looked over my shoulder. I felt a sharp prick on my ankle and started to run. *Had the god snake bit me? I must get back to the room.* Finally, safely back in the room, I was glad everyone was asleep as I examined the bite. *Bloody mosquitos.* I laid back on the bed and tried to stop the room spinning. Kam groaned in her sleep. "Can a god change into a mosquito?" I asked. And promptly passed out.

FILIPOS – An Education

I surfaced in a panic. "Shit, it's gone ten and Filipos wanted me in his office."

"Whatever for?" questioned Kam while munching on an apple. "We've had our breakfast," she gloated.

"Yes. You've missed breakfast, dad," added Lindon.

"I don't have time for breakfast. All I need is coffee." Truth be known I felt like throwing up. "I have to go and talk to Filipos, but after a quick shower."

"Why do you have to talk to Filipos? You missed the water too. It ran out an hour ago," asked Kam.

"That'll be right." I moaned, "Nicotine it is then." And I walked out onto the patio sucking in large quantities of vapour trying to kick start my system. I sat gazing into space under the stupidly hot sun. I was trying to piece together the events of the previous evening.

Kam asked for the third time, "Why have you got to see Filipos?"

"I was talking to him last night, and I slagged off the hotel."

Kam frowned at me. "You drunken fool. He probably wants to kick us out."

"No, he doesn't. I think. I don't really remember, but I think he wants me to give him ideas about how to improve the hotel."

"But you've never worked in a hotel."

I shouted into the darkness of the suite. "Lindon is the water back on yet?"

"Nope."

"Oh well, only one thing for it." I put my e-cig down, dropped my bed shorts and jumped into the pool." Once I stopped my involuntary gasping because of the cold, I dunked my bed hair into the water. My head was still throbbing, and I still felt like throwing up, but at least I was fully awake."

Dried and dressed and three coffees later I was about to leave the room. "Kam, why don't you come with me?"

"No chance. You got yourself into this mess, and you can get yourself out of it."

≈≈≈

I tottered down the steps from 208 and staggered my way to reception. I had to be careful to step over the remains of a frog on the walkway. *Shit, I forgot about that.* A shiver ran down my spine, and I cringed, the way I would when hearing a squeaky blackboard and chalk.

I entered the reception area. The coolness was a relief from the madness that Helios was creating outside. The lightness of the walls, floor and ceiling, maintained a balanced level of light. My hungover eyes managed to keep their focus. I approached the desk in reception, Mikalis was on duty.

"Kalimera Mikalis."

"Kalimera Rod, you want to speak Greek today?"

"No thanks, not this morning." I could barely think after all the beer, let alone speak Greek.

"What can I do for you? Is everything alright with the rooms? Are you enjoying your stay?"

"Er Um, I'm here for a meeting with Mister Filipos," I announced.

Mikalis went pale, as pale as the wall behind him. "Why are you meeting with Mister Filipos? Do you have a complaint?"

"No, No, I was talking to him in the bar last night, and he invited me for coffee this morning to continue our conversation. I'm about an hour late."

"OK, one moment please," and he picked up the telephone. He dialled a single digit and spoke in Greek. A moment later, he spoke again before ending the conversation and hanging up the phone. *Why do Greek conversations always sound like heated arguments?* He gestured behind reception. "Go through. The door before my office is Mister Filipos' secretary, and she will take you to him. Oh, he is OK with you being late, it is the Greek way." It struck me as a bit formal for a coffee.

I gave a quiet knock on the dark solid wood door. "Hello, I am here to see Mister Filipos. Mikalis sent me to you."

"Mikalis?" She looked like she didn't even know him. "Oh, you mean Mister Mikalis," she said stressing the mister. I looked back at her. *I'm sure that's what I said.*

≈≈≈

99

I entered the office. "Mister Filipos." I reached out, and we shook hands.

He sat back down. "Take a seat. Would you like a Greek coffee or a frappe?"

He didn't wait for me to reply. He picked up the phone and jabbered in Greek. Moments later, two frappes arrived. My fourth coffee yet it was only eleven o'clock, and it still didn't sort the hangover out.

"Last night, you told me if it were your hotel, you would run it differently. Now is your chance to tell me how I should run my hotel." He emphasised the word 'my'. I gulped.

It wasn't so much his tone but the words he used. I sensed he wasn't going to be so receptive to my observations as he was the previous evening. At which point his mobile rang, he picked it up and bellowed down the phone. When I say bellowed, I mean bellowed. His volume was a match for Zeus.

In the office, the walls were clad in stained wood panelling. It was a weak attempt to give the room some grandeur. All it did was make it dark and stuffy. The complete opposite to the light, airy and cool marble walls in reception. It had the atmosphere of a sauna. I don't recall if it was the room or the hangover, but I was feeling extremely overheated. He ended the telephone conversation and threw his phone down all in one smooth action. *Jesus, if the kids treated their phones like that, I'd go spare.*

"Problems, problems, problems, all my staff ever bring me are problems," he bemoaned. It would be fair to say that by this point, I was shitting myself. Kam always said I got sucked in by weirdos, but this was something different. I was sat in front of a man whose, volume, tone, and manner scared me. He wasn't a weirdo. He was a monster. To compound the fear, he'd asked me to tell him how to run his hotel.

"Please don't bring me more problems, bring me solutions. Last night you suggested that I needed to sort my employees out. What did you mean by that?" At least he showed an interest in my opinion. Despite my fears, I decided not to sugar coat what I was going to say. It was a risk. *We'll have nowhere to sleep tonight.*

"They aren't doing the jobs you're paying them to do. I've seen staff doing things that would get me the sack at home."

"Tell me examples."

"One morning, there were two men. They were walking the lawns, picking up litter. They walked past more litter than they picked up and spent two hours doing it. Who was checking the work they'd done? You have been paying them to walk around and talk. The lawns still looked a mess."

He picked up his phone and played with it rotating it between his massive fingers as if it were a fidget spinner.

"As I told you last night, too many of them shrug their shoulders." And I took a sip from my frappe. "I've seen staff walking past the hotplates and in full view of the guests, they use their hands to help themselves to food."

I paused long enough for him to digest that point, and for me to decide if I should raise the next issue. "I am suggesting that some of your staff mean your hotel harm."

We chatted for a while longer, and I became more relaxed the longer we spoke. He really didn't know how to deal with the issues. I offered my experience, but I am no expert at being a guest in a hotel full of gods. He continued to show an interest.

"Rod, I know you are on holiday, but would you do me a favour?" he asked as he stood up.

"Of course."

"Can you be my eyes at the hotel? My managers keep telling me that everything is fine."

"I will," I affirmed, also standing, because it was clear he wanted to bring the meeting to an end. *And why do your managers lie to you? They are terrified of you, that's why.*

≈≈≈

"Who's phoning you at this time of night?" Kam enquired as we watched the setting sun.

One quick glance at my mobile told me who it was. I glanced at Kam and raised one eyebrow.

"Hello, Zeus."

"*A certain bird told me you have met with Filipos.*" His tone suggested that I shouldn't have done.

"I did is that a problem?"

"*Only if you mentioned Helios or me and the other gods.*"

"No, I didn't. I decided I would let him raise the issue first. Anyway, I thought he was one of the directors listed on the contract I signed."

"Didn't you read the contract properly, he isn't on the board at Olympian. He's on the contract as the owner of Helios. He will be on the board when Olympian take control of Helios."

I don't know if he meant to, but he'd slipped in some vital information he'd neglected to tell me at the start.

"By the way, can gods become reptiles?"

Kam looked at me as if I was crazy.

"*Why?*"

"Never mind, I was just wondering." The memories of the previous evening were a bit sketchy. I wasn't even convinced I'd witnessed the snake and the frog. For all I could remember, it may as well have been flying pigs or pink elephants. I hung up.

Kam looked at me, quizzically. She had the look of a woman that suspects her husband has just spent the family budget on a gadget. "What's that about reptiles?"

"Nothing. I was just wondering." I felt the guilt of a man that had just spent the family budget on a gadget.

≈≈≈

Given that we were only there for seven days, we also had to spend a lot of time with Mags. We showed her around the parts of the island we'd seen before. It didn't leave much time to be the eyes of Filipos. During that holiday, there was only one other event that seemed as if it might be instigated by the *D80's*.

It was Lindon who came up with the name. We couldn't keep calling them deities or bad gods. He suggested D8, but Alyss pointed out that spelt *date* in text language. In the end, we settled for D80.

We had an amusing couple of hours while Mags was having an afternoon nap. We tried nicknaming each of the D80's. It soon fell apart, when someone renamed Prometheus as Pussy. Lindon and Alyss started winding each other up, and one called the other pussy. We decided that maybe we wouldn't give them nicknames. For the time being, they were D80's.

Two days before our departure, there was an event that had to be the mischief of the D80's. I was sitting under the shade of vine leaves at the taverna, enjoying the break from Helios' attempts to cook tourists. Behind where I sat, I could hear a young couple talking. Their voices were loud, so I couldn't help gate crashing their conversation. He was telling her to go to reception and complain that they had ants in the room.

"We will get upgraded to a pool room, a bloke told me earlier." They finished their drinks and excitedly trundled off in the direction of reception. I necked my frappe. I just had to see how this played out. After all, Filipos had asked me to be his eyes and Zeus said I was to look out for mischief.

As they approached reception, there were maybe ten people all shouting at Mikalis. They were shouting about ants and, of course, they were all trying to get a room with a pool.

One of the complainers loudly announced, "You gave a guest a pool room earlier."

Having already discussed the downside of upgrading with Filipos, it was pleasing to hear that Mikalis wasn't giving upgrades. *Says the man whose family have got two pool rooms.* It's a question of balance if you upgrade a guest someone else will have to be downgraded. You now have two guests with a complaint, and one of those is the fault of the hotel.

I couldn't know but guessed this was the work of Demeter. She was the D80 of agriculture and harvest. I suspected that the *'in the name of Zeus'* trick wouldn't work with ants. There'd be far too many of them. We usually used boiling water at home. I texted Zeus, and he was of no help. His stark reply. "It is the family's job to deal with it." True to form, he wouldn't get involved. I hadn't seen any ants all day, but the number of complainants suggested the gentleman spreading the rumour had been extremely successful. Maybe he was a gender-switched Demeter. Unless of course there was indeed a plague of ants at the hotel. I headed for 208 and the family.

I could hear the girls squealing before I even started to climb the stairs to the suite. By the time I got caught up with the others, they were trying to stamp on ants. If the sirtaki had been playing, I'm sure they would have been in step to the beat. The ants were bigger than the ants we had at home. Not giants, like in *Jason and The Argonauts*. They were about a centimetre long. If what I was seeing was repeated throughout the hotel, then we had a plague of ants to evict. The air conditioning was blasting ice-cold air into the room, and even the low temperature didn't deter the ants. What were they looking for? A swarm that size would be searching for food or transporting the queen.

I did the mountza and shouted the magic mantra. "In the name of Zeus stop." That didn't have any effect whatsoever. Still, it was worth a try. I had only one option left, so I joined in the stomping. While hammering my strongest foot hard onto the floor, I was, maybe, taking out two of the critters with each step. It wasn't a one-sided battle because as fast as I was trampling on them, other little buggers were clambering up my standing leg. It tickled, at first, but stung like hell when they nipped the flesh on my calves. This led me to change my rhythm and use each leg alternately. I even tried jumping up and down with both feet, allowing me to double my kill rate. Unfortunately, reinforcements were entering the fray quicker than they were taking casualties. The pungent stench of formic acid filled the room. But that was the key that unlocked a long-forgotten memory. When I was a young boy living in rural Gloucestershire, we used to disturb ants' nests just to get them angry. We knew we had pissed them off as soon as we could smell the formic acid. Around the same time, we created experimental ant traps. The bait would be a sucked boiled sweet. They would all gather in one place, and that made it easier to kill them.

I turned to Kam, who was stomping like she was at a barn dance. "Do you have any of your barley sugar sweets left in your hand luggage?"

"U-Hu," was all she could manage between stomps.

I located the sweets and placed a few in my mouth. "Lindon, take some euros off the side and go buy some sweets, something to suck or chew."

I placed one of the moistened sticky sweets on the patio outside the room, right next to the pool. Instantly, the column of ants started to break up and change its route. I took another sweet from my mouth. And threw it over the balcony onto the lawn and the same with a third. I reloaded my mouth. Kam stopped dancing and loaded up her mouth. Alyss grabbed a handful of sweets and stuffed them into hers. We fired wet sticky candies out across the lawns aiming to get them to land as far away from the room as possible.

Lindon returned laden with armfuls of toffees and boiled

sweets. The smell of sweetness was overpowering. We patrolled the grounds of the hotel, dropping our stealthy payload of sugar at every opportunity. We left sticky teasers in the flower beds, on the lawns and pretty much everywhere that wasn't near the guests' rooms. I didn't know if it had worked, but the shrieking from terrified guests had stopped. In a later conversation with Filipos, I suggested the lazy litter pickers get a new title. "Sticky Sweet Droppers." It seemed that ants would rather have an easy sweet than work for Demeter. I suspect they knew that they would take fewer casualties. I chuckled inside as I thought: *I'm going fucking nuts. Ants don't ponder that much. Do they?*

It was the start of a strong bond of friendship with Filipos. On the last day of that visit, our luggage packed we were sitting around the private pool watching the sunlight sparkle on the rippling water. It made the tedious wait for the impending airport run more bearable. Loud shouting stirred me from a daydream of how we could engineer an extended stay. "Mister Rod, Mister Rod." Filipos's secretary was stood on the other side of our pool. Her ruddied face with sweat dripping from her nose. She gasped deeply for each breath, like a horse that had won the Epsom Derby and broken the track record. With the long pauses and the accent, she was incoherent. "Thank the gods." Followed by a deep breath. "I have found you." Another long pause while she figured out the English for what she had to say. "Mister Filipos would be honoured if you could…"

Come on, spit it out, woman. "Could what?"

Another gulp of warm Aegean air. "Extend your stay by

two weeks as his guest." And she beamed a broad grin of self-satisfaction as she realised she'd managed to relay her message.

This was a perfect opportunity to hide the fact that Zeus wanted us to stay for the entire season. I looked at Kam, and she gave a barely noticeable shake of her head. I tried to figure out why she was saying no. I looked at the still red and sweaty secretary, feigning disappointment. "Oh, If only I could. I still have commitments at home. But I would love to return in a few weeks. That is if Mister Filipos is agreeable. Please tell him that it is a generous offer. I would love to accept, but the notice is too short. I'm due back at work in Manchester tomorrow morning. I will come to his office shortly and discuss it with him." She turned to walk away dejected. Her posture was more akin to a punter that hadn't picked the Derby winner. Clearly, she was under pressure to get us to stay.

I looked at Kam. "Poor woman. Maybe we should have accepted his offer. One minute she thought she had managed to win Filipos's approval. The next, she has the task of disappointing him. I feel sorry for her." Filipos had solved our main predicament. We could return and stay for the season, and it wouldn't be considered strange. "Why did you shake your head?"

"Because if you'd accepted there and then, it would put doubt in his mind about us. You've told him about your work back home, and he would know you have to turn up to work. If you forget about Zeus and the others for now. In the real world, if you were going to stay an extra fortnight, you wouldn't be able to do it without notice. And if we want to be here for the season, you will have to leave your job."

"Yes, that's exactly what I thought," I bluffed.

≈≈≈

We'd only been back home for a week, and we got a one-word communication on Messenger. It was from Filipos, *"HELP."* It seemed there were all kinds of mayhem going on at the hotel. He wanted us to help, so we took him up on his offer for a free stay at the hotel. I resigned my job and booked flights, just me and Kam. The kids were back at school and were given exemption from their contracts by Zeus. They stayed with Mags, and their task would be to find out what they could about different Greek gods.

Returning for the season also gave us a chance to spend some time with Zeus. In discussions with Filipos, he asked that while we couldn't always be present in reception dealing with complaints, I could do several things to help. He asked us to take charge of the travel site accounts and use them to counter poor reviews. Put management comments on like: *'We are sorry your stay wasn't to the high standard we expect for our guests. This very issue is under review, and its solution will be part of the development plan for next season.'*

I shouldn't have suggested a development plan, but it seemed the sensible way forward. I guessed that with a plan in place, like managing the 'ants issue,' the hotel should be able to minimise the problems the D80's could throw at them. Unfortunately, the task of developing the plan fell to me. There didn't appear to be enough hours in the day to do everything.

Any time spent with Zeus was useful. It was an

opportunity to clarify some key points and to express my fears.

I looked into Zeus' eyes; one of them was shining again. "I'm not sure that we're up to completing the job. We don't have any means of combating the gods. All we can do is try and put right the crap they're causing."

He looked straight back at me. "Trust me. I know you are up to it."

"What happens if it gets nasty? If the gods start trying to kill us. Start firing lightning bolts at us." A phrase I later wished I hadn't used.

With an unflinching stare and a straight face, Zeus replied, "I thought you were clever. Besides you are already dead."

"OK, what happens if they kill me a second time?"

"You come back to life. Stupid Englishman. You are immortal."

I didn't even bother trying to complain about him calling me stupid. "Yeah, they blow my leg off, and then I'm a one-legged immortal."

"Oxi, you are a resurrective immortal. When you return to life, you show no signs of the injury that killed you. They blow your leg off, and it kills you. You resurrect and get your leg back. Simple. You have customer service knowledge, think of it like a returns policy. If the product is damaged within its lifetime," and he laughed. "You get an identical replacement." He added a quick rider. "This doesn't include fair wear and tear." He laughed again.

"This is all too much for me to understand, I still don't think we can do it."

He drew closer to us. "Listen. It is in the board's interest to make sure you come to no harm."

He came even closer. So close, I could smell the goat and wet earth again. "There are only two ways that will end you. If your remains are removed from the tombs in the cities. Or if you enter the tombs." He paused and glared at me. "You *can*, and you *will* succeed."

"I don't know," I moaned.

I started to analyse and digest that conversation. It was way too complex for an ordinary mortal to compute.

"You still aren't convinced, are you?" he queried. I just stared back at him. "Let me show you. In two minutes, I will launch a lightning bolt into the play area. The four children playing there will die. You can save them. All you have to do is stand in the way. The lightning bolt will hit you instead of them."

I managed to compute that and stated my conclusion to the process. "You're fucking mad."

"Ninety seconds left. It won't kill you. Trust me; I'm a god of my word. You won't even need first aid."

"Sixty."

I looked at Kam, and she looked right back at me. Usually full of good ideas, she just shrugged her shoulders.

"Twenty."

Hold on. You just jumped some numbers in that countdown. I thought to myself as I moved directly in front of Zeus.

"One, Zer..."

I felt the most painful sensation ever. But I never saw a flash, and I didn't hear anything.

"Told you so." laughed Zeus.

Kam was just stood there open-mouthed as if she was screaming, but no noise was coming out.

"Fuck, Fuck, Fuck, you didn't tell me it would hurt," I complained.

"Course it hurt, you were struck by lightning, but the pain was over in a flash." And he laughed at his pun. He fucking laughed.

Suddenly he was a bloody comedian. But he did have a point, I felt the pain, and it did hurt. The next thing I know, I am back where I started. Pain-free and nothing damaged, just a terrible smell of singed hair. It was a useful training session. Yes, that's what he called it, a 'flaming training session'. It did mean I was no longer afraid to die or lose a valuable part of my body.

Being worried about Kam's mind if she witnessed her babies dying or not dying, we negotiated for the kids to limit their visits to only once per year. I told him they could be on the substitutes bench if we needed them. He made us promise that succeed or fail, they would return to the island by April 2018. In return, Kam and I would stay for entire seasons. The rumour back home was that we had won the lottery and deserted the kids. But this was OK. It was much better than the truth.

We didn't have to wait long to discover the problems with resurrective immortality. It was during our first physical confrontation. I'm not sure of the room we were in, but it wasn't 208. We'd decided that it wasn't fair to downgrade paying guests to accommodate us. It was poor customer service and would damage the hotel's reputation. Filipos was offended that we were snubbing his hospitality, but we couldn't justify the cost of his special treatment.

The war against the D80's took a new direction and became more real. Kam and I were walking past a block of suites on Socrates Street, a group of guests were on a first-floor balcony. They were loud and boisterous so much so that I glanced up at them. They were apparently enjoying an evening of drink and waiting for the sun to go down. And who could blame them? It is something we'd done many times. I smiled and bid them a good evening.

"Kalispera," I shouted up to them. There was no reply, but the revelry stopped, and all eyes were looking down on us. I shuddered as I felt an avalanche of ice slide down my spine. It reminded me of something my mum once told me. "That sensation is a sign that someone has stood on your grave."

Kam and I looked at each other. "Let's go," she said. And we quickened our pace.

I heard a sudden whoosh as something passed by my face. We later found it was an egg-shaped pebble. Like the ones that people build cairns out of. They would take pictures of the white stoned cairns with the blue sea in the background. It narrowly missed me, but it caught Kam on the brow above her right eye. She didn't bleed from it, but there was a definite cut. I glanced up at the balcony, and the revellers were gone. I knew which balcony it came from. I took Kam to reception to give her first aid.

Mikalis was on duty and ushered us to a back room. One of his staff tended to Kam while he phoned Filipos. Filipos' anger was revealed by the volume of his voice. Mikalis had to hold the phone away from his ear. *Remove those guests immediately.*

Mikalis closed his phone. "Mister Filipos is coming to the hotel, and he wants to remove the guests. Do you know which room they are in?"

"Yes, it's the upper room in the first block on Socrates Street," I stuttered.

He went to leave the room, then turned to me. "There is no blood because of shock. Kam should rest. You stay with her, and I will investigate."

I needed to contact Zeus immediately, too many people had seen the damage to Kam's face. It didn't matter about other guests. They come and go. But Mikalis had seen it, his staff had seen it, and Filipos was about to see it.

Zeus advised, "She will have to live with a scar. It hadn't killed her because it would have healed when she resurrected. You mustn't let her die from that wound. That will mean you have disclosed. She will have a permanent scar, but that is what the mortals around you would expect."

"What about the lack of blood? How do we explain that?"

"Bluff it, I'm sure you will think of something," he encouraged.

I was about to hang up then I remembered to ask for advice about dealing with the guest that had thrown the pebble. "What should I do about the guests?"

His reply was as helpful as ever. "Don't ask me. That is your job. You can deal with it in any way that you see fit." Then he hung up, and I frowned at the phone as if trying to telepath my resentment at being cut short.

I updated Kam. "So, I have to have a scar forever, just

because Zeus says so?" She wasn't happy.

"The only alternative is to resurrect. Meaning you have to die first, and it has to be from the injury." I was trying to show her that despite what Zeus wanted, we didn't really have any other option.

Mikalis returned, and not surprisingly, the guests had denied any involvement. It was their word against ours. He didn't believe them over us, but there was enough of an argument for not involving the police. Not least our non-disclosure agreement.

"I think we should get you back to our room. Do you feel up to it, sweetheart?" I asked Kam.

"Yes. I don't feel any pain, and it isn't bleeding, is it?"

Mikalis expressed his doubts. "I am concerned that there is no blood. Should we call medics in case she is in shock?"

I looked at Kam. Thinking quickly, she lied. "No, I don't need a medic. In the past, when I've been injured, there has been very little blood. Doctors have told me my blood coagulates so quickly it rarely reaches the surface of the wound."

I made a mental note to always carry some fake Halloween blood in case anything happened again.

She continued to try and reassure Michalis. "I just need a plaster to keep the wound clean and closed until it has healed." She smiled at me as if to reassure me that she had it under control.

We were just leaving as Filipos was arriving. He was furious. "Mikalis. What room are they in?"

"Room 137 Mister Filipos."

"P*ame,*" Filipos barked at me as only he could, and he led the 100-metre march to Suite 137. Leaving Kam with Mikalis.

Filipos knocked. No, he thumped on the door to the suite. It swung open, and there stood two Eastern European guys. I guessed they were Russian they were wearing the bright red home shirts of Spartak Moscow. No sign of the females that were on the balcony.

"YOU WILL LEAVE MY HOTEL NOW," commanded Filipos.

"*Oxi,*" they chorused in Greek as they both laughed.

I was worried this was going to escalate. These men were in their prime. It would be fair to say both Filipos and I were quite a bit past our prime.

"YOU WILL LEAVE NOW, OR I WILL HAVE YOU SHOT!"

What the fuck? What was I hearing? *You can't say that to a guest.* If anyone heard that, then the hotel's reputation was the thing that would die. I needed to think of something and fast. We were in a desperate situation, but using a gun wasn't the solution.

I stepped forward. I raised my palm towards the potential gods and shouted. "In the name of Zeus, LEAVE NOW."

This brought the unseen women to the doorway. I had four people doing that squinty thing. My God, four D80's in the same place. It was the godly equivalent of a lion's den. Filipos' idea wouldn't have solved the problem. I maintained my unflinching stare. They barged right past us, and they were gone.

I was sure the D80's weren't gone for good. But at least

the form they took had gone. This was a significant development. They knew that there was something special about me. It unsettled them, but it also disturbed me. Had I raised the level of risk facing the family? Kam would now be recognisable as the woman with a one-inch scar above her right eye.

I turned to Filipos. "Thank you Mister Filipos. I don't think they would have left if you hadn't threatened them. Would you really have had them shot?"

More to the point, could he have had them shot? I thought to myself.

"*Parakalo,*" was his stark reply. I couldn't pick up on his tone. I wasn't sure if he meant '*you're welcome*'. Or was he saying '*please*' as if the suggestion was preposterous? That was unsettling, but I let it go.

The risk of physical harm from the D80's was real. The thought that Filipos considered shooting someone was real. These actions turned what were petty skirmishes into a war of survival. My family were at risk, and that scared me. The event with the stone demonstrated our vulnerability. We needed to be a bit more reclusive and yet we needed to be more proactive. We'd been drifting along waiting for an event to happen and then reacting to it. We were drawn into battles. We couldn't win the war waiting and hoping they would give up. At some point, we needed to launch our own attack.

≈≈≈

Zeus was little help. "You aren't ready to have powers. Besides, how do you know which powers you will need?"

"We don't know. All I know is that we have to be more

pre-emptive. Any advantage of anonymity we have is reducing by the day. We are going around in circles, they start an offensive, commit some damage then we come along, and they stop. But it's too late, they've won, their mischief is complete."

He looked at us. "I understand. I really do. But I don't know what you want from me. Give me a plan. Tell me what you need. Then I will give it to you."

I pondered for a moment. Before responding, "OK. I'll draw up a plan. We also need to stay at another hotel. We can't risk staying behind enemy lines. We need to stay somewhere close enough to get to Helios when needed, but somewhere away from all the madness."

Zeus sighed. "You can stay wherever you like. But you must realise Filipos will be offended because you are rejecting his hospitality."

In his presence, we continued to call him Mister Filipos, and he addressed us as Rod and Kam. It clarified that he had a higher social position than us. It's the Greek way. When he wasn't around, he was plain Filipos. We couldn't adjust to using the name Vangelis.

Staying somewhere other than Helios would have been a real insult to him. We could hardly say we couldn't afford it. He let us stay for free. He'd have been offended even if we tried to pay for our stays.

Proud and forthright, he measured his worth against how people reacted to his hospitality. In our case, the level of service and care he provided was faultless. Sometimes this would slip when he interacted with his paying guests. This was typified when he threatened to shoot the D80's. To him, they were regular guests.

Travel review sites were his bible, and negative comments would send him into an instant rage, followed by days of depression. He and I had similar goals in life. He wanted to leave a legacy to the tourist industry of Rhodes. I just wanted to leave a legacy.

Many times I'd be not so complimentary about things at the hotel. He would sulk, but never rage. Then he would come around and ask how I would put it right. On these occasions, he would never put the solution in place immediately. He would leave it a few weeks then implement it as if it was his own idea. But I was OK with that.

He asked me to oversee hotel feedback to guests' review comments. The negative reviews always involved conducting an internal investigation. And this consisted of him interrogating some unfortunate member of staff or a D80. The outcome was still instant dismissal. If it was a D80, they would be dismissed and come back in a new form to apply for the job they'd just lost.

Some staff were completely innocent, bloody good workers. These of course had been set up by the D80's. It became a mechanism they used more and more to get rid of employees that were good for the hotel. All the while, any cronies kept their jobs and continued to drag the hotel's reputation lower.

As the 2014 season came to an end, I began trying to get Filipos to look at the bigger picture. To use review sites to help him see if a member of staff added value to the hotel or not. I felt the time was right to let him in on the whole immortality secret, but it wasn't my place to do it. The contract made it clear that the only person who could disclose to Filipos was Zeus.

We must have done enough to convince Zeus we intended to fulfil the contract because he allowed us to return to England for the winter.

PROMETHEUS – *Of Humanity*

The 2015 season started full of hope, and we still had three years to complete our contract. We communicated with Filipos in March, and he revealed a deal of his own.

"Rod, Kam this is going to be a great season," he beamed on my tablet screen.

"We truly hope so. You deserve a good year."

"I have signed a contract with a religious organisation. They want sole occupancy of the hotel for two weeks. On the run-up to *Pascha*. And it is just before the tourist season starts. Easy money, they are providing their own staff. It will all be profit," then he let slip the amount. "Two million euros."

Kam was sitting facing me so she couldn't be seen by the camera on the tablet. She mouthed, "D80's?" She raised her scarred eyebrow to signify she was asking a question. His comment told me that they'd made him an offer he couldn't refuse.

I'd not seen him so excited. He filled me in about the deal he'd struck. "The religion is called Argon, and the followers are Argonists." I glanced up at Kam and raised both eyebrows signalling affirmative to her facial question.

This rang alarm bells for both of us. I could hear sirens, bells and horns echoing around my brain. The Argonists sounded as if they had come straight out of a Greek myth.

"What do you think?" he asked.

I couldn't tell him what was troubling me. The decision was his to make. I could see the euro signs in his eyes. If it was my hotel, I wouldn't take the gamble. *Maybe that is why I have no legacy.*

"Well? What do you think?" he repeated.

"I'm not a businessman like you. I wouldn't have handed my hotel over to total strangers. But it is your hotel, and the income will give a good start to the season."

"Yes, I know. We will have a fantastic season." Then his tone changed.

"I'm sorry Rod, because of the sole occupancy, I can't let you stay at Helios until they have left. Please don't be offended."

Inside I was relieved, it meant I didn't have to offend him. "That's fine, and we aren't offended. We were always uncomfortable having rooms that could be earning the hotel money."

"We will let you know where we are staying, and we can meet up with you. We will see you soon."

I thanked the gods that the conversation ended. Any advice I gave would be distorted by my concerns that the D80's might be involved. I couldn't find anything about the Argonist religion on the Internet. I Googled *Argonist.* I Googled *Argonism.* All google returned was:

Agonist, which is too close to an antagonist.

Arsonist, which was too close for comfort given the phoenix analogy.

An organism, we are all organisms, a bunch of cells that exhibit the properties of life.

Not to mention the similarity between the enunciation of *Argonist* and *Argonaut*.

I needed to consult with Zeus on this one. But no matter what Zeus thought, Filipos had already made up his mind and signed before asking for advice. Two million euros and only *Argonists* present on site. It had the potential to end in disaster.

At least we didn't have to break the news of staying somewhere away from Helios.

≈≈≈

I looked at Zeus. "I've got a bad feeling about the sole occupancy thing."

"You are worrying over nothing. If these Argonists have sole occupancy, there will be no guests for them to upset." His attempts at reassuring me were in vain. "If they have paid for sole occupancy, you cannot be there."

"That's already been decided by Filipos. We have to find somewhere else to stay. Can you bestow a power on me that will allow me to keep an eye on events at the hotel?"

He made light of my request. "If I had a euro for every person that asked that, I could give Filipos his two million."

"What about a cloak of invisibility or swiftness of foot so no one could see me," I suggested.

His tone suddenly turned serious. "If I were to bestow you any power, it would be the ability to transform into a small mammal. The cost would be that you would lose the protection of immortality. You become a mouse. You get eaten by a cat. Game over. Is that a risk you want to take?"

It didn't take me long to illustrate my decision. My feelings of horror betrayed by the look on my face.

"I didn't think so," he chided.

With a hint of sarcasm. I looked straight at him. "So we must keep the hotel healthy for three more seasons. Then why don't we hand it over to a group of people we know nothing about. Couldn't we at least explain to Filipos about the D80s?"

"NO," he boomed. I guessed he didn't like my sarcasm.

Well, that was a productive meeting, still no powers for any of us. Impotent again. Insubstantial reassurances and no support for any of my ideas. It was precisely like the job I'd left at home. It made me question myself: *Is this my destiny?*

Kam and I found a small family-run hotel to stay in. We were invited to enjoy the splendour of *Pascha* – Easter, the resurrection. The smell of celebratory meat cooking on spits filled the air. Kam's first taste of goat didn't impress her. It was refreshing to be on Rhodes without the pressures of fighting the D80's.

After Easter, we stayed on the island and moved into Helios for a few days. It was the start of the season after all. Filipos had invited me to spend a few days working with staff to ensure they didn't shrug their shoulders. It also allowed us to weed out cronies from the staff.

We arrived while the last few Argonists were loading cases and boarding their dust-covered coaches belching plumes of diesel exhaust. All at once, the last stragglers turned towards us, and I saw three pairs of eyes look at us and squint. I could hear the horror in Kam's voice as she spoke. "Shit Rod, they're D80's."

"Fuck," I replied as they dashed onto the coach.

I turned and hurried into the empty reception area and shouted. "Mikalis. Where is Mister Filipos?"

"Collecting his payment. He is in the restaurant."

"Come quickly. Something is wrong."

We arrived at the hotel restaurant, in time to see Filipos in tears. A sight I thought I'd never see, a Greek man in tears. He made no attempt to hide his distress. Kam rushed to him and tried to comfort him.

He wasn't upset he was in a rage his bloodshot eyes bulging with anger. He raised his face towards the painting of Helios and did that upwards nod that Greeks do. "THEY HAVE ROBBED ME," he bellowed.

My eyes followed his gaze to the image of Helios. There in one-foot high letters of red paint was the message: *GAMISOU THNITOS MALAKA.*

"Mikalis, what is *thnitos?*"

"Mortal."

It was clear where the origin of the message was. But it wasn't clear who it was aimed at.

It turned out that the last few people to leave had told him the money man was in the restaurant. He'd arrived at the restaurant moments before us, and they'd buggered off with the two million euros.

Kam asked, "Why would they do the sole occupancy thing just to graffiti a painting?"

125

I felt a real sense of doom like a tsunami was approaching. I could even hear screaming. We all headed towards the sounds. I glanced out across the lawns, expecting to see a giant wave sweeping towards the hotel. The screaming was coming from the hotel's cleaners. They had started to clean the rooms ready for the first wave of tourists. They pointed to one of the blocks of pool suites, 208 and 209.

As soon as we entered 208, I understood why the cleaners were screaming. There on the cream wall was the same message, this time in English, '*fuck you, mortal wanker*'. The TV had been ripped off the wall. Dressing table mirror smashed, mattress and chairs were all missing. We found them in the pool. The room looked like it was the scene of a 1980's football hooligan clash. It took Margaret Thatcher and a War Cabinet to solve that crisis.

Our one hope was that room 208 had been targeted because it was special to Kam and me. I had credited the D80's with the ability to make judgments. They were much more indiscriminate. They had trashed over two hundred rooms. What we saw that day, destroyed something in Filipos. It almost broke Kam and me because we'd come to love the place. I would have tried to save the hotel even without the immortality hostage thing. But part of me believed that those events signalled the end. We'd failed in making sure the hotel would still be healthy. Healthy? Instead, it had been mortally wounded. I wondered if it might be better to put it out of its misery and Filipos agreed. It was pitiful. It was the end. We all grieved for the loss.

We spent the rest of that morning going from room to

room, itemising damage and seeing what was salvageable. We discovered that everything ceramic had been smashed including bathroom fittings. There were live wires exposed everywhere. This posed a risk of electrocution to everyone. If something could be damaged, it was damaged. The amount of broken glass was immeasurable, and most of it was in the pools. Throughout Greece, the drainage system can clog when people put toilet paper into it. Not happy with putting paper down the toilet, the Argonists had used bedsheets. It was heart-wrenching.

Seventy rooms were untouched. Over the next few days, we were able to make good another thirty rooms. We threw destroyed stuff out and borrowed salvage from other rooms. It meant we could block off one end of the hotel and its grounds because we couldn't let guests see this.

The cost of putting everything right, totalled exactly two million euros. If only they'd paid, poor Filipos would have been able to recover from it. He couldn't pursue it via legal action. There was no evidence of the contract, and the only contact he had for them was an unobtainable phone number.

As it was during the Easter period, we messaged Alyss and Lindon to join us, but not to bring Mags. They would be useful. Four zombies would be better than two.

The aftermath of the Argonist episode was when we were closest to Filipos. He was vulnerable. He spent much of his time meditating with his phone. He used it mostly as if it was a set of worry beads, constantly twirling it between his thumb and forefinger. He'd given up shouting and blaming. He was a beaten man. He needed help, and I wasn't sure we were the right people to give it. We could help with the material things, like moving stuff around or working with staff and guests. But we had no abilities when it came to helping people in such a low state of mind. He needed a few sessions with a psychiatrist. Not surprisingly, even Zeus didn't have the answer.

I think it destroyed something in all of us. I started to wonder whether there was any point in carrying on? We'd been sent a powerful message, a show of power, a power I felt helpless to combat. Mikalis had been ever-present since our first visit. He was loyal to the hotel and Filipos. He couldn't see a way the hotel could recover and still maintain his reputation for filoxenia. The task was too great, and it wasn't just fatal to the hotel. Poor Mikalis suffered a major heart attack and never recovered. That was the loss of a truly great friend. The whole family were in mourning, and it compounded Filipos' depression.

≈≈≈

"Zeus, we have to help Filipos. He is broken," I pleaded.

"That's not your concern, Helios is dealing with it," he suggested with that same glint in his eyes. Having googled Helios, it transpired that Helios was the all-seeing eye of Zeus. That answered that question. In fact, Lindon had been researching Greek mythology. He'd been sending me anything that he believed might be relevant. I'm sure his motivation was to see which mythological god he could be.

"He's my friend, and I'm concerned for his welfare. What if he kills himself? It will be game over."

"Don't worry so much. If Filipos dies, he will be made

immortal like yourself," he reassured as if he was already planning it.

"That'll be good for him, live forever with depression." I was still impotent, and Zeus was still no help.

≈≈≈

The attempted destruction of the hotel escalated the confrontations. Most events took the form of malicious reviews, tour operator complaints and reclaiming of money. There were some attempts at further damage to the hotel. But, not as open as the Argonist attack. The refitting of the hotel suffered from little niggles. To us, they were small problems. But they were significant issues for genuine guests. We introduced routine inspections at checkout times. Once the D80's realised we were questioning and charging guests for damage caused. They moved to other more effective ways of hurting the hotel.

The next major battle could have been avoided if we'd had a bit of foresight. I didn't make it known, but I suspected Zeus had the foresight but didn't share it with us. I was starting to consider that he wasn't surprised by anything that happened.

The hotel continued to struggle financially, with the cost of repairs and tour operator reclaims, the budget needed to be adjusted. The hotel accountant, or money man, was a cagey bloke called George Papadopoulos. If you picture in your mind a stereotypical image of Scrooge, Papadopoulos was that image. Long thin fingers, an unkempt goatee beard, greasy swept-back black hair. He is the only Greek I'd seen that had a look of evil about him. His thin face never smiled. More than once, I considered whether he was a D80. But he passed the squinty eye test.

Papadopoulos insisted that some wage payments should be withheld or delayed. This meant that some staff weren't to be paid the wage they were expecting each month. They wouldn't have got away with it in the UK. But Papadopoulos told me it was common practice in Greece at that time.

In general, the staff that wanted the hotel to survive accepted this. There was a small minority that decided to stir up a revolt. Papadopoulos refused to allocate money to the staff budget. The state Filipos was in meant he had no will to argue. He just followed the recommendations of the money man. Papadopoulos was his most trusted advisor, and Filipos didn't have the fight in him to argue.

The staff unrest whipped up by the D80's and their cronies, led to a strike. Imagine the situation. Guests were witnessing picket lines and strike meetings in reception. And a Greek meeting is not a quiet affair. At least we knew that the staff who didn't strike were unlikely to be D80's or cronies.

Every guest that witnessed the mayhem was a potential complaint and an operator refund. Something needed to be done, and Filipos didn't have the motivation to negotiate with the strikers. The staff had been whipped into a frenzy of non-cooperation by an individual named Kostas. I suspected he was a D80 but had no evidence, beyond the damage he was causing to the hotel's reputation.

He was in the reception area, addressing an audience of disgruntled staff and bemused guests. He boomed, "We cannot work without payment, we all have bills to pay…" This was followed by a loud cheer from the staff. I picked my way through the crowd to get to the front of the throng. He continued his stirring. "No more work until we get what is owed." Another loud cheer went up from the staff. Almost as one, the guests' faces suggested they'd realised that they were in for a bleak holiday.

I refrained from using the mountza Zeus thing. There would be too many witnesses. "Kostas, stop. We must talk."

He didn't do the squinty thing. "I'm not talking to you. You are Filipos's friend." I heard another loud cheer behind me. My only thought, o*h Fuck, I now have a baying mob at my back.*

"Yes, and Mister Filipos has asked me to negotiate with you. Can we talk in private?" I had to try to gain a position of power. Kostas was a big man with a full head of hair and beard, both of which were jet black. He looked as if he was once muscular, but his muscle had become fat. He still had a look of power about him. He boomed when he spoke as did all of the Gods I'd met. He came across as a Greek version of *Brian Blessed.*

"I want to talk to Filipos and Papadopoulos, not some English Malaka," he replied.

I stepped closer so he could hear me over the noise of his disciples. "I have another friend. You may know him. His name is Zeus."

That was the trigger. Out came the squinty thing, followed by a look of panic. Poor Kostas had nowhere to run without disclosing his godly status.

I rephrased my earlier request. "My friend has asked me to negotiate with you. Can we talk in private?"

"No. we will talk here."

"Why? Are you scared that I'll defeat you? Mister Filipos has asked me to talk with you, and I have the power to have you dismissed and removed from the hotel. Where will your strike be then?" And I stared at him. The crowd quietened.

He stared straight back at me and did the squinty thing again. "I have the staff behind me." They cheered again.

"No, you haven't, you have a few cronies. Oh, I'm sorry you don't know what a crony is, do you?" I paused to think and allow him to examine my soul. *Which one are you?* I tried to categorise where a strike fitted in the scheme of things. I concluded the strike was mischief. "Tell me, Prometheus, what will the strikers think when they know that their leader is nothing more than a man that thinks he is a god? In 2015 you will be locked up to have your schizophrenia treated."

His eye shape changed from a narrow slit to complete circles. If he was under a non-disclosure agreement, I had just put him at risk.

"Very well, we will talk in private."

"Good, let's walk. I love the lawns and the beach at sunset."

He signalled to the strikers to leave the reception. A handful of loyal staff remained to deal with the guests.

"Look at that view, Prometheus. Isn't the setting sun beautiful as Helios shines on the hotel after a day's work?"

"Who are you? How did you know that I am Prometheus?"

"I didn't. I used analysis, you will know it as *analusis*. Its meaning has changed over the millennia, but it allows me to read the clues you gave. It will be the cause of your destruction," I threatened.

His mouth opened as if to say something, but it was clearly just a gormless look as he tried to process my warning. His eyes widened as fear filled the void between his ears. I never thought I would ever be in a position that I could frighten a god. Was it really that easy? Did I have the power to help Filipos save the hotel?

The events of the next few minutes answered those questions. For a split second, I saw the ball of flames leave his fist. As it reached my face, everything went blank. When the smoke cleared, there was the smell of singed hair again. And I was still stood opposite Prometheus.

With newfound confidence, I sneered, "Is that it? Well that failed, didn't it?"

"Who are you? How can you be immortal?" he questioned. I was going to say I was the god of Malakas but didn't know if I'd keep a straight face.

I looked out to sea. "It's almost sunset; do you want all your cronies to see the eagle eating your liver?"

He looked at the remnants of the sun as it sank into the sea, it told him he had to leave, and he was beaten. "What do you want from me?" he asked.

"The strike is over, you understand? You and your cronies will leave the hotel. And in the morning you will come to the reception desk and leave fifty thousand euros in cash. You will be paying the wages of the staff that are still here. Mark it for the attention of Rod Prince."

He left, but I knew we had made an enemy of Prometheus. It wasn't a comfortable feeling. I also knew that he would be back, he wouldn't be Kostas, but he would be back. I learnt something about myself that day. Maybe I could have a destiny.

As I walked back to my room, an eagle swooped low overhead. Its wing clipped the top of my head as it generated enough power to climb high into the darkening sky. Maybe it was thanking me for weakening its prey. Its wings folded as it dived, and I fancied that it had located Prometheus and was preparing to feast.

True to my demands the package was delivered the following morning. The challenge I had was getting Filipos to accept it.

≈≈≈

As the war intensified, my confidence fluctuated between arrogance and self-doubt. I knew a bit about self-doubt, it'd plagued me for years. Working with unemployed learners allowed me to recognise it in others. Each of them was a mirror of myself. As I was heading into unknown emotions, the need to consult with Zeus and Helios increased.

These meetings were a little disconcerting if we met during the night Helios was present. At times when the sun was above the horizon, he was just the glint in Zeus' eyes. At first, I didn't realise it, but I later noticed that in the morning it rose in his right eye. At noon it was visible in both eyes for a fraction of a second. After mid-day, it set in his left eye. I always imagined it must be like having a permanent migraine, with the white light in your field of vision. Maybe not, Zeus never complained. Lindon found the answer while researching the myths. "Helios was referred to as Zeus' eye. One poet, Hesiod, while describing the genealogy of the gods, suggested that Zeus's eyes were the sun."

Gatherings always followed the same pattern. I asked for something, Zeus refused, I offered a compromise and he got angry – meeting over.

"Zeus, I have some doubts about being able to win this war. We seem to spend most of our time firefighting. We are forced to react. An event occurs, and we deal with it, but nothing changes. We then just sit back and wait for the next event."

Zeus looked at Helios then back at me. "So tell me about your plan."

"What's the point? You will only tell me no," I suggested, like a kid that was fed up discussing bedtime with his parents.

"You won't know unless you tell us," Helios encouraged.

I outlined my plan, but I didn't tell them I was making it up as I went along. Lindon had carried out a lot of useful research. Because of his thoroughness, we learnt that Prometheus had upset Zeus.

"I understand that you dished out punishment to Prometheus. He was to have his liver eaten each night, by an eagle."

"Yes, what of it?"

"We also know that it grows, ready for the eagle to eat it again the next night."

Zeus confirmed, "That is correct. But I can't change the punishment." He'd anticipated what I was about to say next.

I've always had an interest in science, and I used to watch Tomorrows World. Though I did fail Biology, Physics and

Chemistry. But somewhere in the back of my mind, I recalled that a damaged liver regenerates. Unless it has suffered too much damage. I didn't know if the same applied to Deities.

I asked the first question. "Does the eagle eat all of the liver?"

"I don't have the faintest idea," was all the help Zeus could offer.

Clutching at straws, I threw the question open. "What about you, Helios? After all, you see everything."

"Not at night I don't, and by the time it is light enough to see, the liver has already mostly regenerated."

"I suspect the eagle, isn't eating enough of the liver, and that if it ate more, it wouldn't regenerate. Without his liver, he will die."

"And then he will resurrect," they both chorused together.

"Yes, I know he'll resurrect. But if enough time passes after the removal of the entire liver, he would resurrect without the liver."

Zeus as enthusiastic for my ideas as he ever was, proclaimed, "It can't be done. He will surely die without any liver left. Then he will resurrect with a new liver."

Helios looked at Zeus and suggested, "We cannot be sure of that. Rod might be correct."

Spurred on by the sun god's support, I asked, "Can you send more eagles each night. To make sure that they eat all of the liver?"

"No, I can't send more eagles. The punishment has been set. An eagle means one eagle. I am unable to change it." And he stressed the words '*an*' and '*one*' as if he was talking to a child.

I thought *here we go again, I asked for something – meeting over.* The repetition was like the constant tick of the clock on the wall.

"OK, can you make the eagle meet a partner eagle and have a large brood of chicks? You know, lots of mouths to feed. Then it would have to eat all the liver."

"Sorry, wrong god." But that time he didn't say it with anger. "You need to talk with my daughter. Artemis. She is the goddess of the hunt, and she is also the goddess of wild animals. I will arrange a meeting. I will also ask Athena to be present. She is the Goddess of Wisdom and Warfare provided she thinks the war is just. Your situation will intrigue her."

"You mean, you think I might have a plan?" I would have been speechless with surprise if I wasn't so excited.

The feeling of euphoria was never going to last. "You have a lot of work to do before meeting my daughters," he suggested.

All of a sudden, we had a new priority. We needed to find out all we could find out about the liver. What would happen if the entire organ was to be removed? How much of the liver had to be destroyed to stop it regenerating? I had to sell the scheme to Athena, and that was supposedly a challenge. It would be her that decided on the probability of the success or failure of the idea. The role of Artemis was to get the eagle to fall in love. Probably more of a job for Eros or Aphrodite to be honest.

Zeus cautioned, "Be careful where and how you do your research. Don't discuss it with anyone on the island, except your family, of course. Above all, do not use a hotel computer to do your research or exchange emails. Meeting over."

I felt a little titillated that he'd, at last, been positive about one of my suggestions.

ARTEMIS – *Of the Hunt and Wild Animals*

Lindon and Alyss returned home to Mags and set about their research. We needed to know how long a person might survive with a chronically damaged liver. Their school was a Science and Technology Academy, so they were able to work under the guise of a school project. This made it easy to suggest investigating a hypothesis. They used a conjecture to do with animal husbandry. This allowed them to be able to link with a local agricultural college which was a recognised route to becoming a vet. They had access to a large group of veterinarians, or whatever the collective noun for a group of vets might be.

The kids were asking questions about different conditions that affected animal organs. It was a vet that suggested they should narrow their research. They needed to reduce the number of variables. There were too many to even start to complete a study for a school project. Somewhere on Google, Lindon had discovered that humans and pigs were genetically similar. I can testify to this, given some of the smells and sights I used to encounter on my train commute to Manchester.

Lindon discovered a study that looked at liver disease in pigs. The study suggested thirteen per cent of pigs had some form of liver disease at the time of slaughter.

Survival rates of acute liver failure in pigs was the title of their study. This let them ask as many questions as they liked about causes, treatments and survival rates. They were able to ask random questions like, "Would this be the same for humans?"

They learnt that a human was more likely to suffer acute or chronic liver failure than a pig. But with medication and treatment, humans were able to recover. Lindon sent me an email. It was an almost empty message with the subject '*call me*'. It did contain what appeared phone number, and that had all the findings of his research. Telephone: 11001-010-111. *Clever boy.*

≈≈≈

I woke to the unmistakable woosh-thump sound of rotor blades overhead.

"What's that noise?" Yawned Kam, before shouting. "I can smell burning."

I drew back the curtains in my half-roused state. "Sounds like a helicopter. Bloody hell it's got a bucket underneath it's getting water from the sea."

I saw a plane a bit further out to sea. It was flying low and scooping up water.

"There must be a fire on the island." I opened the patio doors to go out and try and get a panoramic view. I looked to the left and saw that there were flames and smoke no further than a mile from where I stood. As the sound of the helicopter subsided, I heard the sirens of fire teams passing the hotel.

Within seconds, the ear-piercing racket of the hotel's alarm started. I ordered Kam to get dressed. This, in itself, was another surprise. I couldn't remember the last time I'd ordered her to do anything.

Then Zeus appeared on the patio and interrupted the panic. "Yes, get dressed but don't go anywhere. The fire won't reach the hotel; it is a smokescreen. The mischief-makers cannot know that Athena and Artemis are here. Staff and guests will be evacuated, and we will be given time for our meeting. Stay in your room. We will be back in thirty minutes." He left with a parting shot. "Tidy yourself up, Rod. You don't look good standing there in your boxers."

Thirty minutes later we'd showered, had a brew and nicotine. We were alert enough to be able to greet our divine guests. Zeus being Zeus didn't bother knocking.

"Rod, Kam please meet Artemis and Athena."

Artemis looked much like Alyss, sweet looking, with a face that suggested she was very young. She had the face of an early teen and certainly didn't appear thousands of years old. She had elfin features, a teardrop-shaped face with a tiny nose that would have been at home on a child's doll. Her long silver blond hair swept back into a bobble to form a mane-like ponytail. She had small hands with dainty fingers that didn't match her muscular upper arms. She had broad shoulders and a healthy six-pack, revealed by her sports bra and skimpy shorts. Her skin was pallid and not what you would expect on someone from the Mediterranean shores. She had a scent of the outdoors, like sweet-smelling oregano.

Athena, in her t-shirt and shorts, was a different being

altogether. I'd always given Kam a ten for her beauty. Applying the same measure, Athena was well off the scale. I couldn't say what it was about her, but it was difficult to avoid staring at her. She was a tall woman, and her lilac-tinted blond hair struggled to hide her ample breasts. She had a narrow waist joining a pair of long slender legs. Her hair framed her face perfectly, with her high cheekbones and a clearly defined jawline. Her full lips looked almost like a selfie pout. The same as Artemis, she was soft-skinned with a cold to the look complexion. Not as pallid but still only a hint of olive skin. Her beauty was natural, and not an ounce of make-up was needed. She had a smell that I couldn't identify, but it still overshadowed Artemis' oregano tones.

Kam unsure of the protocol didn't know whether to bow or curtsey, so she did both. Me, I gave up trying, and I could only stare. At least I finally closed my mouth.

Kam broke the silence. "My God. You're beautiful."

She took the words right out of my mouth.

Athena smiled. "Thank you. I have heard so much about you all and the sacrifices you have made for the island."

Artemis added, "Yes the whole of Aegis is grateful. If Rhodes dies all the islands in the Aegean will fall."

We sat around the rectangular table like a war cabinet holding a COBRA meeting. I imagined the table used in Downing street was a little bigger than the one in the suite. Fitting five people around it was just doable. Zeus sat at what would be the head of the table, rather obviously. As it was still morning, Helios was present in the sparkling right eye of Zeus.

Zeus as Chairgod opened the proceedings.

"Rod, I've already outlined your plan as I understand it. Have you been able to firm it up?"

I slid the print of the email across to him. "Yes."

He stared across at me. "I thought you weren't going to use email at the hotel." He scolded.

I defended myself. "Read it. Does it give away any secrets or tell you anything?"

"What is this? It's just a phone number. Now they know how to get to Lindon while he is in the UK."

It was my turn to laugh, something I didn't feel I had been able to do for…well… an eternity. "It's a message from Lindon, but not sent by Lindon," I explained. There's no way it can be traced back to him.

"But what about the phone number, can they not trace him with that?" he queried.

"No, because it's not a phone number, it is the answer to how we can harm Prometheus."

At which, Artemis sat upright. A tell-tale sign that she relished the opportunity of hurting her former lover. It would appear that hell isn't the only place that has no fury like a woman scorned.

Athena wanted to know more and asked, "Can you tell me what is in the message? To us, they are mere digits."

My confidence rose. I clarified, "Is it true that you are the goddess of Mathematics?"

A smile spread across her beautiful face. "Indeed, I am."

"Then, you will understand. The numbers are binary numbers. The 11001 is binary for 25, and it tells me that a liver cannot regenerate if there is less than 25 per cent of it left intact. The other numbers are two and seven. This tells us that death will occur between two and seven days from the point it stops regenerating. This tells us the eagle isn't eating enough of the liver."

Athena smiled again, but I wished she hadn't. Her smile made her even more beautiful. "An interesting plan, but it needs more. We need to know what to do with that information."

"There is more." And I outlined how I anticipated the plan developing.

"Prometheus must resurrect without his liver being able to sustain his life. We need to ensure that the eagle eats more than seventy-five per cent of it. This will stop it regenerating. The eagle can't eat all of his liver. If it does, he will die instantly. When he resurrects, it will include having a new and repaired liver. He needed to die, but not from the injuries to his liver." I paused because I'd got to the bit that might not work.

"Go on," prompted Athena.

"The key to success will be time. I have assumed the survival time is proportional to the amount of liver left. I have calculated that when the liver gets to five per cent, toxins will build up in the body. They will increase so fast that death will occur in hours. Someone then has a small window of time in which to kill Prometheus. Using any means except further damaging his liver."

Zeus became involved in the discussion. "This is where you come in Artemis. As Rod said, the eagle isn't eating enough of the liver to stop it regenerating. He has asked if you can help. Rod, tell Artemis what you need."

"Is it possible to give the eagle a partner so that they have chicks? If they have young, the eagle will need to feed himself, the hen and the chicks. But too many chicks and the liver will all be eaten. Too few and the eagle would still not eat enough."

Artemis smiled, but it wasn't the beautifying smile of Athena, it was more of a mischievous grin. "Yes, that can be done. What do you think, Athena? Has he got a plan that can work?"

Athena put on her glasses. They made her appear more intelligent. "It is likely to succeed. The oracle of Delphi, Pythia, is saying that she sees four chicks. She also sees that Prometheus is living a life of eternal death and resurrection. Each resurrection lasting *four-score-and-ten* minutes." She took her glasses off.

I mused to myself, *Bloody hell, glasses you can communicate with.*

Zeus looked at me and smiled. "I knew we could do it."

I looked at him and raised an eyebrow. He corrected himself by saying, "I mean, I knew you could do it, Rod."

"Thank you. The only problem is that someone has to kill Prometheus within that short time. I'm afraid it won't be one of the family," I warned, making it clear that we didn't want to murder anyone.

Artemis with childlike excitement volunteered. "I'll do that. I'll be present while the eagle is feasting. When I see it has eaten enough. I will kill the cheating bastard."

Her last comment made Zeus frown. "Artemis. Mind your tongue."

"Sorry. But I have waited for millennia for this

opportunity. First I will send some beautiful female eagles. They will be ready to nest."

Zeus asked, "How long will it take for there to be chicks. We cannot risk too much time in case the plan is discovered."

A discussion took place, and Artemis told us the hens would be sent immediately. I hoped the eagle was randy and liked the look of at least one of them.

"Three months is the earliest that any chick will hatch. Nest building, mating, egg-laying and incubation cannot be any shorter," calculated Artemis.

"Athena and Artemis, thank you so much for your help. We all know what we must do. This will not be discussed any further until after the deed is complete," clarified Zeus and he closed the pow wow.

Kam and I were left in the suite alone, except for the sound of alarms and helicopters. Twenty minutes later, and there was silence. The fire was out, and the hotel resumed its business.

≈≈≈

For the first time, the family and our divine friends could see hope. It was the first proactive action we'd taken. We needed to keep our feet on the ground, at least the family did. It was only a plan, and we all know what Robbie Burns wrote about the best-laid plans.

Zeus warned us that if the plan worked, we would all be seen as a severe threat to the D80's.

As a family, we'd set ourselves the target of St Rhodes day - Nov 10th, 2017 to win the war and defeat the D80's. This gave us around 28 months to plan and put in place our attacks. Lindon needed to step up his research. He'd asked not to go to university. He couldn't see the point if he was going to spend the rest of eternity living on Rhodes. Kam and I had to admit there was little point, and the higher priority was researching the D80's. At eighteen, he was close to leaving school. Alyss was sixteen, and wouldn't get to take her A levels. She joined Lindon in gathering information. They continued to live with Mags. It was lucky that she enjoyed their company, and it helped to keep her young.

Kam and I had almost taken up permanent residence on Rhodes. We did take holidays in the UK, mainly when we felt in danger. It became a safe haven.

The thirteen weeks waiting for the chicks to be born, seemed to take forever. I'm sure all mothers would agree that the last trimester is the one that seems to drag on the most in a pregnancy.

Athena had insisted that to ensure there were no hiccups with any of the babies, some eagles' eggs should be put in an incubator in Athens. This meant that Artemis could balance the number of mouths the eagle had to feed.

Before the eggs showed any signs of hatching, the hotel had closed for the season. Both Kam and I worried about the health of our friend Filipos. He needed the break afforded by the closed season. If only we could tell him what was going on. He would learn that none of the disasters was his fault.

My worry for the winter was that the D80's would leave the island because the hotel was empty. I felt more comfortable knowing where they were and what they were up to. Zeus reassured us that they would remain near the hotel. They would try to disrupt the winter repairs. It didn't matter where Prometheus went, because the eagle would continue to eat his liver to feed its family. Given all the trouble that the hotel had in 2015, I was nervous that the plan would fail. That outcome didn't bear thinking about.

I did manage to use the time to talk to Filipos. I'm no counsellor, but with encouragement, he did start to open up and communicate. He still didn't have the fire he had when we first met. I did have the opportunity to justify why letting us stay at the hotel for free was bad for the hotel. Having an open-door policy and staying whenever we liked wasn't helping the hotel. When I told him that we would be staying in Helios less often, I thought he would be offended, and he was. In his frame of mind, he assumed it was because he'd failed us.

I looked at him. "Your offer is extremely generous, but it doesn't help you or the hotel."

"Where will you stay? You are family, and you should stay here." I remember my mum using the same argument when I told her I was leaving home at eighteen.

I reassured him. "Nothing will change. I will still come to the hotel, and I will still help. I will still be your eyes on the staff. We will be staying just minutes away in Kremasti."

"Ah, you have a new love. Olympian Dreams. I have seen the pictures on Facebook," he lamented. He thought that I was rejecting his hospitality. Knowing we were going to stay at the swanky Olympian only made it worse.

"It's not my new love. It's that every time you give me a room, some poor guest has to be moved out. It costs you money. Money that you need to recover from the damage done by the Argonists. Please see that I don't wish to offend you. Everything I do, I do it for you."

For the rest of that closed season, we had little contact with him. I missed him. Yes, 2015 was a dreadful year, and I felt I'd lost a dear friend.

On the first of November, we went to Athens. It was a kind of downtime progress meeting. We'd planned to spend Christmas together with the kids. Having experienced Greek Easter, we'd long wanted to experience the Orthodox Christmas. It was also an opportunity for Lindon and Alyss to meet the goddesses. We contacted the kids, and they flew to Athens from the UK.

Artemis told us that the chicks were expected to hatch a few days after we were due to return to Rhodes. It was decided that Lindon and Alyss would remain in the capital with Athena. Artemis was going to travel to Rhodes with us and pose as our daughter, using Alyss's passport.

We needed to try and find some gold to create a golden tip of an arrow or a knife. Artemis thought that one gram would be enough to make the sharp point she wanted. It didn't have to be pure gold, but it couldn't originate from Greece. The gods wouldn't permit it.

Athens had a good supply of jewellery shops. I imagined most of their stock originated from Greece. As Artemis needed it immediately, Kam and I discussed our wedding rings which were made of welsh gold. Mine was the heaviest at three grams. I donated it to the cause.

The fashioning of the tip was left to Artemis because she would know exactly what she needed. She would do it once we'd returned to Rhodes. At least I got to wear the ring for a little longer. As Prometheus was unlikely to be in any shape to resist, she would use a dagger to make sure of the kill.

The family returned to Rhodes on Guy Fawkes night. The relevance of the date was wasted on Artemis. When we arrived at Olympian dreams, Artemis had a planning meeting with Zeus and Helios. I wasn't privy to this because according to Zeus, I didn't need to be. They'd decided that Artemis was to spend the rest of her stay close to where Prometheus dwelt at night.

Once the assassination was complete, the four of us would return to Athens, where we hoped to be safe from divine retribution.

≈≈≈

A few weeks after we returned to Rhodes, Zeus summoned us to a meeting at Olympian. He had news of Artemis and Prometheus.

Zeus flicked on the office TV screen and started a video. It showed Artemis making a bloody good impression of David Attenborough whispering in the undergrowth:

"The chicks have started to hatch," she breathed.

"I know this because the amount of liver eaten has increased each night." She clearly didn't want to use the word cock. "Unfortunately. Daddy eagle hasn't been eating enough. This leads me to believe, or hope that there are still more chicks to hatch. My concern is that older chicks will demand a greater amount of liver. As the remainder hatch, the eagle may try to eat the entire banquet. I will bide my time."

And the screen went black for a moment. As it faded back in, we could see:

> The eagle flying down for its next feast. The beast started its work, clawing and tearing at his flesh to get to the bloodied liver.

Artemis must have been wearing some kind of bodycam to give us closeup point of view. I almost felt sorry for Prometheus. But given the threat he posed to us, any sympathy I felt was soon overcome. The video jumped ahead:

> Dawn started to break. Prometheus was lying prone on the ground. Artemis approached him, and his skin had clearly begun to take on that hue of jaundice. He opened his eyes, and they were bloodshot and yellow. The camera peered into the cavity where his liver once was. We could see that there was hardly anything left of it.

We could see that there was hardly anything left of it. But I was relieved to see there was some of it still visible.

> "Goodbye, uncle Prometheus," she teased in her childlike voice.
>
> He laughed at her. "It's not goodbye. My liver is regenerating. I am resurrecting. The way my brother's punishment intended." He laughed again.
>
> "That is where you're wrong. The eagle has eaten too much for the liver to regenerate." She threw some nectar at the liver to cauterise it. It stopped bleeding and scabbed over in its diminished state.
>
> The gold-tipped knife glistened. She plunged it upwards into the exposed cavity of his abdomen. The heart stopped beating. How could it beat? She worked the knife to slice it into many thin slices. The cause of his death was the destruction of his heart. Artemis stood back to reveal Prometheus filling with

> colour. He was resurrecting. The opening in his abdomen started to seal over what remained of his shrivelled liver. He regained a healthy skin tone, as he groaned, realising the error in his calculations.
>
> "What have you done? There will be no one to care for the humans," he pleaded.
>
> "You haven't done very well at looking after humans so far. You are redundant. You aren't worthy of being an Olympian god."

Zeus fast-forwarded the video a little.

> As the sun rose higher, Prometheus's skin colour returned once more to a jaundiced yellow. He screamed in pain as his liver failed to sustain his life, and another death came swiftly.

"She estimated it was around a 90-minute cycle," relayed Zeus. "He now continues the repetition of resurrection, death from chronic liver failure and resurrection again."

I felt sorry for the eagle chicks that would go hungry that night. They'd probably die. In the final scene:

> The camera pointed towards the sun. The closing words of Artemis: "Helios, your descendants have excelled."

Zeus looked at us. "That was two days ago. Your plan was successful. Helios has seen it. Prometheus lives as an invalid for as long as it takes you to fly to Athens. You will be rewarded. Now go and enjoy your Christmas together."

"But what about Filipos? I fear he will let the hotel fade away over the winter, and it's too early."

"Don't worry about Filipos. Enjoy Athens. All will be well by Christmas."

ATHENA – Of Wisdom and War

We met Artemis at the airport and had an uneventful flight to Athens.

"Are you guys really related to Helios?" asked Artemis.

"I think so. We don't have any evidence, but he and Zeus told us we were. They even gave us immortality."

"You must have impressed my dad. He hasn't done that for over two thousand years."

When we arrived back in Athens, Alyss and Lindon were there to meet us at the airport. Alyss was full of the stories that Athena had filled her head with.

"She's invited me to live with her in Athens."

"Well that's not going to happen you're only sixteen."

"I'll be seventeen in a few weeks."

Kam interjected with her usual delaying phrase. "We'll talk about it."

That made me realise how Filipos must have felt when we told him we weren't staying at Helios anymore.

Lindon, on the other hand, had spent his time in Athens visiting historical sites. His hope was that he might gather information to support his research. He didn't say so, but I suspect he was also looking for some freerunning locations.

As the date neared to Alyss's birthday, Kam and I did discuss the idea that Alyss had requested to stay with Athena. Kam convinced me that it might not be a bad thing if she was nearer to Rhodes. Mags was approaching eighty. With sixty plus years between her and Alyss, it couldn't have been much fun for either of them. Lindon seemed to think that Athena was good for Alyss.

"You guys do realise that Alyss has seemed a lot happier while we've been in Athens," Lindon declared in aid of his sister's request. "I think Athena is good for her. They have been getting on really well."

The family celebrated Alyss's birthday by eating out at a restaurant in the Plaka area of Athens, sited right underneath the acropolis. "Please, can I stay with Athena?" she asked for the hundredth time.

Kam relented. "Dad and I have discussed it, and we think it will do you good to stay with Athena. So yes, you can."

Alyss squealed, and she looked at Lindon. "Thank you. Thank you," she shrieked. Clearly, they were in cahoots.

"There are conditions. While you are in Athens, you will be enrolled in a language school so that you can improve your Greek."

"I will, I promise. Athena has already started to teach me about the language. I am learning lots about the culture."

"You need to make some mortal friends, too. You'll have the opportunity to meet some at the language school. I'm sure Athena will want some time without babysitting you."

"But Athena is much more fun. She's even let me taste ambrosia."

As inquisitive as ever, her comment interested Lindon. "What was it like?"

"I can't describe the taste, but it was beautiful. I felt like I was in a dream state. As if I was on drugs."

Her comment raised some concerns. I mimicked her comment, and my eyebrows mimicked the concerns. "Whoa, rewind. Drugs?"

"No silly. It gave me a sensation the way I imagine drugs would make me feel."

We had an ad-hoc discussion about drugs. How they were bad for you and how your body came to rely on its effects. Alyss pointed out that nicotine was a drug. "You and mum take a drug several times a day."

Kam and I looked at each other without saying anything. We knew Alyss was right. What could we say?

I took a deep breath and promised her. "My New Year's resolution will be to give up vaping."

Kam agreed, "And I will give up smoking."

With Alyss's birthday out of the way, we had just two weeks to wait for Christmas to arrive. It also reminded us that Kam and I had both missed celebrating our own birthdays. We agreed it didn't matter if we were going to have an eternity of birthdays. But first, we had to remove three more D80s. We put the war to the back of our minds.

We couldn't believe the difference from the Christmases we were used to. The celebrations pretty much filled up Christmas Eve. Christmas day was more about families getting together to catch up and relax. We went to the cinema and saw *Avengers: Age of Ultron*. I had to laugh; it was like watching a training video on how to battle with superheroes. A thought crossed my mind, our battles with the D80's would provide material for a book or film. I made a mental note to ask Zeus if it was allowed.

New Year's Eve 2015, we'd had a Facebook message from Filipos, *Eftychisméno néo étos se sas kai pollá chrónia*. Which translates to Happy New Year to you all and for many years. We sent the same message back to him. As much as social media would let me, I detected that he was brighter. It is the first positivity he'd shown in a long while.

The first day of the New Year arrived. It was hard, but Kam gave up the fags, and I gave up vaping. We were sure it was our newfound state of immortality that gave us the power to succeed. It is something we had tried many times before in our mortal life, and we had always given in to temptation. That time we just stopped. I suppose it was a crutch we no longer needed.

I called Zeus. "Filipos seems brighter, with a bit more ambition."

"That's because he is brighter. He is also more motivated. You will see the difference for yourselves when you come back to Rhodes."

"When will a room be available at Olympian Dreams?"

"We will start preparing for the new season at the end of January."

I looked at the family. "Who is up for Rhodes on the first of February?"

It was almost unanimous. "Not me," chimed Alyss. Just in case we'd forgotten she was staying with Athena.

"OK. Zeus, we'll see you on the first of February."

"I wait for you." And he ended the call.

I was ready for heading back to the island. The weather in Athens wasn't too different from what we get in the UK. I needed to feel the warm sun on my skin again. By Rhodian standards, it would be cold for the natives. For us, a solid ten to fifteen degrees centigrade was warm. Alyss, as agreed, stayed with Athena. Though she did promise to come and visit during breaks at the language school. Kam would visit Athens regularly. Kam, Lindon and I headed for Rhodes.

≈≈≈

Arriving at Olympian Dreams was an enjoyable experience. So many friends we'd made took the effort to greet us. Such a difference from the polite nod we would get at home. Here was a group of people that celebrated our arrival.

We met with Zeus. He greeted us with: "Welcome back to our beautiful island. Where is Alyss?"

Kam responded first. "She's staying in Athens. She's with Athena and learning Greek."

"You should have asked for permission," he admonished, like an old school headmaster. "Athena has work to do, and I don't want Alyss distracting her."

I was slightly irritated by his tone. "In that case, give your permission now."

Then he did that squinty thing on me. I just glared at him.

"Do you think being with Athena will do her good?"

"I er… we do," I responded still glaring at him.

Then as if waking from a dream, he shook the squint off his face and changed the subject. "I have news," he announced with excitement. "Filipos is recovered. He is looking forward and not back. He is now on the board of Olympian Dreams with a twenty per cent stake."

"I thought you told us he would never be able to afford it," I queried.

"He received an offer he couldn't refuse. Financial input for Helios and a share in Olympian."

"You mean he's sold it? Who to? How do we know the backers aren't deities?" I could hear my own panic in my voice.

"Stop with the questions, and I will explain."

"Helios and I have formed a company. I had the idea for the name. We've called it D80 Ltd. It's a good name, don't you think? The company has bought sixty per cent of Helios Hotel. We now have a controlling stake."

"You mean you've driven him so low he wanted out at any cost."

"No, let me finish. The company have wiped out the debt caused by the Argonists. Filipos has personally received five million euros, and a seat on the board at Olympian." He looked at me as I tried to digest the figures.

I opened my mouth, ready to speak, but he interrupted me. "The good news for you and Kam is that you both have a twenty-four per cent stake in D80 Ltd. That is your reward for defeating Prometheus. What do you think about that?" And he thrust yet another contract in front of us.

Caution was telling me to study the contract. There wasn't

a lot to read. It was the Articles of Association for D80 Ltd. It didn't appear to add anything to our roles that weren't already covered in our earlier agreement. I did note that it absolved us of any financial responsibility to D80 Ltd. We also got another salary. I'd have felt better if we had a twenty-six per cent stake each. As it stood, we could still be overruled by Zeus and Helios. We signed.

"How much does Filipos know? Does he know about us being on the board of D80 Ltd? Does he know we're immortal?" I asked.

"Will you stop with the questions? He is on a need to know basis. He needs to know nothing. All negotiations were conducted via an agent. We can't risk the renegades knowing anyone from Olympian is involved. Trusting anything to a mortal would put us all in danger."

"So, nothing's changed," I stated.

"Yes, it has. Filipos is happy. Your wish has been granted."

"Yes, the hotel is part mine, but no one knows about it. I'll still be impotent."

"No, you won't. Filipos listens to you, and he trusts your advice." The meeting closed.

≈≈≈

As time journeyed into March, the spring flowers bloomed. Everywhere was so green. It's something we never saw when our visits were limited to the summer season. Rhodes has a much shorter winter than we get in the UK. The air was full of the various scents as pollen was lifted into the air by the breeze. As I'm sure, Shakespeare meant to say. 'Rhodes, by another name, would smell as sweet.' I genuinely believe that Rhodes has a unique smell all of its own. So different from the variety of fumes generated by man back home in the UK.

I had several meetings with Filipos, and the difference in him was immense. He asked me to oversee the recruitment of staff at the hotel. This suited me because it reduced the opportunity for D80's to gain employment at Helios. Kam applied for – and got – the role of Head Housekeeper and this allowed her to be at the hotel a little more. She was also able to watch out for malicious damage to hotel property. It was her job to log any damages. No-one questioned her going into rooms with a hi-vis jacket and clipboard.

We were in an ideal situation. I had some control over who was employed at the hotel. Kam would have access to guests' behaviour that was inappropriate. To all intents and purposes, Filipos continued to run the Hotel. The fact he had a sleeping partner called D80 Ltd didn't bother him at all. It was good to see him with a spring in his step. I knew he was better when I heard him bellow down the phone to a supplier.

Lindon was able to conduct his research while at Olympian and volunteered to help with the animation team at Helios. We were looking forward to a good year. It had to be better than in 2015. It certainly couldn't be worse.

"Dad, do you think we will succeed?" he asked.

"Of course. If I didn't think that, I'd give up now. There's always hope."

"There is always hope because it's locked up in Pandora's box."

I looked at him. "What do you mean?"

"When Pandora opened the box, all that was left when it was closed, was hope. It's from my research. I'm worried that we have only got two summer seasons left." He was concerned, and this pleased me as it was a sign of his growing maturity.

I'd been pondering over the same thing while we were in Athens. Seeing the flowers arrive in Rhodes so early was just what I had been waiting for. I knew we'd seen flowers as early as April before, but I didn't realise how soon they started to show. Seeing blooms around the island in February was a real bonus. It gave me hope, even if it was locked up in Pandora's box.

"Do me a favour, son? Can you concentrate your research on Demeter for the time being?" I asked.

"Of course, any particular reason?"

"Nope, I've got a theory, and I want to check it out. Give me all that you've got on her already and don't forget only use the computer at Olympian."

I seemed to recall that in early 2015 I watched a TV programme called *'Secrets of the Bible: The Ten Plagues of Egypt'*. In the program, there was a hint that the plagues could be explained by science. It was suggested that a volcano erupted on one of the Greek islands. I think it was on Santorini. The program suggested it was the instigation of the ten plagues. This was around 1600 BC. I needed some idea of the time that the Olympians came to power.

≈≈≈

It wasn't long before Lindon passed on what he'd found. "Here's what we've got on Demeter." And he handed me a

161

single sheet of paper.

"Is this just a summary? It isn't much."

"That's because there isn't a lot. We already know she's Zeus's sister. But did you know they had a kid together?"

"Let me get this right, Zeus is our CEO. He is married to Hera, who is also a director. Zeus has a kid with Demeter who's a D80, and she's his sister?"

"Yep, but it gets better. Their kid, a daughter called Persephone, was abducted by Hades, Demeter's brother. He went on to marry the kid, his niece, that is."

"So, the entire board of Olympian is connected to Demeter in some way," I clarified. I was looking for reassurance. "OK, what's your view? Are we being conned by Zeus? Are the D80's a power of good?" I asked.

"No and no. Everything I've found out is in the public domain. The board would expect us to know it. No, they aren't keeping anything from us." My son's comments were reassuring.

"There's more. The events of the abduction led to Demeter overseeing the seasons. Persephone is reunited with Demeter for a few months each year, and that's during the spring and summer. Pretty much during the holiday season in Greece," he added.

I looked up from the summary. "Yeah, I can see. OK, so we know that already. What I need to know is have you uncovered any hint of when this all happened?"

"Yep, it was about 1600BC."

"That's exactly what I wanted to hear." The jigsaw in my mind started to fall into place.

"Anything else?" I asked.

"Yes. Demeter is also known for founding the *Eleusinian Mysteries*. These were big festivals held every five years. Everyone that took part was sworn to secrecy, so nothing is known about them. But Demeter doesn't get a mention in any other myths."

"Is Persephone a goddess?"

"Yes, she is. She is the daughter of two gods, and she is the goddess of the spring."

"In which case, she is also a D80," I proclaimed.

"I have considered that, but she isn't named in the contract. I guess if she was then Zeus would have included her as a *bad god*."

"But didn't you say that Zeus was her dad?"

"Yep. And because of that, I've put Persephone on the back burner. Hades will be the best source of information on her."

We needed to try and identify Demeter. I clung on to the fact that we were heading towards the season when she would be with Persephone.

Going to Helios for a few days was easy, given that Filipos was expecting me to spend time with his staff. It was late April and the season had begun. My role was to assess the staff's customer service skills. I arranged to work with small groups across all departments. Groups of four doing role-play. With a mixture of languages, this made for an amusing time and lots of shrugging shoulders. We used the ample space that was the restaurant. It was always empty between meals. The painting of Helios had been restored, and it had the Argonists' graffiti removed from it. That my search for bad gods took place under the gaze of a good god, was rather fitting. It gave me strength.

I wanted to work with all the staff. I needed to be able to ask each employee a straightforward question. I built it into the role-play I'd developed. Posing as a guest, I had the opportunity to question every one of them. "Do I know you?" I would ask them as I stared deep into their eyes. I was looking for that squint.

My search had mixed results. I managed to identify a housekeeper who was calling herself Despoina. I suspected this was Hestia. At least Kam could keep an eye on that one. But it let me know that if I was correct, then Demeter wasn't posing as a member of the hotel's staff.

I had to turn my attention to the hotel's guests. It was difficult because we didn't have a clue about what we were looking for. Meanwhile, I accessed the hotels booking system. I was looking for bookings that had two women in the party. It was like trying to find a grain of salt on a sun-kissed beach. It could be two women in separate rooms. I ended up suspecting half of the guests at the time. I thanked the gods that the hotel wasn't full.

Kam hadn't noticed any attempts at sabotage in any of the suites. This is often the first sign that a D80 is at work among guests. All that kept me trying to find her was the thought that maybe Demeter hadn't appeared at the hotel yet. We didn't even know if Demeter and Persephone's time together had begun. Perhaps they would be staying somewhere else. Maybe my theory was completely wrong.

I messaged Zeus. "Do you know if Demeter and Persephone are at Helios?"

"Dunno, M8," was his bleak reply. He'd obviously ignored my request to drop the use of text-speech.

I was starting to get disheartened and doubt myself. Lindon came to the rescue.

"I think I've found Demeter and maybe her daughter. Let me show you. Come and see." He took me to the animation pool and showed me two women sunbathing on the lawn in front of Suite 124. We didn't get too close. It couldn't be obvious that we were looking at them. If he was wrong, I would have been labelled as a pervert.

"You watch them, if they want to get a drink or something, they'll leave their sunbeds, and within seconds the sun disappears behind a cloud. What an awesome way to reserve your lounger."

They reappeared, and the sun did too. I wasn't convinced. I needed more proof that one of them was Demeter. They looked too happy, like real guests. My experience was that the D80's were miserable sods. I walked to where they were tanning themselves. They did have beautiful bodies and the voice in my head shouted *pervert*. In my defence, I might be immortal, but I'm still human. As I got near, they both rotated and laid on their stomachs, and that view was equally enchanting. It did make it more difficult for me, though. Because of the presence of her cellulite dimples, I guessed the lady on the left was the mother, Demeter.

I stared at them. "Excuse me, do I know you?" *Pervert* went the voice in my head again. They both turned on to their

165

backs. This revealed mountains and valleys of flesh. The older woman looked like she was in her forties. She had blonde wavy hair, the colour of wheat at harvest time. It was cut in a bob. Although she'd been laying in the sun, she was surprisingly fair-skinned. She must have been using a high SPF sun cream. She had a slight baby tummy, but not a single stretch mark was visible.

"I don't think so," she replied through her thin lips.

"Maybe," added the other woman. She looked younger. She could be the daughter. She had the same full lips of Zeus and Athena. *Could this be Persephone?* If this was mother and daughter, she got her mouth shape from her father. Her hair was much longer and was swept up in a loose bun. It was mousy in colour and appeared to be wavy. She had a look of Athena about her, and they could easily be sisters and cousins. She looked like she was in her late teens.

I looked for the squint. Like an idiot, I hadn't factored in the sunglasses. What an absolute bloody fool. All I could see was a bloody reflection of myself. I apologised and made my exit. They did rotate again to return the vista to the original view, and the thong-clad bum cheeks.

"Well, is it them?" asked Lindon when I got back to him.

"I don't know." I looked skyward as if asking the gods for guidance. I counted for a few seconds. "Do you fancy having a bet with your old man?"

"Depends if I have a chance of winning."

"I bet you twenty euros they'll leave their loungers during the next ten seconds, nine, eight, seven, six, five, four," I counted. And the ladies got up and walked towards their room.

"Wow, how did you know they'd do that?" asked Lindon, impressed by my ability to predict the future.

"I thought you were clever," I teased. "I looked up at the sky and saw the cloud coming over. The ladies aren't controlling the weather. The weather's controlling them."

As the clouds cleared, the sun came out, and so did the mountains and valleys.

"You have work to do Mister Animator. I'm going to catch up with your mum."

≈≈≈

I told Kam about Despoina being Hestia and employed as a housekeeper. It also gave me a chance to find out if the ladies in Room 124 had been creating problems. Kam hadn't noticed anything. She did say that Despoina and her friend had been cleaning that block. She agreed to check it at the end of cleaning the following day.

"Never mind tomorrow. We could spend the evening in the bar tonight. I want to meet the ladies from 124, if they're out," I offered, inviting my wife out for an evening of god hunting. Such a romantic gesture.

As anticipated, the wholesome twosome appeared in the bar. I could hardly approach and ask them that same question. I toyed with the idea of saying, *you look different with your clothes on*, but that is a cliché and might earn me a slapped face. I ran an idea past Kam, and she thought it was a good one.

"I'd like to apologise, for earlier would you like to join my wife and me, we have a large table to ourselves?" I didn't stare.

They glanced at each other. "Yes, thank you, that would

be nice."

They collected their drinks and joined us. We introduced ourselves, and they were mother and daughter, Mrs and Miss Fox. Maybe the daughter was divorced because she had a ring of even whiter flesh on her left hand. I apologised again and asked them how they found the hotel. The tone of the conversation changed immediately. All that came out of their mouths was pure poison.

"The hotel is the worst I have ever stayed in. It's filthy, and there is a disgusting smell in our room. The staff are rude, and the food isn't fit for dogs. The entertainment is rubbish. It's too far from Rhodes town." And that was just a polite summary. I almost wished I hadn't asked. I guessed she was trying to sway our opinion of the hotel. It didn't work. I stared, and she squinted. They got up and left, they were clearly flustered, to say the least. I knew I had the right woman. It was Demeter. I checked her booking; it was for two weeks, and she was on day three. It meant I had time to put a plan in motion. I needed to meet with the board of Olympian – except for Filipos, of course.

DEMETER – *Of Harvest and Agriculture*

This was my first opportunity to meet with Hades and Hera. I noticed how beautiful Mrs Zeus looked for her age. She had a mother's face but didn't look older than twenty-five. Lindon said she was a MILF, but I didn't have the foggiest idea what that meant. Zeus was the youngest of his family, yet he looked the oldest. Clearly being King of the gods is a stressful job. Bearded Hades looked a similar age to Zeus.

We got the introductions and greetings out of the way. I opened with, "I thought you would have told me about the relationships between you guys and Demeter."

"It's public knowledge. Everyone in Greece knows of the myths. They have studied the gods all their lives," ridiculed Zeus. As it was morning, Helios twinkled in just Zeus' right eye. The rest of his family nodded in agreement with him.

"Yes, but I'm not Greek. I'm a stupid Englishman. Remember? Anyway, no matter, I need to know more about Demeter."

Zeus glanced at the others, and then back at me. "What do you want to know? We will share everything with you."

"Anything that isn't in the public domain. Any family secrets. Information about the Eleusinian Mysteries."

"We can't tell you anything about the Eleusinian Mysteries. We were never privy to those events. If we had been, we would still be sworn to secrecy," cautioned Hera.

Hades shuffled his feet before adding, "They would have always been conducted while Persephone was with Demeter. Other than that, I know nothing." He didn't make eye contact, and that made me feel uneasy.

"Can I speak with Hades alone please?"

"No," was the stark response from Zeus.

"OK, I understand, but I have my own theories about the mysteries."

"What are they?" asked Zeus.

"They're still only theories. I'll let you know when I have developed them a little more."

Zeus and Hades glanced at each other.

"Hades, what do you know about her relationship with Persephone?"

"Demeter dotes on her daughter. She loves her more than any human could imagine, but she is controlling. She won't let Persephone out of her sight except for the few months each year that Persephone comes home to me."

"And what about Persephone? Does she enjoy the months with you? Or is she glad when she can return to be with her mother again?"

Hades looked at me, aware that I was questioning the love his wife has for him. "She is happy. I have told her many times she is free to spend as much time with her mother as she wishes."

I looked at him with a quizzed expression. "What about the four pomegranate seeds that force Persphone to be with you?"

"All bullshit. We made up the story so that Persephone had a reason to come back to me for part of the year. She hates how her mum controls her, but she is weak-willed and doesn't want to upset Demeter. If Persephone had her way, she would spend longer with me. We are living happily in the underworld. We share a secret that we have kept for thousands of years. It is not in the myths, and only the two of us know the truth," and he paused, glanced at the rest of the board, and then continued. "I didn't abduct Persephone. We eloped."

At this revelation, Zeus and Hera looked shocked. This was clearly one closeted skeleton they weren't aware of.

"Hera you look shocked, what has shocked you?"

Before she could speak for herself, Zeus offered an answer. "We are shocked because we believed that Hades had abducted Persephone. We believed the same as everyone else."

This room suddenly stinks of bullshit. I couldn't prove anything, but there was a lot of lying going on in the meeting. I took the opportunity to probe a little further. "Would Persephone know the mysteries?"

Hades laughed. "Definitely, but she wouldn't share the knowledge with anyone. She is fearful of upsetting her mother. As I said. Demeter is a controlling bitch."

I thought for a moment. "Can any of you tell me anything that Demeter has done? Other than reclaiming her daughter from the underworld, control the seasons and hold secret celebrations every five years."

Silence, not a single utterance. I half expected them to say no comment the way an accused might do during a police interrogation.

"Ok, that's it. I don't need anything else for now. I'm sure you want to continue the meeting without me. You have lots to discuss, but they are family matters." I gave my farewell and best wishes before leaving.

I had somewhere I wanted to be, and that was in Kamiros.

≈≈≈

On the trip from Ialyssos to Kamiros, I had an opportunity to consider the risk I was about to take. I've never been a big risk-taker. At best one pound each way on the Grand National which always failed of course. The words of my dad echoed once more. "If you don't take risks, you will never amount to anything." This was balanced by his disrespect of liars. "If you surround yourself with liars, you surround yourself by fantasy. You might as well live in a novel," were his most significant words of wisdom. Something he expounded when he'd once found out I'd lied to him. And he wondered why I didn't like taking risks. To me, telling a lie is still taking a risk. So why had a roomful of gods just made a sizeable ante-post wager?

I headed for the reception desk to get hold of Kam. I needed to have an update on the state of Demeter's room. My worries were confirmed when Kam told me it was no better than the way the Argonists had left it. *Why didn't Despoina report the damage?* I needed to let that go for the moment.

It was evening before I managed to catch up with the Foxes. As luck would have it, they'd separated for the evening. Miss was at the fakir show. Lots of flames and walking on red hot coals and broken glass. The look on her face betrayed the pleasure it was giving her. I guessed it was a reminder of home. Mrs Fox didn't appear to be in the mood for such underworldly activities. I sent a text to Zeus asking him to tell Hades that Persephone was alone at the fakir show and I needed him to keep her occupied. Zeus replied, "H's cumming M8." *Bloody text-speak again.* Within seconds I caught a glimpse of Hades. He was among the cheering crowd. He managed a wink in the microsecond we made eye contact. The dirty sod. He was signalling exactly how he was going to keep Persephone occupied.

I hadn't felt my heart pound this fast since my first date with Kam. It was the adrenalin preparing me for the risk I was about to take. I hoped it wouldn't end up like my last Grand National bet. It fell at the first fence. There was a bit more than two quid on the table here.

I pressed the bell on Room 124, nothing not even a bing or a bong. That figures, they will have broken it. I knocked a little too hard, and it stung my knuckles. The door swung open.

"What do you want?"

"I am concerned about the damage to your room," I said, using my best customer service voice.

"What about it?"

"I am worried that a previous guest has damaged the room, and that might be why you had so many issues with the hotel."

"Yes, that's exactly why. It's a dump."

"I am concerned that we have let you down and the hotel would like to put things right. We always want to act when a guest hasn't experienced the wonderful *filoxenia* we pride ourselves in."

She smiled. I knew that despite posing as an English woman, she understood some Greek.

"I particularly like to ensure that our English guests have the best of experiences. Will you allow me to put it right?

"OK, impress me. This isn't a chat-up line, is it?"

"Most certainly not, I am a customer service professional," I announced, showing an uncharacteristic flourish of confidence. That's not to say that in different circumstances, I might have fancied a trip down the hills and valleys. But I was a happily married man.

"Well if you stopped looking at my breasts, I might believe you," she flirted.

"Forgive me, but it isn't intentional. I am just trying to avoid staring into your eyes," I lied. God, here I am lying already. I reassured myself *it's a symptom of being a risk-taker.*

"So, are you going to give me one of the bungalows? Or give me my money back?"

"I can't do that, but I can upgrade you to a pool room. Would you like one of the first-floor pool rooms? Let me show you the room I have in mind." I'd already checked availability, and I had the perfect room for them.

≈≈≈

"This is Room 208, it is charmed, and it is my favourite

room at Helios. It is much more spacious, as you can see. There are two bedrooms. You and your daughter would be very comfortable here," I encouraged as I showed her the extensive living area.

She seemed impressed. Even more so by the pool as I flicked the underwater lights on. I could see her excitement by the increased difference between the hills and valleys as she took deep breaths.

"Please look around and make sure there is no damage before you accept the upgrade." I knew that I was rendering any sabotage attempts of 208 impotent. She couldn't create damage, without us knowing it was her.

My heart was still pounding as she looked around the lounge and the bathroom, which had a shower and a jacuzzi bath. It was pure luxury.

"Both bedrooms are beautiful. You have a chance to pick which will be yours before your daughter gets to choose," I smiled at her, she smiled back. I had her. I felt like an estate agent that had managed to offload a slum to an unsuspecting buyer.

She reached for the handle of what was the master bedroom. That was when we both heard the noise. My plan went out the window. My horse had fallen at the second fence. The noise was the unmistakable sound of a woman having an orgasm.

Demeter burst into the room, and I followed milliseconds behind. I couldn't believe what I was seeing. Jesus Christ, I should have shared my plan. My life returned to type. Despite the best of planning, I was in white water rapids. So much for proactivity. I had to react fast.

I exclaimed, "Miss Fox, what are you doing?" and I paused before adding, "in this room?"

At almost the same moment, Mrs Fox echoed what I'd said. "Persephone, what are you doing?"

I could have answered that question for her. No matter who she replied to, there was no doubt that this was a voluntary liaison. Persephone was on top.

What is it with my plans? This needed some quick thinking because there was no plan B.

"Mrs Fox, please. Let's wait in the lounge, and give them a chance to get dressed," I suggested, not wanting to make eye contact with her or look too long in her daughter's direction. I didn't know if Hades was the jealous type.

We stood away from the bedroom door, surrounded by a painfully awkward silence. We waited, and we waited. I resisted the urge to call out to them. I didn't want to be the one to break the silence. At least the lovers couldn't jump out of the window without hurting themselves. *Bugger, they're immortal.* It was a relief once they'd joined us. The delay allowed me to try to gather my thoughts. I needed to regain control of the developing situation.

It was Demeter that broke the silence. "Mister Prince, you can leave us now. This is a family matter."

"Mrs Fox. I'm going nowhere. I have a duty of care to all our guests, and that includes your daughter."

"This is a family matter," she hissed with venom.

"Correction, this is a hotel matter. Your daughter is in a room without authorisation, and I don't believe the gentleman is a guest. He is trespassing."

Hades frowned at me as a form of objection to my accusation that he was a trespasser. At that moment he and Zeus would have passed off as twins.

I went to the front door and locked it. "Nobody's going anywhere."

I stared at Hades and spoke to him with the only name I knew him by. "Hades, are you two going to tell Demeter what you told me? Will you expose your lie?"

The revelation that I knew their godly names shocked Demeter. The look on her face was a picture I will always remember. I stared at her, and she squinted.

"Who are you? What lie? What do you know that I don't? Are you Zeus?" Her voice trembled as she asked the last question.

"No, I'm not Zeus, but I know you are a deceitful liar, and it seems your daughter is too. You should be very proud of her."

"What do you mean? We are not liars, we are gods, and I demand your respect."

I pointed at different places on an imaginary diagram on the wall. "Let's look at your family tree. We have you, and you are sandwiched between two of your brothers. A rather friendly threesome."

I moved my hand back and forth as if to illustrate the proximity of the siblings.

"On the left is brother Zeus. Who happens to be your daughters' father and uncle at the same time. On the other side, we have Hades. Who is your daughter's husband and her uncle. You're obviously a close-knit family. Though it does make for a messy family tree diagram."

"This is all public knowledge. It is in the myths. How are we liars? We didn't create the myths."

"Oh you did, and you capitalised on them. Persephone was never abducted. She has been lying to you for an eternity. She and Hades eloped. She lied to you."

Hades looked at me in horror. I'd revealed his secret.

Demeter looked at Persephone with tears in her eyes. "Is this true? How could you? We are meant to be together for always. Only you and me. Just as we had always planned it."

I interrupted her. "And what of your deceit?"

She looked at me through her tears.

At last, the plan was back on track. I did something I hadn't done for a very long time. I stood straight and tall, and I puffed out my chest with authority. I'm sure I grew six inches taller.

"You are a liar and a phoney." I felt a little guilty because it was unusual for me to talk like that to a lady in distress. I had to remind myself that she was a D80.

I continued to push my guilt away as I tried to bully her into defeat. "You are no more a goddess of the seasons than I am. When Persephone eloped." At which she winced. "Yes. When your devout daughter left you. You threatened to bring famine to the people by turning their land barren. You got lucky. A massive volcano erupted at Thera, and it cast dust and debris high into the sky. It shrouded the whole of the Mediterranean and the lands around it into darkness. As the dust fell to earth, it turned the waters red and killed everything it touched. It made the land barren. Your claim that it was because of the loss of Persephone is an act of deceit and a lie."

She lunged at me. All the while, screeching like an attacking primate. I felt her hand tighten around my throat as she bit hard at my face. I thank the gods that Hades was there. Because he'd fired a lightning bolt straight at my head.

As I resurrected, I saw Demeter motionless on the marble floor. Persephone moving towards her. Now she was crying too.

Hades looked at me. "She isn't dead. She has lost consciousness. The blast threw her against the wall."

"What the fuck did you do that for?" I stared at him.

"Did you want to resurrect with half your face bit off?"

He did have a point. The horror of that thought stopped me from answering. I was trying to hold my breath because the stench of singed flesh and hair was disgusting.

"Persephone, you have a decision to make. This is your chance to stand up to your mother and be true to yourself. Do you love Hades?"

"Yes, with all my heart. But I love my mother too," she sobbed.

With a paternal tone, I turned towards her and held her hand. "Sweetheart. We all love our mothers, but sometimes we must stand up to them. They brought us to life. They loved and tended us so that we may go on to lead a happy and independent life. We can't let them live our life for us. It is unhealthy when a mother isolates you from the love of others," I paused to let that sink in. "Loving Hades doesn't mean you must love your mother any less. I want your

179

permission to let her see that."

"Don't bother. I get it." Demeter sobbed, and she got up from the floor. "I long to see more of her. I don't like her being away for so long."

"Then why don't you go and live in the underworld with her?" I suggested, and Hades looked at me.

Between sobs, Demeter sniffled. "He wouldn't allow that."

Persephone looked at Hades. "Would that be possible?"

I looked at Hades and raised my eyebrows. I stared over my spectacles, imitating a schoolmaster defying a young lad to misbehave.

"Of course it would. I can set mum up in a nice location. Somewhere near to where we live." Demeter scowled at her brother because he'd just referred to her as mum.

"At bloody last. I'll leave you lot together to rebuild your relationships. Before I go, can I ask one thing, ladies? Tell me of the Eleusinian Mysteries."

"They were celebrations. I gathered together learned scholars. They knew the truth of the natural progression of the seasons. I promised them wealth and happiness. I bribed them not to reveal the secret that you have now uncovered."

I can't believe I was right. It was a guess, and I was never any good at poker. "I'll keep your secret, as long as you stay away from this hotel and live in the underworld. That way, you will keep your mythic reputation."

"Now, in return, tell me who you are. How are you immortal and I know nothing of you?"

"Me? I'm Rod Prince, a good friend of the owner of this

hotel. Which means I will go to great lengths to ensure the hotel continues to thrive." I was unsure of whether the non-disclosure agreement extended to D80's. I wasn't going to risk letting her know I worked for Zeus.

I enjoyed telling the board how my mysterious plan had worked. Hades was happy for me to omit the part where he and Persephone fucked up, in every sense of the expression.

Zeus appeared impressed. I suspect he expected me to fail. As I did.

I'm sure that inside, he was a bit miffed I hadn't shared my plan for his approval.

I felt my inner confidence growing for the first time since my dad died when I was a teenager. So long without self-belief. He would have been proud of me. I could take risks and succeed. I'm sure he would have forgiven me for lying on that occasion.

Zeus assured me that Hestia and Poseidon were going to present a much higher risk.

He gave a sinister warning. "To fulfil your destiny, you have much bigger and more dangerous battles to face."

You just had to piss on my parade. I thought to myself.

≈≈≈

Alyss and Athena flew in from Athens. There was to be a meeting between the family and the godly members of the Olympian Dreams board. The point of the meeting was to discuss the progress we'd made so far. I had to justify why I hadn't shared my plan with anyone. I couldn't provide an answer. Other than I didn't want to look stupid when it failed. I got a rollicking for going it alone. A 'well-done Rod' would have been appreciated.

"Of course I went it alone. You're all brothers and sisters. You've thrown me into a monumental battle of sibling rivalry," I paused for a second. "Besides you keep telling me it's my job to solve it, so I did just that."

I didn't trust any of them.

The most unnerving point was that I kept having flashes of self-confidence. I'd raised my voice to Zeus but chickened out at the last phrase. "I'm sorry I know you're right."

I detected a softening in his tone and facial expression as he sympathised with me. "You must remember I am your employer. When you go maverick, you jeopardise everything. Your selection was because of your unassuming manner." And he glared at me. The stare undid all the earlier softening. Back home, we called it a *bullshit sandwich*.

I merely grunted. Another employer that doesn't recognise innovation.

Then came another microsecond flash of confidence. I used sarcasm to ask a question. "OK, boss. What do you want us to do next?"

"That is your job. Bring me a plan." And the arrogant fucker glared at me again.

I raised an eyebrow.

He clearly noticed my irritation. "I understand why you're upset."

My voice raised a note or two, or maybe even an octave revealing the anger I'd tried to hide. "Exactly," I spat, "you're paying me to do a job, and yet you are micromanaging me. You could have saved yourself some money and solved the problem yourself."

"No. I need your ideas, but above all, I need to know what you are doing."

"There you go again. You are controlling me. I need your trust. I need to be free to do my job. It slows everything down if I need to pass it by you first. You have to let me make my own mistakes."

The corners of his eyes dropped, and he wore the face of a crying child frustrated that he couldn't express himself adequately. "There is too much at stake."

"Don't you think I know that. My wife and kids are the stakes. Do you have such little trust in me to think I would risk harming them? I'm not a risk-taker."

My last comment fed him the words he needed to express himself. He bellowed "Well that's a lie. Given your performance with Demeter."

My confidence crawled back under its stone. It knew its place.

"We will leave you to it, come up with a plan. Let me know when you have one." And he stormed out slamming the door. The rest of the board looked at me. They knew I was right, but not one of them spoke up for me. And they left too, but not before Hades smiled in my direction and said, "Rod, talk to Athena. She will explain."

Athena stayed in the boardroom. "Ignore my dad. He is terrified you don't need him. You have demonstrated so much power, and it worries him. The entire family is frightened of you. They are concerned that if you manage to win this war, there is nothing to stop you from becoming a threat to them.

They are worried that dad has created a monster he can't control."

"But I've never been a threat to anyone." I felt the most depressed I'd felt since finding out we'd been killed. "I just want to be appreciated. Isn't that what we all want?"

She held out her hands. "We all do. That's the problem. You and Dad have the same needs, but you have a different way of achieving your goals. He is used to demanding what he wants and getting it. By using your mind to try and understand your adversaries, you are unsettling him. He doesn't understand you. Your approach is alien to him."

I was embarrassed. I was holding hands with the most beautiful woman of all time with snot starting to trickle from my nose. She passed me a tissue. "Spend some time with your family. I'll catch up with you later."

And she left. I took a deep breath. *Soppy git, fancy getting upset in front of Kam and the kids.*

Kam held out her arms. "If you want to tell him to stick his job, we'll understand."

"What? And have the bully think I'm a loser. I wouldn't give him the pleasure. Anyway, we've got a plan to develop. Any ideas?"

We each took a separate side and sat at the boardroom table. "OK, let's brainstorm," cajoled Lindon.

"Yes, and you can chair it," I wearily responded. I was too tired to run the meeting. "I would rather just shout out ideas."

"What do we know about Hestia and Placebo?" questioned Alyss.

Lindon was quick to correct her. "Stupid kid. It's

Poseidon. I thought you were learning Greek."

"OK. Po-side-un," she retorted, over-pronouncing his name."

"They're brother and sister of each other and the rest of Zeus' clan." It was all I could contribute, given my feelings for the lot of them.

"All that sleeping together is a bit weird if you ask me." And my wife looked at me for confirmation that I was OK.

Lindon outlined what he'd managed to find out about them to date. "Hestia is the goddess of the hearth and the home. Some say she is the representation of society in general. The hearth is the source of sacred fire which is the source of life and prosperity to society. Her influence is waning a little as fewer homes have a real fire. I suspect she hates central heating. She hasn't been known to leave Olympia. Which means she hasn't figured in any myths. Other than the story that Poseidon made a play for her. She swore on Zeus' head that she would remain a virgin for all eternity. This was so that she could remain at the heart of every household. There you have her, that's Hestia, any ideas? Anyone?"

Like all good brainstorming sessions, it soon descended into chaos. But it also lifted my spirits. Without anyone saying anything, it became a competition to see who could offer the most outlandish suggestion.

"Feed her up, make her too fat to move."

"Nope, won't work, she can shapeshift."

"Do the same to her that we did to Prometheus."

"We would need to train another eagle."

"What about using flame retardant material."

"Could be worth thinking about."

"Already considered that," informed Lindon. "Most fire-retardant chemicals are harmful to humans. They've been linked to obesity, and we've already discounted that."

"She has sworn to remain a virgin. Why?"

"So she doesn't have to stop home with the kids." Someone joked.

"Suppose someone took her virginity. Would that destroy her?"

"No, but it would piss Zeus off. He would lose his head."

"What if she fell in love with a girl? She could stay kid-free. How could we use that?" queried Alyss.

"Dunno, but it's worth thinking about. Write that down."

"What about diplomacy? It worked with Demeter."

"You mean blackmail. Write that one down too."

The suggestions got more and more extreme. I suggested we take a timeout. "We should take some time to think about things. I don't think feeding her kryptonite or to encase her in concrete is going to do it."

POSEIDON – *Of the Sea and Storms*

We'd decided to have a night off and eat out. Opting not to visit any of the hotels on the north of the island. We opted for a beautiful taverna we'd come across in a village called Fanes. *To Kyma*, The Wave. It sits above a beautiful harbour and has one of the most beautiful sunsets of the whole island. It's not far from Kamiros, but far enough that we were able to forget all about the war for a while.

"Anyone mentioning a D80 has to jump in the harbour fully clothed," I joked. It was a night off, a night to let our hair down. The Wave had been run by Paraskevi and her husband for longer than we'd known of it. They were an elderly couple and had a thriving business. The food was fantastic. All home-cooked. Paraskevi was a petite woman that still had a youthful smile and a mischievous twinkle in her eye. I imagine she was beautiful in her youth.

She pulled up a chair, to sit with us as she always did. That was part of her charm. Instead of standing over us to take our order, she would always sit at the table with us. She considered us as one of the family. She had good old-fashioned Greek values and treated every guest as a friend. During our first meal there, she was trying to take our order. The kids were preoccupied with their phones, and she slapped her hand down on the cloth-covered table. "Put your phones down and tell me what you want to eat," she commanded. Amazingly, they did as they were told. We all had a lot of respect and admiration for her. We were intrigued by the time she'd told us that Paraskevi is Greek for Friday. She was named after St Paraskevi, the name day for this Saint is 26th July. She would never tell us her real birthday, so we always sent her best wishes on that date. It was easy to remember because it was the same date as our wedding anniversary.

"Paraskevi, what can you tempt me with?" I asked.

"My family visit tomorrow. I have made Moussaka for them. You want to try some?"

"Mmmm, yes please, I would be honoured."

That summed up Paraskevi, generous Greek hospitality.

"How is the season going?" I asked.

"Oh, you know, visitors come and go."

"You're looking tired, and we are barely into the season." The dark rings under her eyes were the clue.

She looked out across the harbour to the sea, and did the Greek upward head flick, almost like an upside-down nod. I liken it to pointing with your nose.

"The water comes, I don't know how long the harbour will live, or the beach."

"What do you mean?"

"The sea is wearing away the land. It seems much worse this year. We used to be able to park the car below by the harbour. But now … the water rises over the harbour wall, and there is not even enough room to park a moped." She looked sad; the shine had gone from her eyes.

I stared at the others, they stared back, and they knew what I was thinking.

"I wish this place was mine," signalled Lindon.

"You can buy it. Then when it falls into the sea, you will be sorry."

This wasn't like Paraskevi. By nature, she was cheerful, positive and always smiling. But that night she looked worn down by events.

"It's not only here, but it is also all along the northwest coast. I'm surprised you haven't noticed it at Helios," she mused. Then she snapped out of it. "And how is Filipos these days?"

"He's better, and the fortunes of the hotel are looking bright."

"Ask him if he has noticed the sea coming. *Diávrosi*. What is the word in English?"

"Erosion," translated Alyss.

I looked at her in surprise. The Greek language lessons were paying off.

"Yes, tell Filipos, the island is eroding."

So much for having a night off. Still, the food was *poly nostimo,* but we didn't expect anything different.

It was clear that, as the threat was to the whole island, we couldn't take nights off. We had a new dilemma. Who is the greatest danger to us, Hestia or Poseidon? I felt hope returning, as I realised that this was the first time we weren't reacting to a godly event. At last, we were able to control when our next battle took place.

Kam suggested, "Maybe we should take some time out and use it to visit other parts of the island. We could try to understand the involvement of the D80's."

"Yes, and it will allow us to keep moving. I feel like we are sitting ducks being around the hotel all the time."

Lindon agreed, "If the good gods are worried about us the bad ones will be looking for a chance to get us. If they don't know where we are, they won't be able to plan anything."

"Kalo schedio," said Alyss as Paraskevi appeared with the bill.

"What is a good plan?" asked Paraskevi.

"We're going to tour the island, and be tourists for a while," said Kam.

≈≈≈

We had just settled for a meze meal at Gitonia Mezedokafenes. Our favourite eatery in Ialyssos. This was to be the start of our R and R. But who should walk in and fuck everything up? That's right Zeus. Not only him but an entire band of business-suited strangers I'd never met. I nodded in acknowledgement, determined that he wouldn't join us at our table. The owner, Lambros, who obviously couldn't read my mind, sat them at the table next to us. Pulling two tables together to make room to accommodate them all. Zeus, of course, sat at the head of their extended table. His seat just happened to back onto where I was sat.

"Have you brought me a plan?" said Zeus. He spoke as if talking to his business guests, but our table knew it was a question for us.

I swung round on my chair through ninety degrees. I was sidewards and behind him. "Why all the theatrics? How did you know we were here? If you wanted to speak to me, you could have summoned me, the way you usually do."

"Questions, always questions. I didn't know you were here. It is a coincidence."

I grunted to signal I didn't believe him. "No, we haven't bought you a plan, and we're going to take some time out to visit other resorts on the island. Is there any reason we shouldn't visit the places of our interment?"

He had a particular tone that he used when he wanted to mock me. He demonstrated it once again. "What do you mean take time out? You have a deadline?"

"We need time to be together as a family and think of the way forward. The idea is a little creepy, but we thought it would do us good to see where we're buried. Is there any reason we shouldn't?" I repeated.

"I am surprised you didn't ask sooner. There is no reason at all, but don't disturb anything. Your tombs must remain intact. You will find them unmarked near the acropolis of each location."

He was about to list the four locations, but I interrupted him. "I'm sure we know our own names. But if they're unmarked how will we know the exact locations."

"You will feel it when you are close." And he turned his head and smiled at me. That was unusual in itself.

"Thank you, is it really a coincidence you are here? Who are your friends?"

"Yes, it is pure coincidence and who these gentlemen are is none of your concern."

His last statement really concerned me. But I let it go, I was on private time with my family. For thirty minutes, I tried to listen to his group's conversations, but my Greek wasn't up to it. I whispered to Alyss, "Can you hear what they are saying?" She just shrugged her shoulders and brushed her hand over her hair, as if to signal it was going over her head.

≈≈≈

As we were in Ialyssos, it was logical to visit the acropolis in Ialyssos first. Visiting the tomb of our youngest offspring was an unpleasant experience for Kam and me. It was tempered because Alyss was alive and stood next to us. But it gave us an insight into what might be waiting for us all. As we stood outside of the gates to the Monastery of Filerimos. Looking at the cylindrical stone pillar, I couldn't help picturing all the happy times we'd had together before our death. I put my arm around Alyss' shoulder to remind myself that she was still alongside me.

"Dad, why do you let Zeus talk to you like that? Asked Alyss.

"Because he's older and wiser than me. He pays our wages. Let alone the fact he could take back our immortality. Then who would be stood here looking at your tomb, no-one? I hope that by serving him well, we'll create a legacy. Something for people to remember us by."

"You mean to be remembered for saving Rhodes?"

"In a way, yes. But it's more about knowing our purpose in life. Understanding why we are here. It's like the battle. If we don't know what we have to achieve, where do we begin? We're actually creating a myth about the Prince family."

"*Mythos,*" she said.

"Yes. I could do with a pint right now."

"No dad mythos is the Greek word for myth."

"I don't think he is wiser than you. Older, yes. Wiser definitely not," she laughed with a hint of wit.

To try to let her see the seriousness of our situation. I reminded her that under that heavy cylindrical stone was fourteen-year-old Alyss killed on 23rd May 2013.

"But I don't feel sad at all. I know you and mum feel sad looking at my tomb. But I have a feeling of ecstasy being in this spot. A bit like when Athena gave me ambrosia."

The very thought that we were dead cut deep into my emotions. Remembering that none of our mortal friends knew where our bodies were or even that we were dead. *What kind of legacy is that?*

"When I was with Athena, she told me her dad's testing us to see if we are worthy. She doesn't think he'll let us fail."

"Think isn't enough sweetheart, she may know her dad well, but I reckon he has set us up to fail."

"Why do you think that?" She was showing an interest now.

"Because he is the King of gods. He could banish the lot of them to the underworld. He doesn't need us. He is using us for some reason of his own."

"You don't like him, do you?"

"He is OK as a man or a god. But he is a bad manager. I've met his type before. The minute something goes wrong, he will blame us, and then the game is over. When it goes well, he takes all the glory. I am only trying to keep us immortal for as long as I can."

That little exchange seemed to appease her curiosity. My little princess is growing up. I looked at her, and for the first time, I realised she had become a beautiful and intelligent woman. This brought a lump to my throat, and I kissed her forehead. Appropriately, there were many beautiful peacocks with their eyed tails, to watch over Alyss. That returned a smile to my face.

Lindon always had perfect timing and then was no exception. "Did you know the peacock is associated with Hera. You know. Zeus' missus."

"Nice one son. Keep up with the research."

At the top of Filerimos hill, where the cross is, we had a spectacular view below us. I imagined it must be like the view the gods see when they look down from Olympus. It gave me a sense of power as I looked down over my kingdom. *Steady on Rod – you're getting a bit ahead of yourself here.* I thought to myself, and I smiled inside.

"Hey guys, if we are the Princes of Rhodes, surely that down there is our domain." And I shouted at the top of my voice, "I am the King of Rhodes." To which everyone joined in.

Alyss finished off the hilarity by screaming, "Zeus is a pint of Mythos." And we all hugged before heading back past the thirteen stations of the cross. A tree-lined avenue, representing Jesus making his final journey to Calgary. The sound of peacocks screaming, provided a suitable soundtrack for that fateful event.

≈≈≈

We decided to rotate around the island in a clockwise direction. Kam chose the route, but she had a knack of making me think it was my idea. This meant the Acropolis of Rhodes was our next visit. We headed towards Monte Smith. It was a rather fitting resting place for me as it's very close to the stadium. I was a sprinter in my teens. My greatest legacy to that point was breaking the schools one hundred yards record the year before the UK went metric.

If looking at Alyss' tomb was eerie, it wasn't the same as looking at my own grave. I almost felt a sensation of euphoria. But, where Alyss' stone was cylindrical. Mine was ironically shaped like a dice like you might roll in a game of chance. Just an unmarked cuboid of stone, sitting under the shade of a spine laden hawthorn tree. It was where I perceived the front of the acropolis to be. Rhodes Acropolis was the temple of Apollo. And I imagined the splendour of what would have been the focal point for the worshippers of Rhodes.

I'd hoped for a tombstone of white polished marble and gold lettering: 'Here lies the King of Rhodes.' Instead, my legacy was marked by what appeared to be a numberless concrete dice. No chance of throwing a bloody six with that lump of rock. Again, we were able to look down on the activity below us, the fast-moving traffic travelling along the main road through Ixia like an army of ants on a mission.

"What would happen if we lobbed a handful of sticky sweets down there?" joked Lindon.

Kam wasn't usually the type of person to draw attention

to herself, but she let out an extra loud shout. "Who cares. I'm the Queen of Rhodes!"

The tourist alongside us gave a funny look as he tried to distance himself from us.

Lindon's resting place was next, but it was getting late. We decided to stay in a Rhodes town hotel for the night. We could party a little as all good tourists do. And in the morning we could catch a boat to Lindos.

Staying in Rhodes town allowed us to catch up with friends. We had an ouzo filled night, and it was a chance to be proper Brits abroad.

At the hotel, we were pampered. It was a grand but small hotel, situated just behind the municipal buildings. A stone's throw from Mandraki harbour. They spoilt us in our short stay, and their breakfast was fantastic. It was a silver service dining experience, and the waitresses were very attentive. It was clear that they weren't D80's.

There were a couple of small issues that arose, and I did wonder if the D80's were at play in Rhodes town too. The events were too minor to be attributed to gods, but it still crossed my mind. As we readied ourselves to set off to find a boat, I put all concerns out of my mind. We were tourists out to have a good time, and we didn't want to waste it thinking about the war.

We strolled along Mandraki harbour, accompanied by a cacophony of sounds. The sound of halyards slapped against the masts of yachts by the breeze. Greeks shouting greetings to each other as their working day began. The hornet-like noise of mopeds, with helmetless riders, making their way to work in the tavernas in Old Town.

It was good to see so many smiling tourists. It made me consider that our sacrifice was for the benefit of a lot of people. We opted for a small cruise that went direct to Lindos, without the swim stops. The day-return tickets were ridiculously cheap.

The weather was beautiful, the forecast was fine, and we were heading to the south side of the island. We would be travelling along the calm Mediterranean. I say the weather was beautiful, but no, it was baking. Helios was obviously having a good day. It reminded me of that first sensation when I got off the plane the day we died.

The engine started in a cloud of diesel smoke. There was only four of us plus the captain who could best be described as a Greek Bob Marley. His dreadlocks hung down to the middle of his back. He was well toned and obviously worked out. He had a full beard that stretched down to his solar plexus. His olive leathery skin was devoid of any body hair. I smiled to myself as I wondered if he shaved it off or used some type of depilation cream. I guessed he was in his mid-thirties.

We introduced ourselves. He informed us his name was Leonidas, and he invited us to call him Leo. He told us he was named after the king of Sparta. I wanted to say, *and I am the King of Rhodes,* but I thought better of it. He offered us refreshments, a delicious sweet tasting punch. Alcohol-free, of course. Alyss likened it to the Ambrosia she had tasted in Athens.

Leo raised his glass and toasted. "Yamas."

The family chorused as one, "Yamas, Leo." And we all

sank our drinks in one.

Leo proceeded to top up our glasses. "Where you stay?"

Without a thought, I told him, "Helios." Before Kam corrected me.

"No, we're staying at Olympian Dreams."

Leo expressed familiarity with both hotels. "You notice the difference? I know people at both hotels."

We sank another shot of the delicious punch. The sirtaki played quietly in the background through the boat's sound system. We exited Mandraki harbour, passing the buck and doe deer on their pillars. Leo set a course to take us around the tip of the island. We passed the cruise ships that were bringing in day tourists.

We were headed towards what we'd always termed the calmer coast. We were proved mistaken as we passed Faliraki and Kallithea, the wind picked up, and clouds rolled in. The swell started to make the boat rise and fall. It was like sitting in the middle of a child's see-saw, as the boat began to rock. This was unsettling, we'd always known this as the warm side of the island, and the water was generally calm.

As if from nowhere, waves started to throw the small vessel about. More unsettling was the laughter from Leo. The boat was lurching from side to side. Kam looked at me and muttered, "Now you know why I don't like boats." The consumption of ouzo last night didn't bode well on my nautical stomach. The bowl of punch slopped its sweet contents all over the deck.

Leo laughed as he spoke to us, "Malakas. Didn't you read the name of my boat? The Poseidon. Let this be a lesson to you. Stay out of my business."

Shit, it's Poseidon. I felt a chill run down my spine, as I saw a massive wave to our left. It was already forming a white crest, and then it broke right over the boat. I felt it roll us over, sending all four of us into the not so clear blue sea. I felt my lungs fill with water, the way they did when Alyss pushed me into the pool. Each breath made me cough and ingest even more water. I couldn't see the others. The mixture of salt and sand stung my eyes. I was still caught up in the rolling wave and was unable to orientate which direction was up. This seemed to go on for an eternity. Was this to be my perpetual outcome. Like Prometheus enduring a never-ending circle of life, death and resurrection. The prospect of being under my dice at the acropolis seemed a comfort compared to the terror I was experiencing.

As I surfaced, my eyes were still stinging. Self-preservation hampered my vision and stopped me from seeking the rest of the family. Water filled my ears and filtered any external sounds. My pulse thumping inside my head, magnified. Through my salted and gritted eyes, I could see the shadow of the boat as it loomed large before me.

There was a sudden blinding flash. Once my eyes adjusted, the boat was gone. The sea had calmed. The sky cleared and Helios shone once more. As my senses recovered and my ears ejected their saline bath, I could hear Kam close to me coughing and spluttering. I scanned the water around me, trying to find the kids. I could see Lindon about thirty metres closer to the shore than I was. He was swimming towards us. As he stopped, I could see him lift Alyss' head clear of the water.

"Kam, it's Alyss," I shouted as if she'd already asked what Lindon was doing. Kam, who was a stronger swimmer than me, was already moving towards them. They were both still alive but shaken. At the time, it hadn't crossed my mind that they were as immortal as Kam and me. We reached the shore and sat under the now burning sun. I passed out at that point.

It was the smell of leather that started to rouse me. Something tickled my face, and I opened my eyes momentarily. Kam's hair was blowing in the breeze and flashing across my face. I was incoherent as I muttered, "Yousmellofleather." And I blacked out again.

The next thing I remember, I was being shaken awake by Kam. "Rod, wake up, you've had a bad dream."

"What? Poseidon was a dream?"

"No, you were groaning about being attacked by a leather spider. We are in George. Zeus saved us from the sea."

I opened my eyes fully, and sure enough, we were in George.

"Where to, Rod? Do you want to continue your downtime, or do you want to get back to work?" And he had the arrogance to give a contemptuous smile. *Sarcastic bastard. And I'm supposed to be grateful for being saved from the sea.*

"Just drop us at Aegean Spa. We've got stuff to pick up." He could see I wasn't in the mood for his bloody games. *I've always hated being woken up.*

The whole event made us aware that immortality doesn't bring fearlessness. We'd all experienced the terror of drowning and dying, and I didn't like it. It wasn't a pleasant sensation.

Discussing it later, the others agreed with me. It reminded us we needed to do everything we could to avoid being in that situation again. We'd taken a break from the war, but the war hadn't taken a break from us. We'd taken our minds off the fight. We all needed to remain alert with no more distractions. I blamed myself, I didn't have to mention Helios.

It transpired that Zeus had been watching over us. When he saw the danger from the boat's propellers, he intervened. The blinding flash was his lightning bolt. Having a guardian god gave us some comfort. But he warned that he wouldn't always be there for us. He'd been told of our predicament by Helios who saw the storm brewing. If it had happened during the hours of darkness, one or more of us could have suffered mutilation. The outcome would have been severe and permanent. More so, than the still visible scarring on Kam's face from the stone-throwing incident.

The whole family took a knock to its confidence. At least I know I felt less confident. We postponed the visit to Lindon's tomb, and we headed back to Kamiros with our tails between our legs. Once back at Helios, we could catch up with Filipos, and we'd be able to visit Kam's tomb.

≈≈≈

Kam's place of rest was the easiest to find. Right next to the entrance of the archaeological dig at Ancient Kamiros. The tomb was in front of a flowerbed of what appeared to be red roses. Recently laid concrete was all she had for her stone. The scented flowers, an appropriate memorial for her. She confirmed that she felt the same exhilaration that Alyss and I had felt at our tombs. Lindon resented the fact that he'd missed out. "When can we go to Lindos? I want to feel that sensation."

"You will once we are sure it's safe. Let's gather our energy first," I assured him.

"I really do feel like the Queen of Rhodes stood here with the Bougainvillea petals at my feet," said Kam. Clearly, I'm not the green-fingered member of the family. I thought there were too many tourists around to shout anything.

Uncharacteristically it was Alyss that announced her royal lineage. "I am the Queen of Rhodes!"

Another visitor joined in. "I am Spartacus!" And before you know it, everyone was shouting out mythical or legendary names. There was even a Robin Hood in there somewhere. Alyss blushed. The congregation cheered. Then Lindon brought the theme back to mythology. "I am Kratos!" Everyone stopped and stared. I guessed they weren't too sure who Kratos was.

≈≈≈

I noticed a greater sense of caution amongst all of us. For my part, it was caused by the events following the visit to my tomb. It was good to be in Kamiros, at Helios. I somehow felt secure there, despite our protector being at Olympian Dreams. There was something about the place that made it feel like home.

Sat at the very edge of the hotel's lawns. I once again heard the sound of the gentle rolling of the pebbles. It was almost like a lullaby. I looked out at the blue sea, and all I felt was peace. It was times like that when I disappeared into my own private thoughts. It was how I tried to make sense of what was going on in our lives. I put my headphones on and played my *Spotify* playlist *Greek Sirtaki*. It always took me through the entire spectrum of emotions. Some tracks would make the hair on the back of my neck stand on end, and some would make me feel melancholy. But it gave me hope and inspired me. It reminded me why I loved Rhodes and why our challenge was a worthwhile cause. It was my destiny to be at Helios. Somehow, I sensed my legacy was going to involve the place.

It eased the memory of the battle with Poseidon, though I will never forget it. A valuable lesson learnt. How could somewhere so beautiful be in such danger? The blue Aegean Sea had become a god's playground. Something so precious left for the spiteful and dangerous Poseidon.

Moreover, how could we defeat him? Questions I pondered over as I listened to various versions of the sirtaki. The next track started, the *Zorba Sirtaki Mix* version by *A.T.H.E.N.A.* As the sound filled my head I glanced down, and what I saw made me shudder.

Paraskevi was right. The bank I was sitting on seemed so much nearer to the hotel than I remembered it. I stood up, the track still blasting in my ears. I ran to the far end of the sea-facing lawns. There I knew there was a concrete path running from the hotel to the beach. The path was still there, but it stuck out a metre into thin air. The land below it had gone. The last time I walked along that path was less than twelve months previous. A closer look showed me that the metre sticking out into thin air wasn't a true reflection of the erosion. There was another metre of the path broken away, and it was laying on the pebbled beach. Two metres in twelve months.

The sea was swallowing the land the hotel stood on. I needed answers to so many questions. Was the rate of erosion constant or accelerating? Did Zeus and Helios know about this?

≈≈≈

I made a panicked phone call. "Zeus. Did you know that the land the hotel is standing on is eroding?"

"What do you mean, eroding?"

"The waves are washing the land into the sea. The Aegean is a lot closer to the hotel than when you recruited me."

He didn't need prompting as he answered my first question. "Why did I not know this?"

"You tell me. You're the all-knowing, and all-seeing god. You said if Helios falls Rhodes will fall. Now I know why. If Helios descends into the sea, what is to stop Poseidon swallowing the entire island?"

"How could this happen without us knowing?" He asked again.

"Simple, all the other things that we've been battling were distractions. Once the hotel goes, it will only be a matter of time before Kam's tomb disappears into the sea. The island will be lost," I said. What a Malaka, I couldn't believe I'd been working for someone so powerful and stupid all at the same time. I just hung up the phone and cut him off.

I turned to Lindon who had already started to research on his phone. "Rhodes is on the edge of a deep abyss that disappears deep into the Mediterranean. It is only its size that stops the Aegean pushing it into the abyss. If it is getting thinner by two metres a year, how long before the Aegean wins? The north shore moves out to a maximum depth of five hundred metres. The south shore drops to a depth of over four thousand metres," said Lindon.

"That explains why the hot side of the island is so calm, *Still Waters Run Deep.*" Quoting my favourite song by the Four Tops.

"Exactly. Luckily the waves come from the west, and they hit the island at an angle."

"So, Poseidon has set up a system that will erode the island from the north-west?"

"Come on, dad. You're letting this powerful god thing go to your head again. Remember what you showed me about Demeter not controlling the weather? This is the same. Poseidon is doing nothing, but he is taking the credit for a natural phenomenon. Poseidon or not, erosion is a major problem for Rhodes."

"When he swamped the boat, it seemed real enough," I reminded him.

"I'm not saying he has no power, but it suits him to take the credit for the erosion. Yes, he can muster up the occasional storm or big wave. But I'm sure he isn't responsible for the erosion."

I looked at my son and felt an overwhelming sense of pride that I cannot express. I had a lump in my throat. I remembered all the times I had told him off for wasting too much time on the Internet, for being irresponsible and not thinking ahead. He'd grown to be a level-headed young man.

"For now, we should keep this to ourselves. I know Zeus doesn't like us keeping things from him. But I'm still worried about the blood ties between the gods. We have to keep our focus. We can't let minor events distract us from the bigger issue."

"I'm sure you're right," Lindon agreed.

SANCTUARY – A Safe Haven

We resumed our rest and recuperation. We couldn't forget about the war, but we needed time to regroup and be a family once again. We decided on a grand tour of the island. It meant we could resume being tourists again.

We visited all the locations we'd grown to love. We didn't even try to put the war to the back of our minds. We didn't dare forget about Poseidon or Hestia again.

The malicious reviews about the hotel continued. But responding to reviews was demoted to a customer service issue rather than a wartime activity.

We visited seven springs – *Hepta Piges*. It allowed us to once again experience the 200-metre tunnel. Walking through ankle-deep ice-cold water. A perfect antidote to the hot temperature under the heat of the sun. Kam was more scared of the long dark tunnel than the water. We laughed as we remembered the details of the last time we visited. Alyss used her phone as a torch and dropped it in the water. She didn't laugh at the time.

We picked the right season to visit Butterfly Valley –

Petaloudes. All the tree trunks were covered in butterflies. In fact, they're moths – Jersey Tiger moths. They were at the stage where they no longer ate. They clung to the trees to conserve their energy.

For this reason, it is illegal to make loud or sudden noises. It would cause them to fly, wasting valuable energy needed for the next part of their life cycle. I felt the same as a Jersey Tiger moth at that moment. That's what the tour was about. Resting before we moved on to the closing stages of the war. One way or another, the end of the war was closing in.

We visited the castles at Monolithos and Kritina. Monolithos was a shadow of its former self. I bet Zeus could remember it in its heyday. The most striking thing I remembered is when you looked through one of the damaged portals. If you got the angle right, the shape it made, mimicked the outline of Rhodes. I found it inspiring and took it as a sign that Rhodes will survive the war. I remember hoping that the family would too. Monolithos was built in the 15th Century by the Venetians and had seen a few sieges and battles.

Kritinia was constructed in the 16th century and has lived the same violent life that Monolithos has. Kritinia was built by the Knights of the Order of St John. I wondered if the gods had been involved in the battles over these castles.

As we were in that part of the island anyway, we visited Emponas. We visited the wineries and enjoyed the free wine tasting. Kam chanted her favourite mantra. "It would be rude not to." The wine flowing meant we had to stay the night. I thought about all the tourists that come to the island and stay in a hotel or complex. I pondered how they miss so much of real Rhodes by not venturing out.

I'd suggested to Filipos that he encourage his guests to take these tours or visits. He saw that as a threat. As if his guests would fall out of love with his hotel. He was selfish and wanted to keep the tourists all to himself.

We avoided doing the whole tour in one day. There was too much to miss. I've always been amused by guests that say somewhere is too far away. It's a bloody small island nowhere is too far away. It is only fifty miles long and twenty-four miles wide. If Poseidon had his way, it would be a lot less than twenty-four miles wide. Its coastline is shorter than 140 miles and shrinking.

We went to the most southern point of the island and revisited Prasonisi. We saw the tide high for the first time. All we could see was an islet. We were robbed of the spectacular double-sided beach we'd seen before. Was this a symptom of the erosion issues affecting the north coast? Or was it a high-tide event? It was the first time we'd experienced it. I suspected it was the work of Poseidon.

At the northern end of the island, we visited Rodini park, and the ancient tomb cut into the rock face. We needed our graves to be better kept than the one at Rodini. The highlight of Rodini was the opportunity to see freshwater turtles in their natural habitat. We also had a chance to enjoy the shade the overhanging trees provided.

Perfect timing at Kalithea springs allowed us to see a wedding taking place. Kam and I looked at the possibility of renewing our wedding vows there. Then life on the island kind of took over. We blamed Zeus for that.

The bride and groom went straight from the wedding to the Monastery at Tsambika. It's known for endowing its visitors with fertility. You can often see couples visiting to ask for fertility. Mothers take their new-borns there to thank God for the pregnancy bestowed upon them. When we visited, the car struggled up the steep slope. Amid the smell of burning rubber and smoke, a memory came to mind of the dying Eos. I decided to park at the bottom of the steep incline and walk up the hill.

We didn't take any more boat trips, we didn't dare risk it. Kam didn't like boats even before the Poseidon episode. There was no chance she would ever travel by boat again. And this meant a visit to see the beautiful coloured houses of Symi was off the agenda.

We visited Lardos, Afandou and Pefkos. All magical resorts that people visit year after year. One benefit of these resorts for us is a large number of compatriots that visit and return. It is a chance to meet up with old friends from England. So many places to eat delicious food. Kam and I have always considered this the hot side of the island. Temperatures outstrip the north-western side of the island by at least a couple of degrees. The beaches are sandier, and the Mediterranean is calmer than the Aegean. Sometimes we chose to be on that side of the island. It is, after all, where Lindon's tomb is located.

No visit to the southeast side of the island would be complete without a visit to Lindos. Lindon reported the same emotions the rest of us had felt when we'd looked over our own tombs. It invigorated him.

He was fortunate, no slab of concrete or shaped stone for him. His tomb was under the raised floor of a Taverna in Lindos. His tribute was a black and white pebbled mosaic of a ship. No wonder he felt ecstatic when he was there, his tomb was the only one that was indoors. Most likely a tribute to the amount of time he'd spent locked in his bedroom playing on his computer. The taverna was named after the Greek for someone that chooses things from a wide range of sources. Lindon being Lindon picked up on the word chosen. He was full of it. "Ha-ha, I am the chosen one," he repeated too many times.

Alyss managed to calm him down. "Yes but you still aren't Kratos, are you?"

We met up with a friend, Elti, for coffee in Archangelos. The real gem there can be found in the back streets of the town. The church and all its beautiful gilding.

On route back to the west coast, I wanted to visit Damatria, an inland village. It's believed to be the only village of Rhodes dating back to the Doric era in the 11th century BC. Recent excavations have revealed continuous habitation for three thousand years. Zeus will have been a youngster about that time. The village was named after the sanctuary of the goddess Dimitra. I wanted to visit Damatria because the goddess Dimitra is, of course, Demeter. Sister of Zeus and mother of Persephone. I wanted to make sure she hadn't fled to Damatria after we'd defeated her. She hadn't.

The kids insisted we visited Faliraki and the famous waterpark. The largest water park in Europe. They went to the water park; Kam and I went to the beach instead. It is more than three miles long. And we weren't at risk of drowning.

Our favourite relaxing place has always been the village of Trianta, not only because of the proximity of Alyss' Tomb. It is the location of our favourite food outlet. Authentic Greek cooking and meze. Its customers are discerning locals. Not a tourist in sight. Trianta has managed to keep its character of a typical Rhodian village.

And of course, no tourist should ever visit the island without seeing the old town. Getting away from the shopping streets. Touring the back lanes and witnessing locals going about their daily chores. I suggested that these back streets had been the scene of many a battle between different nations, different religions and maybe even mortals and immortals.

We finished up at Kamiros and revisited Kam's tomb. She too felt invigorated from the closeness to where her former body lay.

I took this as a sign and visited Rhodes on my own so that I could visit my tomb. There was a discernible raising of my energy levels and enthusiasm. I could almost feel the adrenaline and endorphins flooding my system.

≈≈≈

"Alyss, how did you feel when you visited your tomb?" I asked.

"It was weird. I felt as if I could achieve anything. It was as if all my cares and worries disappeared. But I did feel sad when we visited yours, mums and Lindon's tombs."

I looked at Lindon. "What about you?"

"The same as Alyss, but elation when at my tomb. Despair at the others."

I didn't need to ask Kam; I could see by the look on her face that her experience mirrored that of the kids. This reflected the emotions I'd felt at the Acropolis of Rhodes. We needed for us all to be in perfect fitness for the war. As individuals, we needed to be away from the tombs of the rest of the family. At the same time, we needed to be near the energy of our own tomb. This suggested we should split up and live apart. None of us wanted that, at least in the long term. Spending our eternal immortality alone was not a choice any of us wanted to make. We needed to find a single place that was as close to our own tombs as possible, to maintain the power that we felt. At the same time, we needed to maximise the distance from other family members tombs.

After hours of discussion and brainstorming different theories with Lindon, I thought I'd found a potential location.

"There's one last place I'd like us to visit before we return to Olympian Dreams," I informed the family.

"Where?" echoed Kam and Alyss in unison.

Lindon didn't query it; he just gave a knowing smile. I guessed he had an idea from the discussions we'd had earlier.

"My secret. Think of it as a magical mystery tour," I sang the last part mimicking Paul McCartney.

We set off to visit one of the mountains of the island.

Kam's face dropped. "Oh, no. We aren't doing the wine roads again, are we? My bloodstream couldn't stand it."

"No. It's not Emponas it's a different mountain," I pointed out as I drove the long and winding road.

As we approached the town we were headed for; the sky clouded over. I could hear rumbles of thunder rolling towards us. I thought to myself, someone doesn't want us to visit this place. My spine tingled with a sense of foreboding. *Had I made a mistake in my calculations? Was this another Poseidon moment?*

As the car climbed higher up the mountain, the sky cleared, and Helios was once again able to look down upon us. What a weird experience it was a thirty-minute journey. We had started out under a clear blue sky, and we arrived under a clear blue sky. For the middle twenty-five minutes, we were under a thunderstorm. With torrents of water cascading down the mountain road.

When we reached the hidden gem in the mountain, I managed to find somewhere to park. It was alongside a tiny little church and a graveyard. The headstones and memorials all in white marble put our own tombstones to shame. We had nothing as grand as the stones we saw here. Most had photographs of the deceased on them. I would've liked to have had our pictures on our tombs. Instead, we had anonymity and non-disclosure.

Given the day of the week and the purpose of our visit. The patron of the church was the most appropriately named Saint. Her Saints day was also mine and Kams wedding anniversary. There was a perfect synergy about us all being at that church at that moment in time. Not many people can pinpoint the exact location of where their soul is happiest. I'd just found mine.

"Oh my god, this is beautiful," announced Kam.

"Bet there isn't much activity here," bemoaned Alyss, clearly comparing it with Athens.

Lindon clearly knew what I had been aiming for. "I bet there aren't any D80's here either. This feels like a good place to hide."

It was the first time we'd visited, so there were new things to see. New tavernas to try and new friends to make. I've always liked the phrase: *A stranger is just a friend you haven't met yet.*

I was interested in watching the emotions shown by the rest of the family. They, of course, didn't know they were the subjects of my observations. We strolled through the streets to get our bearings. We looked at everything in wonderment. The sun beat down on us, and I got a sense that all was well in our world.

As we came to the edge of the town. We were met by stunning views across the valley below. Alyss and Lindon were the first to show any emotion. He put his arm around her shoulder. "Hey, Sis. You really are growing into a beautiful woman now you've stopped being a brat."

"You're not so bad yourself for a man. I like it when you put your arms around me. It makes me feel safe."

They looked at each other like I hadn't seen before. The siblings appeared as one.

I put my arms around Kam, and she made a similar observation. "Look at those two. The days of bickering and teasing seem so long ago."

"Yes, I know. Do you remember when Alyss aimed a golf ball at his head while he was sunbathing?" I reminisced.

"Look at them now. It's only a few days ago that he rescued her from the sea," added Kam.

For the first time for a long time, I felt we were united as a family. A proper team with common goals. The period of temperamental teens seemed like an eternity away. And this was such was an appropriate term. We were immortal souls destined for an eternity of family life. At that moment, I hoped for better family relationships than the Olympian family had.

I could feel the positive sensations starting to rebuild my shattered confidence. I'm not sure the others realised how low I felt for putting them all in danger. I could feel the tide turning. Was it the company or the location? Was I right about this place? Was it where we could maximise each other's contribution to the cause?

By being there, everyone's mood seemed to lift. The thought crossed my mind that we should buy a property and achieve our dream of retiring to Rhodes. After all, it would be a long retirement. If we were to be prisoners of the island for an eternity, it would be the best prison in the world.

"We can't stay in hotels forever," suggested Kam as if she'd read my mind. "I need the loo. Let's find a taverna where we can have a frappe and get out of the sun. It's nearly lunchtime. We can have a bite to eat."

We walked back towards the centre of the town and stopped at the first taverna we came across. It was a beautiful place. Inside, the walls were decorated with a range of agricultural implements. Hoes, rakes, sickles and scythes with their long wooden handles. Images of locals from bygone times were interspersed throughout. It reminded me of a traditional English country pub, except for its size, it was huge by comparison. I guessed it was a converted hotel or guest house. It had a lounge, a public bar and an eating area. It even had a pub garden. The garden had a wooded pergola that acted as a support for grapevines. There were even bunches of fruit already growing on it. None of the plastic stuff you get in an English pub garden.

Kam laughed as she looked at me. "Fantastic, a dartboard. I bet I can still whip your arse, Mister Chairman of the darts committee."

I guessed that she'd remembered the time that Moses had banned her from the league for calling him a fake. He was the league secretary, and I was the chairman. It took a lot of persuading to get him to reinstate her. I couldn't help thinking about the similarities between Moses and Zeus.

"OK, we'll have a doubles game later. Boys versus girls," I challenged, laughing at the same anecdote.

"Ha-ha Moses?" she confirmed.

For the first time that I could remember, Kam ordered Greek dishes. She even had a Greek salad with olives. Now, that was a development.

"You don't like olives," I pointed out.

"I know, but I think I like them now."

I looked at Alyss. With her plate of roasted vegetables. "Athena must be influencing you. The last time I saw you eat a vegetable was when you were eleven." We all laughed about the time that she wanted to be a vegetarian and gave up meat, but she didn't like vegetables.

"Yes. Athena has taught me a lot, and I admire her. I like vegetables now because Athena wanted me to try them."

Kam and I looked at each other in amazement. Alyss and vegetables had never gone together. Ever. "In fact. I have something to say, and for the first time, I have the confidence to tell you. Promise you won't go mad."

"I don't think I could get mad about anything at the moment. Sitting in this place has made me feel really positive."

I looked at her and noticed the beautiful young woman she'd become.

"Of course we won't get mad. You can tell us anything. Like dad said, we feel positive in this place."

Then a chill ran down my spine as Lindon reverted to type and put his tuppence worth in. "Hahahaha. She's pregnant," he mocked.

"Knob head," shouted Alyss. "I'm not pregnant, don't judge everyone by your own standards."

I laughed but inside I was relieved. I could do without another life to protect. "Lindon shut up. You're not helping,"

"What is it? What do you want to tell us, sweetheart?" invited Kam, in a quiet and calm tone.

"Well, I am far from pregnant. In fact, I prefer the company of females..." She paused as if waiting for some kind of reaction or waiting for the penny to drop. "Did you hear what I said? I'm a lesbian." She was clearly frustrated that we hadn't shown a reaction.

I responded first. "And your point is? What made you think we'd get mad? None of us has ever been judgmental or homophobic."

"Aren't you shocked?"

"No, I'm looking on the bright side. You won't be an unmarried mum for an eternity."

"Don't joke about it. I'm serious. I'm a lesbian."

"I'm not joking about it, sweetheart. I'm just letting you know that we're alright with it. Isn't that right, Kam?"

Kam nodded. "Of course."

The look on Kam's face signalled disappointment.

Disappointment that she wouldn't be a maternal grandmother. She didn't say so, but I knew it. She would never have the traditional matriarchal photograph that Mags had. Mother, daughter, granddaughter.

"Don't you want to know how I'm sure I'm a lesbian?" invited Alyss, clearly bursting to tell us more.

"I want to know how lesbians do it," joked Lindon.

"No, you don't. Not while we are sat at the dinner table," I intervened.

Alyss couldn't contain the answer any longer. "That's not what I meant. I've already got a girlfriend, and that's how I know."

"So long as it's not some bloody weirdo you've met on the Internet. I'd be more concerned about that than about you being a lesbian."

"No, it's a real-life person." And she tagged on, "I think."

"What do you mean, you think?" queried Kam.

"I think she is a person. Kind of."

When the penny dropped. It was like a 2000lb World War Two bomb going off in my head. "It's Athena, isn't it?"

"Yes. How did you know?"

"I don't know. I think I read your mind."

I looked at Lindon. "Awwww. What's the matter, son? Did you have eyes on Athena yourself?"

"Damn right. She is the most beautiful woman ever."

Athena had obviously taught Alyss a lot more than we'd imagined. I felt reassured that someone so powerful would care for Alyss. It is another ally that would want to ensure that she and the family were safe.

I felt good, elated. We had a three-hour session in the taverna, and not a single drop of alcohol was needed. We had several games of darts, boys versus girls. At three games each we called it a day so that everyone was a winner. Happiness fuelled the best day we'd had in our immortal persona. Throughout the extended lunch and darts tournament, we discussed our emotions, and it became clear that we all had a similar sensation of euphoria. Many times, during the conversations, someone would finish what someone else was saying. Being there had brought us together and put us in tune with each other's thoughts.

We'd become one. I revealed to the family why I had taken them there. In my earlier discussions with Lindon, I'd set about trying to find lines and geometric shapes that would tie our four tombs together. I confirmed that we all felt closer, safer and more confident. I'd guessed correctly, and that is how I'd found this place.

"This will become our sanctuary, and no one is going to get to find out where it is. The last thing we want is D80's crawling all over it."

I asked the server to come over, and we introduced ourselves to him. He introduced himself as Giannis. Unusually for a Greek man he had long fair hair. He had a serious look about his olive-skinned face. He appeared to be in his mid-twenties, and he clearly worked out. He would have looked at home on Fistral beach in Cornwall.

"Tell me Giannis have you ever been to England?"

"No, I have never left Greece. Why would I? This beautiful country has everything I need," he smiled.

"Have you always lived on Rhodes?"

"I have been here for many years, but I have spent most of my life near Athens. Was everything OK with your Food?"

I'd detected a timely change of subject, so I ordered drinks. We needed to have a celebration drink to mark Alyss' coming out. Four large Mythos was the order of the day. I love the way it's served in an ice-frosted glass. So refreshing.

"Yamas, here's to our baby girl, now all grown up," I announced to the clink of thick glass tankards.

I looked at Alyss. "You can't let Athena know where we are. I don't want any of the deities knowing of this place."

"I will never tell her," she promised, "but I think it's too late." And she nodded towards the door.

"Bloody hell. What did we do to deserve this?" I asked, not sure who I was asking or even expecting an answer.

I was shocked and taken by surprise. Athena walked right in and hugged Giannis, and she didn't even acknowledge us.

APOLLO – The Most Complex God

Athena greeted Giannis. "Brother, it has been too long."

I immediately glanced at Lindon. He looked back and raised an eyebrow.

Giannis gazed into Athena's eyes. "I know. You must come to the island more often. Have you seen Artemis? She came to stay a few months ago. She was pissing about with the local wildlife. She's still a daddy's girl."

I looked at the others. Like me, they had a *what the fuck* look on their faces.

"Yes, I have seen her. We visited Dad together," she replied

He grunted. "How can you call him Dad? I haven't seen him since the colossus fell. It will be a lot longer still unless the bloody family sort themselves out. Malakas," he scowled. And he clearly wasn't happy with his family.

He must have sensed we were staring at them or having a what the fuck moment. He glanced in our direction, and this caused Athena to look over. As soon as Athena spotted Alyss, her eyes lit up. That was reassuring. She proceeded to drag

Giannis towards where we were sat.

"Let me introduce my half-brother Apollo. Artemis' twin. This is his taverna."

It was Giannis' turn to have a what the fuck moment. His sister had just announced his real name. He squinted at me, and I glared at him. I didn't know whose side he was on. *Twin of Artemis*. I could see the likeness, but facially they were at least ten years apart. I wondered if you always stayed the same as you were when you first resurrected. That would have suited me to be eternally stuck in the prime of life.

I raised an eyebrow. "You told us your name was Giannis."

"Of course I did. That's because I am Giannis. Everyone knows me as Giannis. I live here, and it is my secret place. Athena, who are these people? Why have you brought them here?"

"Relax, silly. They aren't mortals. I know them, and Artemis has met them. She completed a task for them when she was here," she revealed. This appeared to placate him a little.

I could tell he was still cautious about us. Lindon solved that problem. "Apollo. The protector of Rhodes."

"Yes, that's right. You are both smart and good looking," said Giannis. That put a smile on Lindon's face.

"I read that some people worship you as the god of the Sun."

"I am the god of the Sun." He defended his position by stressing the word 'am'.

Then I put my foot in it. "I thought Helios was the god of

the Sun."

"Bah. Helios is a Titan, not an Olympian. He is the Sun god which is different. All he's got that I haven't is a bloody chariot. The Olympians beat the Titans and banished them. That chariot should be mine. Anyway, they can all get stuffed. I want nothing more to do with them. The only gods I have anything to do with are Athena and Artemis. The two most beautiful women in the world." He turned and hugged Athena again.

I swallowed deeply, Unsure how he would take the news that we were descendants of Helios. More so, I had real concerns about the timing of Athena's appearance. She clearly didn't come here often. Why now? Why, while we were there? Alyss didn't even know where we were going to be. I looked at Lindon and Kam, and they knew what I was thinking.

Athena looked into Giannis' eyes. "I love you, brother, and I will always be here for you. But I have news of my own to tell you. This is Alyss. A very good friend of mine."

Alyss interrupted her. "It's OK. I've told them."

Athena blushed and looked at Kam. "Oh. Are you OK with it? I mean us?"

"Of course."

"In that case. Apollo, meet my new partner Alyss."

Giannis moaned. "You get all the pretty girls. I liked the look of her myself."

Now it was Alyss who blushed.

The protective father in me made me clear my throat out loud. No father likes a lad hitting on his daughter. God or no bloody god.

Athena introduced the rest of us and explained our relevance to the protection of Rhodes. She told Giannis about how Zeus had given us immortality. "Dad has been using them to protect the island. Protect it from Prometheus, Poseidon, Demeter and Hestia." I was alarmed by the word 'using'.

Apollo interrupted my thought as he became angry and started to shout. "What the fuck. I am the protector of Rhodes. Why didn't he come to me?"

"Oh yeah. Like you would have offered your help, or even, that he would ask for it. You haven't communicated for centuries."

"I know, I know, but I am *the* protector."

"Well, you still can be. You can help dad and the sane part of the family."

"I will, but only if they know nothing of it. Above all, no one must ever know of this place. I stay here for a reason." He looked thoughtful for a moment as Athena's last comment finally sunk in. "Are any of them sane?"

"We're with you on that," I agreed. "You say this is your sanctuary. I am sensing it is ours too. We would like to use it as our place of safety. Is that in order? Because we are at one with the place. It gives us more strength."

"*Vevaios.* Of course. From what Athena has told there is a reason that you gain strength and comfort from this location. It is near a focal point from the alignment of your tombs."

I swallowed deeply. "Before we go on. I must tell you something that Zeus told us. Something Athena hasn't shared with you."

"If it's OK with Athena, it's OK with me." He had a laugh just like his father, though not so loud.

Athena looked straight at me. I think she'd guessed what I was about to reveal. But it had to be done if we were to build a connection with Giannis. Any relationship had to have a foundation of truth. And truth builds trust.

"Zeus told us that we … Ummm … we are descendants of Helios." I didn't so much blurt it out, it was more of a stutter.

It was reassuring that he'd read my nervousness. "We are all bloody descendants of the Titans. It doesn't mean we have to like them. I won't hold it against you." And this time he laughed as loud as his dad. "We can share this sanctuary. We have a common goal, and I'll be able to help you. But remember this location and my involvement must never be revealed."

I felt like I should spit into the palm of my hand and shake on it. The way I'd seen Irish travellers swear an oath to each other. Giannis beat me to it and spat right at me. It made me jump, and I frowned at him. The look on my face told Athena I didn't have a clue what that was about.

"In ancient Greece, when someone spits at you like that, they are giving you good luck and warding off evil," she informed us.

"In parts of the UK, we do this to share an oath." I gobbed into my right hand and shook with Giannis.

He proceeded to spit at the others, and they each spat in their hands before shaking.

I'm glad he didn't suggest becoming blood brothers. I was

thinking back to some old western. A cowboy and some native American tribesman cut the palms of their hands before shaking. That would have been a step too far.

We remained at the Taverna late into the night. I got plastered again. We all did. It was good to hear the family tales that Athena and Giannis shared with us. Some of it repeated from myths that Lindon had told us about. Other stories didn't appear in any myth that he'd discovered. Lindon was mostly interested in these.

He and I thought the same thing at the same time. I know because of the way we looked at each other. *If we survive this, we could write a book of myths about these undocumented events.*

It was getting late, and I was too drunk to drive. Our new team member extended his hospitality and gave us shelter for the night.

"Whenever you are here, this is your home. I have plenty of room, and you are family." Almost an exact repeat of the phrase Filipos used when he spoke to us about the hotel.

≈≈≈

Given recent events, I had a good night's sleep. We'd, at last, managed to find somewhere that gave us complete peace of mind and safety. We could relax.

In the morning Giannis had rustled up a full English for us. Though Kam opted for Yoghurt, honey and apricots. The rest of us made sure that nothing went to waste. I don't know how Athena kept such a stunning figure because she ate twice what I could manage. I kept that thought to myself.

For the rest of the day, we held discussions about the war we'd been having. Giannis was impressed that we'd managed to survive. He cheered when we described some of our victories. He offered encouragement when I explained how useless I felt after the battle we'd lost to Poseidon. He was so much help to my recovery. He listened and empathised. As all good counsellors do, he let me talk but made a lot of encouraging noises. I decided I liked Giannis. He was happy to help, and he gave the outward impression that he was genuine. I had no sense that we were being used as pawns. Pawns in a mythical game of chess. The way I felt about all the other gods.

The others decided that they wanted a break from the counselling session. They preferred to use the time to get to know the area better.

Without the others present, I felt better able to voice my doubts and concerns. How could I, a mere human, compete with the mighty Olympian gods? The conversation turned to godly deeds and powers and how the gods would or could use them.

"Bah. Don't believe everything you read. The world is different now. When I was born, it was easy to get people to believe you were making miracles happen. All you needed was a brain and the ability to tell a well thought out story."

"What we call fake news now?"

"Yes, that's it. In a time when communication wasn't as advanced as it is now, the spoken word was all there was. You needed a friend to go to another community and tell what they had seen. Another friend goes to a second community and swears what they had seen. Before you know it, you are a god with superpowers. Then the poets and playwrights take over.

They adapt and embellish the stories. They then travel throughout the land, putting on plays and reading their poems. Then you know you have cracked it." He smiled. "Every lover I ever had was because of my fame. I don't have any more power than you do. I might be a better archer, but I have had years to perfect my technique."

"But what about immortality? It seems real enough to me," I queried.

"Immortality isn't some magical power. Yes, it does exist. It's in your blood. When a human dies, their spirit lives on and generally transfers to a new being. It's called reincarnation. Some blood types stop the spirit from moving on by reincarnating into the same body. The fortunate ones are those that have resurrective immortality. That is the type that we all have. The body rebuilds itself and repairs damage."

"So I was born with immortality?"

"No, you got it when you almost died in the taxi crash. Which I don't believe happened, by the way. I believe you were drugged and taken to a medical facility. There you would have had all your blood replaced. It is the blood you were given that gives you resurrective immortality."

There goes that Johnny Nash song again. "Why were we picked?"

"Only Zeus will know the answer to that question."

I looked at him puzzled. What he was telling me seemed too fantastic to be true. But then again, so did the idea of a war with the D80's. He could see I was doubting what he was telling me.

"You ask anyone who Apollo was. Trust me. I'm a god of

my word". And he laughed at his poor attempt at humour.

My mind was working harder than my overheated phone, and I knew what happened to my phone when it overheated. It rebooted. Any remnants of the hangover I had soon disappeared.

"Let me get this right. Gods have no more power than I have. They merely thrive because they have something in their blood. They have built their mythology by creating fake news. Then convince others that the stories are facts."

"That's about it. Most of the myths were created by the great poets and writers of the time. You could make yourself a god of anything. Though it is more difficult nowadays, because of the Internet. We now live in a global village, so you have no other village to go to where you can start to build the myth."

"But I could show my ability to resurrect."

"And you would really want to do that, would you? Have the world, and it's top scientists poke and prod you to figure out how you could resurrect." Then he hit the button fair and square on the top of its rounded head. "I don't know you, but I think you are a more private person than that." I looked at him my thoughts all over the place. I remained silent, and I knew he was correct. "Why do you think you've been searching for a sanctuary?"

"What about the closeness of my family and being on the same wavelength? I thought that was a power I got from being here."

"Come on. You are a bright guy. You have lived together all your kids' lives. You are close, and you are bound to understand how each other think."

Again I knew he was right. "Ah but…" I paused because I once hated a boss that always used that phrase when I had a good idea, "what about Zeus' lightning bolt?"

"Have you actually seen lightning? Or just a flash and a loud bang? I'm sure even Lindon knows the science behind that. Listen to me, and think about it. If you created a flash and explosion in front of people who'd only experienced that from lightning. Then they would call it lightning."

I was trying to recall any other events that I couldn't explain with science. What Giannis was telling me was exactly what I had used to defeat Demeter.

"What about the underworld?" I queried thinking I had caught him out.

"North pole, South pole, Sahara Desert. Anywhere that hasn't got a large population."

"Then why is the underworld seen as a punishment?"

"Would you want to live in that level of hot or cold for an eternity?" He'd made his point.

"What about our tombs and the power we get from them?"

"I'm sure your spirit is entombed. I doubt you will find any bones to dig up. They are still inside your skin," then he sniggered, "if they weren't inside you, how would you stand here? You would be a slug." At which point I sniggered too.

"What about Helios being the light in Zeus' eyes?" I queried. "I have seen it."

"No. You haven't. What you have seen is called *photophobia*. Sensitivity to light. I think the same word is used

231

in English, but it is Greek. Bright lights make your eyes water. Dependant on which way he is standing, his left eye, right eye or both eyes water. He could ease it by wearing sunglasses, but he is a stubborn fool. He wants to maintain the myth that he sees everything happening in the world through Helios."

"And that is why the D80's squint when they are looking at me. They want to see if I have watery eyes."

"Exactly, and there is every chance that if you are angry, nervous or excited, you will have watery eyes. The squinting god will retreat quickly because they will think you have control of the blood supply that keeps them immortal. That is the only power my father has."

It was as though we were living in some kind of fantasy world. We continued this analysis for longer than I can remember. We'd missed dinner by the time the others returned.

"We've got a surprise for you. We've found somewhere to live. Somewhere for sale," announced Kam. "You must see it. We all love it."

"First, I have some news of my own. You're never going to believe it," I didn't have a clue where I was going to begin. I didn't get a chance before it all kicked off between the gods.

Athena looked at Giannis. "What have you told him?"

"Everything."

The older of the two siblings gasped. "What have you done?"

"Exactly what you should have done. You are supposed to be the goddess of truth, wisdom and fairness."

"But…"

"But nothing. We are all in the same boat. This poor family are being used to sort out a family quarrel. Where's the bloody fairness in that? You say you love Alyss, but you let her get caught up in all this shit. They have a right to know."

"Dad is going to be pissed with you, Apollo," she shouted.

Kam, Alyss and Lindon looked utterly lost. Kam looked at me as if to say, *what the fuck's going on?*

"We'll leave you guys to it, and catch you later. I should look at the house they've found." And we beat a hasty exit.

≈≈≈

The house was all we could have hoped for. Nothing out of the ordinary. It would allow us to blend into the local community perfectly. It wasn't right in the centre and not too far out to draw attention to ourselves. The neighbours on one side were English, so there was nothing to make us stand out. On the opposite side of the narrow road, there was another Taverna. This gave us somewhere else to go when we wanted to discuss things without Giannis present.

I feared the most significant issue would be Greek government red tape. This was likely to be a much bigger battle than we currently faced with the D80's. After viewing the house from the outside, we went to the Taverna. This one was much smaller than Giannis'. And it was near the museum of agriculture.

I didn't think it appropriate to go back to Giannis too soon. I was famished and ready to eat. It made sense to have our evening meal in the tiny taverna. It also allowed me to bring the family up to speed on the depth of the deception we'd been enduring. We ordered a meze meal for four.

233

I concluded telling the family of my discussion with Giannis. "… He says that it's all fake news and rumour." They were as stunned as I was. I still hadn't managed to digest it all myself, and they had so many questions. I could answer some basic queries, but most of the questions needed Giannis to answer them.

Lindon was the first to start to look forward. "This is to our advantage. They have no powers. They are the same as us."

I thought out loud. "Even more, the gods aren't as intelligent as we are. They don't know technology the way that Lindon does. The longer we keep what we know a secret, we can maintain the element of surprise."

Kam added, "Yes. The longer we keep it secret, the longer we stay safe."

Alyss was clearly blinded by her love for Athena. "Athena will protect us."

I still had my doubts about Athena and expressed my concern. "I'm not so sure that she'll keep our secret."

"Blood is thicker than water," said Lindon. He was confirming what I was already thinking.

Inside I noted that day as a turning point. We'd found our sanctuary, but we had learnt something that could potentially destroy us all.

Lindon raised an important point. "Once Zeus is aware that we are in on his secret. Our battle will be with all the gods. And he has one power that can destroy us all. He has control of the immortal blood supply."

"We can't let them see us as a threat to their secret society.

Because that is all that they amount to." Kam hugged me to let me know she sensed that I was invigorated and ready for the challenge ahead. We all were. That day I felt the veil of self-doubt lift. Once more the Johnny Nash lyrics from *I Can See Clearly Now* became my new earworm. I literally felt like a god. I felt that not only was I their equal, but I was more superior.

Kam raised the issue of Poseidon and erosion. I pointed out that it was happening all over the Greek islands. It was being taken care of by the Greek government and international scientists. Poseidon was just capitalising on it and taking the credit for it. All we had to do was convince him to give up the war with Zeus.

"Is that all?" queried Alyss with a tone of sarcasm.

"Yes, we all need to understand that they're just ordinary people. That they have immortality, but so do we. Remember we have something that they haven't. A close family, all working towards the same goal. They would sell each other out if it suited them. They are all liars and conmen. The only one we've met that's like us is Giannis."

"What about the big wave that almost drowned us?" queried Kam.

Lindon provided the answer before I had a chance to try and figure it out. "He drugged us or hypnotised us or something. Remember he gave us a drink when we were on the boat, and that was just moments before it happened."

"Oh, that's right. I'll give him bloody *yamas*," threatened Kam.

At least Alyss was beginning to see that she couldn't

assume Athena would automatically take our side. "Do you think Giannis and Athena will help?"

"Giannis? Yes. Athena? I hope so. We will find out when we get back to Olympian," I pondered out loud.

We got on with our meze, chased down by the odd ouzo or two.

≈≈≈

Smiling at Giannis, I asked, "Is it safe to come back?".

"Of course. You know what us Greeks are like. Athena could pick an argument with herself if she didn't get her own way. She has always been spoilt by our father. At least she's still here." And he grinned back at me.

Kam looked at me. "The same way you spoil Alyss. Bloody dads and daughters." I had to remind her that she too was a daughter and probably spoilt by her own dad.

Athena entered the room. "I am sorry for my behaviour earlier. Apollo thinks I overreacted. But he has put you in so much danger by telling you the Olympian secrets."

"We realise that, but I also think it gives us an advantage. The danger won't be real until the board know what we've been told."

"That is the problem. The board already think you know their secrets. Remember how furious my father was when you went it alone with Demeter? How you figured out she wasn't controlling the weather or the seasons. Now you will understand why he was angry with you."

"He can't be sure. Otherwise, they would already be dead mortals," reassured Giannis.

"No. Neither can we. We must assume that he knows that

we know that he knows," I rhymed.

To which Alyss had a fit of the giggles. "That sounded so funny. *To me, to you.* It sounds like the Chuckle Brothers."

"Oh, sweetheart. There is nothing funny about the situation you are in," said Athena.

Lindon saw an opportunity to have a dig at Athena. "Leave her alone. That's how she deals with difficult situations. She always did it when dad was telling her off."

That is the first time I'd ever heard Lindon defend Alyss. Imaginary or not the place and the situation really did bring out the best in us.

In an attempt to deflect the rising tension, I intervened. "What I want to know is how we can defeat them and win the war? Until they're gone, they'll continue to create problems for the island."

Putting on her glasses and goddess of war tone, Athena responded with a declaration. "That is for you to conclude. First, you must decide what constitutes victory. Then you must calculate what consequences you can live or die with."

"So you aren't going to help?" I queried, showing my disappointment.

"You don't need my help. You already have all the answers you need. However, I would like to take Alyss back to Athens with me. She will be safer there."

Alyss interrupted her, "No. The family are stronger when we're together."

Lindon put his protective arm around her.

Kam agreed with the goddess. "She could be right. Alyss would be safer in Athens."

I looked at Alyss."The choice is yours, sweetheart. You must decide what is best for you."

"Nope. I'm staying. I feel safer when we're all together."

Athena was clearly disappointed. "So be it. Then I will stay on the Island as well, but I will stay with my father."

Giannis looked at her. "What the fuck would you stay with him for?"

"He is still my father, and I will be close enough to see what is going on. I will leave tonight. Come, Alyss, let's go for a walk."

"What about you, Giannis? Can you help?"

"Not physically. But I can advise and support you. I can't be seen to have any involvement. I need to protect our sanctuary at all costs."

"You could shapeshift," I pleaded with a hint of desperation in my voice.

He laughed. "Rod, I wish I could. The gods aren't able to shapeshift."

I assured him. "But we've seen it."

"No, you haven't. What you have seen are gods that have people they trust to be able to take their place. Remember you told me how you got some of your D80's to back down. Think about the words you used."

I thought for a moment. "In the name of Zeus. Ah, I get it, they thought I was representing Zeus."

"Well you were, weren't you?"

"With luck, I still am. The longer that he trusts me, the more time we have."

"Yes, and you must also return to Olympian Dreams soon

before he starts to wonder about you."

Kam looked at me as she offered a solution. "The kids and I could return tonight with Athena. If he asks about you, we can tell him you're spending more time in Rhodes. That you're gaining strength from being near your tomb."

"Perfect, but don't go with Athena tonight. Go first thing tomorrow. Athena arriving and your return mustn't appear connected. I will get a friend to take you," offered Giannis.

Kam and Lindon left to find Alyss.

"OK, Giannis. Cards on the table. The gods aren't going to get up and leave because Rod Prince says so. You know as well as I do that I'm going to have to blackmail them. I will have to threaten to reveal their deceit. As soon as I make the threat, we are doomed. They will drug us," I paused as the full horror swept over me, "and then kill us."

He looked deep into my eyes. "Pretty much, yes. But that is the worst case."

"There must be other ways?" My tone turning my statement into a question.

"Of course, and as Athena has already told you. You already know how to defeat them. Artemis did it to Prometheus."

"What? Chain him to a post and get an eagle to keep eating his liver until he didn't have enough to regenerate?"

"You are going to have to stop believing everything you are told. Did you actually see that happen? Or was it what someone told you happened?" and he grinned.

"We saw a video."

"A video of what? Did you see the eagle eating the liver?"

"No, we saw his open gut and his liver had reduced in size. We saw Artemis slicing his heart into little pieces."

"How do you know it was an eagle that reduced the size of his liver? All you saw was Artemis use a gold-tipped weapon to finally kill him."

I frowned as I thought about how we knew about Artemis defeating Prometheus. "More deception. Now I understand. But how did she get him to stop? How did she defeat him?"

The tone of his voice became sinister. "The way I could kill you now if I chose to."

Fear tingled my spine, and the hairs on my neck stood on end. "I th-thought you were an ally."

He laughed a little louder. His laugh was too similar to Poseidon's before he attacked us. "Look around the taverna. Tell me what you see on the walls."

"A lot of old farm implements and tools."

"Look a little closer. Can you see what is different about the tools? What else do they have in common?" He presented this riddle as he pulled a penknife from his pocket.

I trembled like a contestant on mastermind, and I gulped. "All I see is rusty old tools."

"Not all rusty." He got up, leaving the opened knife on the table.

He adjusted the spotlight above the dartboard and directed it at one of the tools. Then I saw it, a flash of light, as a scythe glistened and reflected the light. I glanced down at the knife on the table. Everything sharp or pointed had a golden tipped point or edge.

He removed the darts from the dartboard and sat back

down. He leaned forward and stared straight into my eyes. He lifted a dart so that it was all I could see. My eyes hurt because they were focussing on an object that was too close. But I could see it had a golden point.

"If the golden tip of any of these object pierces your skin your immortality is gone. Game over. You are mortal. The only way you can get immortality back would be another exchange transfusion."

I looked down and inspected the penknife on the table. Its small blade had a streak of gold running along its sharp edge. "Good God. No wonder Zeus wants me kept in the dark. I could wipe out every immortal."

"It won't be as simple as that, but yes, you now have the knowledge and the means."

"But I'm not capable of murder. None of us is."

"Use your knowledge and experience well, and you won't be murdering anyone. All you are doing is making them mortal." He reassured me that once the god was mortal, the natural ageing process would take over and do the rest.

"But they are bound to put up some kind of struggle. And then they will try to kill me."

"Of course. Which is why you have to proceed with care," he cautioned as he left his seat again. "You want a beer?"

"Of course." And I laughed first for a change.

He returned with a couple of Mythos in ice-covered glasses.

"I have a gift for you." And he handed me what appeared to be a silver coin.

"I can't accept it. You've already done enough."

"Take it. It isn't solid silver. It is plated, and there are two of them. They have no monetary value. Their strength is in what they hold."

I looked at the worn image on the silver disc. "Who is the image on the coin? Need I ask?"

"Ha-ha it's not a good likeness, is it? It is the amulet of Apollo. While you have it in your possession, I have no choice but to be your ally. I am sworn to protect the holder of my amulet because it holds my spirit. But I am on your side anyway. There is a second amulet, and that holds the spirit of Zeus. It is hidden, and it must remain hidden. He must never find it. If he regains possession of it, we will all be lost. If you are in mortal danger from Zeus, then one of you needs to collect it. You will find it in its hiding place. When you show it to my father, he will have no choice but to protect you from harm."

"Couldn't I show it to him anyway?"

"No, because Poseidon's new mission would be to destroy you and steal the amulet. He would still be out to destroy our families. Yours and mine."

"Can't I have it for emergencies?"

"No, it is your very last resort. If you must use it, there will be a cost. That cost will be my immortality. He will know who gave it to you. My possession of it is the only reason the feud between us hasn't already cost me my life. So please only seek it out if one of you is under the worst threat."

"So I use the Zeus amulet, and he is sworn to protect my family and me. But you will die? Jesus. I don't want that responsibility."

He gave a nervous laugh. "Yes, you do. If the choice is between Kam, Lindon, Alyss or me. I know who you would or should choose, but please be careful. I'm sure you know of the story of Pandora's box. The amulet of Zeus will be sealed in a box in the same way. Once it is removed, it will control all of our destinies."

He proceeded to tell me exactly where I could find the keeper of the box. He made me learn the exact phrase I needed to say to retrieve it. If I got it right, the amulet would be handed over without question.

I looked at him. "Let's both hope it doesn't come to making that choice."

He handed over the darts. "Quite. Now get yourself out of here. You have plans to make, and a war to win." Then he warned, "Oh, and be very careful when you play with those darts."

GOLDEN TRIDENT – *A Present*

Before returning to Olympian Dreams, I stopped off in Kamiros. I wanted to catch up with Filipos.

"Yiasas, Mister Filipos."

"Please call me Vangelis, my friend," he greeted.

"How have things been with the staff and guests?" I asked, knowing the answer would give me a clue to his state of mind.

"Bravo, all is good, and yes I am well. I don't need to shout anymore."

"That's good to hear, let's walk and talk. I love strolling around your hotel."

My reason for visiting was a selfish one. I feared that with the battles ahead, that visit may be my last one. I'd gone to say goodbye to the place I'd come to know and love.

He looked me straight in the eye. "Something troubles you, Rod. Can I help?" His look suggested genuine concern.

"No, my friend, I have some hard choices to make. And I'm fearful of making the wrong decision."

"Listen. Every decision you have made to help me has been perfect. You must learn to trust yourself, make a decision and stand by it."

"What if it is a wrong decision and it hurts someone I care about. How do I live with that?"

"You just do. If you believe the decision is the correct one. You must follow that path. To not do so is a deception. Stay true to yourself. I remember a crazy Englishman that told me the same thing not too long ago." He looked at me and smiled.

I mused to myself. *Oh, Filipos. If only you knew what was at stake. If I screw up, the family lose immortality and maybe die a painful death. You dear friend will lose your life's work.*

I looked straight at him. "It's your turn to listen now. Do not trust anyone involved with the board of Olympian or the company that has taken control of Helios. Aren't they called D80 Ltd?"

"Yes, that's right, but they saved me."

"Dear friend. Be careful – trust no one. You have my number."

"Now, I am concerned. Are you leaving the island?"

"No far from it, but I must go and make my decisions."

We hugged and double kissed. I had a tear in my eye as I walked away from Helios.

≈≈≈

At Olympian, Kam had left a note in the room for me. 'All OK. Come to board room kiss-kiss'. When I got to the board room, I had a welcoming committee. The godly family were there. It was late, so Helios was there too. I eyed him up suspiciously. I glanced at Athena and Zeus.

"What is wrong, Rod?" Asked Zeus.

"Ah, don't worry about me. I have been in Rhodes visiting

my tomb. It makes me melancholy when I have to leave it," I lied as I kissed Kam.

"I understand. Welcome back to Olympian. Come, let's celebrate your return. Did you enjoy your tour of the island?"

"I'm sure Kam has told you, it brought the family closer together. We are refreshed for the final push in the war," I smiled.

"Let's hope so." And he smiled, not something I had seen him do very often.

He cracked open a large bottle of ouzo. Oh God, not ouzo shots. The trouble with ouzo it has such a strong taste and smell; you can never tell if it has been spiked. I hoped my worries were needless. I had to resolve my suspicion issues. I was in danger of blowing everything wide open by the way I was looking at everyone. When Kam had a chance, she looked at me, and that look told me to relax. Not sure if it was the ouzo or Kams reassurance, but I finally settled down.

"Praise to the Princes of Rhodes," toasted Zeus.

"May they succeed in the coming conquests," added Athena.

"Indeed, the saviours of Helios and Rhodes," was Helios' contribution.

"To close-knit families. Yamas," I toasted, suspecting that would irk Zeus, but I really didn't care.

"Yes, you are right, I envy you that quality," lamented Zeus clearly regretting the state of his own family.

We sat, and I poured another round of shots. Helios was first to withdraw; he had an early morning start.

Everyone else was getting slightly tipsy, and tongues were

starting to loosen up.

"I understand our families may come together," announced Zeus.

I looked at him, puzzled for a moment. "Oh, you mean Athena and Alyss. Yes, we could be in-laws."

He grunted. "What do you and Kam think about this whole lesbian thing?" He sounded almost disdainful. The ouzo appeared to have lowered his inhibitions, and Athena glared at her father.

"We are good about it. If Alyss must live for an eternity, it would be good to be forever happy." I stood and raised another toast. "To Athena and Alyss long may they have joy and love."

I didn't return the question. To be honest, I'd had a few drinks, and I didn't give a shit what Zeus thought. I had to hope he couldn't read my mind.

I poured each of us another shot. Athena and Alyss were the next to drop out swigging ouzo, but they did remain in the room.

I glanced at Athena before asking Zeus, "How many children do you have?"

"I gave up counting after the twins were born."

Athena knew where this was heading, and I don't think she liked it.

"Twins, I didn't know you had twins. I always wished Alyss and Lindon had been twins."

"You shouldn't wish that. One will always be a disappointment."

"What were their names?" I asked goading him because I

already knew the answer.

"You have already met Artemis. She was always such a sweet child. Our relationship is like the one you have with Alyss. I would die for her."

"It's easier for me to say that now I have immortality," I laughed.

Zeus smiled.

"And what of the other twin, is it a boy or a girl?" I inquired, feigning ignorance.

The rest of the room was silent. It reminded me of the head to heads I would have when playing a crucial game of dominoes. Not like darts with all the cheering and shouting. Dominoes was a tense mix of luck and strategy. Like the war, we were in.

"A boy," Zeus countered.

"What's his name?" I launched another attack.

I could see Zeus was finding this painful. I poured another shot.

"Apollo," he muttered with a broken tone to his voice.

I stood and raised my glass. "Here's to absent family, Mags, Artemis and Apollo."

"I will drink to Mags and Artemis, but I won't drink to him. To me, he doesn't exist. He is dead."

I was so itching to say he does exist, and that I'd seen him. But the ouzo hadn't loosened my tongue that much.

"I'm sorry to hear that, what happened? How did he die?"

His tone changed. "That conversation is closed. I will not discuss it. I also ban you from using his name in my presence."

"Sorry," I apologised because he seemed genuine in his

hurt.

"Anyway, we have other business to discuss. We still have two more D80's to beat," interrupted Lindon.

"You now have only Poseidon to worry about," revealed Zeus. "Hestia has no will to fight now that Demeter has gone to the underworld with Persephone and Hades. Which reminds me, Rod, we have a vacancy for Director of Staffing at Olympian. The job is yours if you want it."

"I'll think about it. It might be better suited to Lindon if the offer extends to him."

"We can discuss it later. There is no rush. Athena is filling in," added Zeus.

"What news of Poseidon?" I asked, not wanting to reveal my hand about the deceptions.

"He continues to erode the coast. If you don't succeed, the hotel will be destroyed by the sea."

"I believe we can meet our target. If it's just Poseidon. I hope to have defeated him by the end of this season. A full twelve months ahead of schedule. Our personal target was St Rhodes day - Nov 10th, 2017. We are on target to complete it by this St Rhodes day. But first, I need to draw him into the open. Tomorrow we start our planning."

"Excellent news, we can use my office."

"I don't mean to offend you. But I'm afraid the planning's going to be between the Princes. No gods required," I stated in a non-negotiable way.

"But, but. I told you to run your plans by me first."

"We will. But we don't need your help with developing the plan. Sorry."

That seemed to reassure him. There was no way I was letting that deceitful creep know what we were doing and how two-faced we were in return.

"It's getting late, I'm sure we're all tired, and we've had a lot of ouzo and need to sleep it off," I slurred.

"You certainly do. You haven't stopped talking since the second shot," admonished Kam.

The celebration ended. We left the gods in the boardroom I was sure they had lots to discuss, without the presence of humans.

"Lindon, tomorrow you will tell us everything the myths have written about Poseidon. Somewhere in those myths, we will discover his weakness. Run a quick check on myths involving Apollo as well."

"But we now know they are only myths," he reminded me.

"What they did is the myth, their personality is real and may shine through the myths of time." I hiccupped, and it would have been a brilliant pun if it'd been intentional.

I sat on the bed as the room rotated. "Goodnight all." And I drifted off to sleep in the hope my subconscious would answer any remaining questions I had.

It was a restless night. I must have fought around a dozen battles with Poseidon. Each time trying to stab him with a gold-tipped dart. Each time something would stop me from succeeding. I woke in the morning an absolute wreck. It was only 8 am with an ouzo hangover. *Why did I do it?*

"Drink water. Rehydrate," advised Kam.

"What and reactivate the ouzo."

"That's another flipping myth. Haven't you learnt yet?"

I grunted.

Lindon had got up first, and he'd sent a text. *'gone 2 Johns 4 tech c u at 11'*. We knew what he meant. He wanted to use the Internet but not at Olympian. I replied, *'No 11:30 at Irene's Gold'*.

≈≈≈

We left Alyss with Athena at Olympian Dreams. Kam and I sat at Castello House, a roof-top restaurant above Irene's Gold. We sat and enjoyed our usual frappe, with milk, and no sugar. I don't know if it was lack of sweetness or the addition of milk, but it always got strange looks from the local waiters. We declined ouzo. Lindon arrived at eleven-thirty on the dot. One of his greatest qualities was timing.

"OK son, the meeting's yours. What do you know about Poseidon?"

"Loads." And he laughed.

"Go on then, impress us."

"First, I have some juicy gossip about Apollo. He's bisexual. He has appeared in lots of myths with male lovers." And he laughed again.

"Nice one. But we won't hold that against him. And I laughed. "Maybe that's why Zeus is pissed off with him. Tell us about Poseidon."

"He's got a quick temper, and he's very much like Zeus in that respect. He's always on the lookout for a pretty woman. He isn't bothered if they consent or not, he just takes them."

"Has he got a weakness? Other than women, I'm not using your mum or Alyss as bait."

"Yep two that are documented, he suffers from fatigue.

He tires easily, especially when he's away from the sea."

"Don't we all?" joked Kam.

We laughed.

"Are you ready for the big one?"

"Come on. I need to know," I was getting impatient for something that could help.

"He's known for being easily tricked. He's the original Mister Gullible."

"At least we have something to work on."

We spent a good few hours at Castello's brainstorming. We came up with lots of ideas, some ridiculous, some with a lot of potential. The points they all had in common were the same four key points. One. We needed to trick him away from his realm, away from the sea. Two. To keep him away from the sea until he suffered from fatigue. Three. Pierce his skin with gold. Four. Stop him getting the blood transfusion that would re-immortalise him. Kam was the first to spot the loophole in all the plans.

"How do we stop him from getting the transfusion? He might become mortal, but if he doesn't die for twenty years, that is twenty years that he could get the transfusion."

She was right. Once he was mortal, he had to die and as soon as possible afterwards. I don't know that any of us would be capable of committing murder.

"Artemis is capable of it, she did it with Prometheus," Lindon pointed out.

"But if we involve Artemis, we involve Zeus. He will know that we know about the whole gold piercing the skin thing."

"What about finding where the immortality blood is

stored. Because they surely must have a supply," said Kam.

Lindon did a quick calculation "It won't work. The remaining gods will donate a pint each. Then they've got enough to transfuse him."

"Hang on, hang on, let me think... How many gods are there on the island?" I was never able to concentrate and listen at the same time.

"From the board, there's only Zeus, Helios and Hera. Because Hades, Demeter and Persephone have gone. Hestia may still be here. Poseidon's here, of course. There's Apollo, Athena and possibly Artemis, and that is the ones we've met."

"Any more? Who would know for definite?" I sensed we were about to have a breakthrough moment.

"Why does it matter?" asked Lindon.

"They will need to complete a hundred per cent blood exchange. They will have to use a stockpile. Without a stockpile, there won't be enough immortals to donate a usable quantity of blood. If we have calculated correctly, there are only seven gods on the island and that includes Apollo. Without a stored supply of blood, they will only be able to donate six pints to Poseidon. That wouldn't be enough," I thought out loud.

"Even better if more than one god lost their immortality," recalculated Lindon.

"What if they all lost their immortality?" asked Kam.

"That won't happen. There are only four of us. I know we have surprise on our side, but I think the best we can hope for is Poseidon and Hestia. If she's still here and if she isn't, then it will leave one less pint of blood available."

Lindon added the fly to the ointment. "If they can each donate a pint a month in two months they'll have enough. He'll still have to die. Even worse, they capture us and drain all our blood. That is enough to do a completed blood swap for four D80s. And what about the cronies? They might be immortal too."

"Jesus," I sighed. "We need to think about this a bit more, but it's a start. The first thing we need to do is to find out if they have a stockpile of blood. We now have a new war to win. Whoever controls the blood supply, will be the ultimate winner."

"Hold on. Mum, didn't you think that Hestia was a cleaner called Despoina? Is she still at Helios?"

Kam deflected the question in my direction. "I don't know. Your dad's the one that went to Helios."

I wasn't much help. "I didn't ask. I was too busy saying my goodbyes to the place. Why what are you thinking?"

"Poseidon is easily tricked. If we let Hestia overhear the right conversation, we can lure him into a trap."

"Nice one, son. I like that. But first, the heavenly blood bank needs a large withdrawal or transfer to our account."

"First we need to find it," pointed out Kam.

Another restless night lay ahead.

≈≈≈

True to form I must've had a dozen eureka moments throughout the night. I always wake up with solutions. That night was no exception. I thought I'd found the answer. I needed the rest of the family to play *devil's advocate*. I hoped that at least Lindon would spot the holes in my plan. The last thing we needed was a watering can plan. I needed the holes plugged so tight nothing would leak through.

Having said my goodbyes at Helios the previous day. We travelled back there to have our meeting. Athena wasn't happy when she thought she was coming with us. I couldn't let her. This was a family only meeting – she wasn't family yet.

"Vangelis, do you have a room we can use for a meeting?"

"Of course Rod, you know I do, you are family," and he smiled. "Would you like 208?"

"Er no. An office will do. But no one must disturb us."

"You can have my office. I have some business in Rhodes town." He handed me the key to his office.

As soon as we entered the room, I unplugged the computer, the telephone, the copier. Everything that was occupying a socket had to be unplugged.

"Christ Dad, you're not bloody James Bond."

"I know son, but I've lost my trust in everyone not called Prince. No more chat, if you want to say anything, you write it down. Don't forget we're in the god's lair. Hestia and Poseidon pretty much live here." I handed out pens and paper. This made it easier to remember not to talk.

I scribbled: *I had a dream last night.*

Lindon wrote on his piece of paper. *Let's not have a conversation about it. Just write the plan and who is doing what.*

Who do you think you are? Zeus?

No, I am trying to save time.

OK but I need you to look out for weaknesses in the plan.

One: Mum finds out if Hestia as Despoina is still here.

Two: Lindon, remember the conversation we had the other day about gold plating.

He nodded.

I want you to get hold of a half-litre of gold plating solution. See if the guys at Irene's could sell you some. Offer them five hundred euros, tell them I want to plate a trident. If not, it will be eBay, but that could take too long.

Three: Your mum and I will let Hestia hear us talking about a golden trident we are making. It will adorn the Helios beach bar.

He nodded again.

Four: Kam. You go to the pharmacy. Tell them you need some vitamin B12 and four syringes.

Kam scribbled: *why B12?*

It's the one thing you can get without prescription that will allow you to get the syringes. If they ask - you have a thyroid problem.

And the meeting went on like this for the entire afternoon. We discussed around thirty points, and I got writer's cramp. It was so long since I'd held a pen. There was some swapping of pieces of paper, to iron out any flaws the others had spotted.

Alyss, had mixed feelings because her role was to go back to Olympian to be with Athena. That partly pleased her, but she would have preferred to be with the rest of us. She had to be able to keep her eyes and ears open. It was safest away from the action. I warned her that if the plan worked, Poseidon would head to Olympian, to Zeus, to the blood bank and immortality. This would put us all in danger. Not least because she would be behind enemy lines. I would rather she was with Apollo, and that she should try to arrange a visit to the sanctuary with Athena.

I plugged the electrical equipment back in as we had found it. I called Filipos and asked if we could stay for a few days, and he gave us 208. Before we left the office, I put the scribblings through the cross-shredder. Kam bagged the waste up and took it to the incinerator.

We collected the room key from reception, and by chance, Hestia was there. Kam exchanged pleasantries with her. She explained that we were back from our break, and she was about to resume her Head Housekeeping role. Hestia wasn't happy, but we didn't care. It meant Kam could know where she would be when we wished to set the godly trap.

≈≈≈

We didn't have to wait long for the plating solution. The guys gave it to Lindon without question and didn't even let him pay for it. They just wanted a sign near the trident promoting Irene's. At twenty euros for twenty millilitres, they handed over five hundred euros worth of plating solution. Now we had our own stockpile, and we had to protect it. I hoped the local grapevine would spread the rumour about a golden trident appearing at Helios.

Kam knew Hestia would be cleaning the Kafeneion. We made our way there, and sure enough, there she was, cleaning tables the way she was when she first tried to karate chop me. I smiled to myself at the memory. We ordered two frappes.

Kam started. "I think that is a brilliant idea. A surprise for Filipos and he'll love it."

"I do have my uses. To have a golden trident above the beach bar will give it a bit of atmosphere. Imagine the brochure photograph. Blue sea and sky in the background.

The sun glinting off the trident. It will be an image to bring in guests from all over the world. The hotel will be assured of success."

"You do realise that Neptune will want it."

"Ha-ha, That's the Roman version. We are in Greece, and here he's called Poseidon."

"Whatever. He isn't real anyway," she proclaimed loud enough for the entire hotel to hear.

"I wish he was then I would sell it to him for the right price. Make a tidy profit out of it."

I looked up in time to see Hestia disappear around the corner of the nearest block of suites.

Kam looked at me and smiled. "I better brush up on my dart throwing. I need to see if I still have what it takes."

AMBER BLOOD – *Thicker than Water*

We made our way to the dimly lit games room. Kam flicked the switch, and the dartboard illuminated as the light flickered into life. Kam beat me five times straight. I blamed the writer's cramp, but she was always better than me.

She laughed and bragged. "I knew I would beat you, even though you had the golden darts."

I grunted.

Warm air infiltrated the cool of the room as Lindon joined us. "How did it go?"

"Your mum is still the goddess of darts."

"I meant with Hestia." And he tutted.

"Well, she was within earshot for the performance. She didn't hang around. I guess we can expect a visit soon. We must all stay together until contact has been made," I commanded.

"Yes, we are stronger that way, and I can make sure you two don't screw it up." But he did laugh.

"More importantly, do you have transport?" Kam asked

"Yeah, a motorbike."

Always worrying about the safety of the kids, she wanted more reassurance. "I hope you have a crash helmet."

"What and look out of place. Besides, I'm immortal. Duh."

I raised an eyebrow and looked at him, and he knew what that look meant.

"Sorry, Mum. But I'll be OK."

"Lindon you can mark the board for this next game. I still need to beat your mum. Then you can play the winner." I took to the oche again. "If our visitor comes today, you should leave as soon as he arrives and ready yourself."

The door to the centre opened with a crash. The noise made me turn in time to hear Poseidon ask, "Who is the man with the golden trident?"

My heart rate increased. "That'll be me,"

"How much?"

"It's not for sale."

"I will have that trident. You know who I am. I can pay whatever you want. Or I could just take it."

"What will Zeus have to say about that?"

"Why don't we cut the crap. You know I don't give a toss about Zeus. I know you have been employed by him to save the hotel."

"Well done. It seems you know it all. What do you think Zeus will say to me if I sell it to you? It would be easier for me if I lost it."

"Yes. With all that plating solution you bought, you could make another one. I would still pay you. Why don't we flip a coin for it? Winner takes all. Tell him you lost it and make him another smaller one."

"I'm not going to let you win it on a toss of a coin."

"Pick a sport. It makes no difference. I will beat you anyway." He was goading me with his superhuman arrogance.

"OK. Here. Now. What are you like at darts?"

He laughed. "You want to play darts against a god, and you think you will win?"

"No. My wife will play you – and beat you."

He roared with laughter.

Kam rattled off the format. "Three legs of 501. Straight start. Double to finish. No bust allowed." And she launched a dart at the board. Just catching the wire of the bull and missing it.

Suddenly she had his attention as she signalled this wasn't going to be a walkover. I looked at Kam as if to say *don't frighten him off*.

"Hold on. If I win, you hand over the trident. Yes? What if she wins? What do you want?"

"You walk away. Stop your battle with the island, and take Hestia with you."

He took a dart from Kam. He sighed and looked at me. "In that case. If I win, I get the trident, and you walk away from the battle. You leave me to finish what I set out to do." And he launched his dart at the board. He hit it dead centre. If we'd spun the board like a Catherine-wheel the dart would have appeared motionless. I had a rush of doubt and adrenaline. He was good. For a moment I doubted Kam could beat him. He collected the darts from the board and handed them to Kam.

"Lindon give Poseidon your darts. Then go and buy some Mythos for the celebrations."

I stood behind Kam and our victim, so as not to be in their field of vision.

He played his first three darts. "One Hundred aaaaand Eighty," he roared.

I didn't have to try to look suitably worried. I even let out a loud sigh. The way you would if you thought your world was about to come to an end. Kam dropped one of her darts, and it landed at my feet. I handed it back to her. I made sure she saw my look that told her it was a different dart. She stepped up to the oche, and her first dart hit treble twenty. *That's my girl*. Her second hit treble five. *Bugger*. Her third hit single twenty. She collected her darts.

Poseidon was laughing as he took to the oche again. He fired his first dart, and it hit another treble twenty. He steadied himself to throw his second dart. He pulled his hand back so that the flight of the dart was level with his eye-line.

Kam was looking at the board as I lunged, gold-tipped dart in hand. I felt resistance as it contacted his skin. A little more pressure made the skin yield as the dart pierced his neck, and the gold tip entered his body. He turned, and as he did so, Kam threw her gold-tipped dart, and it lodged in his cheek. I still had my dart in my hand.

I could tell he didn't know how to react at first, but he was clearly pissed off. The dart in his face was wiggling from side to side – if I hadn't been so scared it would have been a comical sight. Then he roared so loud it hurt my ears. "What the fuck?! You cheat! I will destroy you for this!"

The rush of adrenaline made my voice falter as I said, "You have something more important to worry about than killing us."

He launched himself at me, getting his hands to my throat.

The dart in his cheek fell to the ground. Kam picked it up and held it close to his face. "Look at the tip. It's coated in gold. You are no longer immortal."

He stared at the tip, and he stopped trying to strangle me. "Bastards what have you done?" He turned and crashed through the door. He sprinted away from the games room. His dreadlocks were flailing about like rows of caterpillars turning themselves into shiny chrysalises.

We didn't try to chase him. That was Lindon's job.

I heard his motorbike engine start up in the distance. Kam and I made sure we had the golden darts and headed for 208. We had to be patient and wait for Lindon to do his work.

The next couple of hours were tense. We could do nothing but wait. Although we'd once again taken the initiative, we had no idea what the response would be. We were also separated. I would have felt a lot better if we were all still together. Unsure of where Lindon's pursuit of Poseidon had taken him. We also had no idea where Alyss and Athena were. Had they followed my advice to go to Apollo for safety? I started to have doubts. Had we been premature in initiating the plan? Had I missed anything in the planning? Bloody Johnny Nash was having a field day inside my head. There were still '*More Questions Than Answers.*'

Kam heard the roar of a motorbike engine first. My hearing was never the best. It was a relief to see Lindon approaching across the gardens.

"We are going to have to stop him riding that bike across the lawns. Filipos will go nuts," I cautioned. He dismounted and was about to start shouting. Telling us what he'd discovered.

"Shush. Come up here," Kam admonished.

Once he was safely in the room, I asked, "Did you keep track of him? What did you find?"

"Oh yeah, I followed him. Like you guessed, he went to Olympian. I heard lots of shouting but couldn't make out what it was about. I think we'll find that Zeus knows about us."

"Did you find it?"

"Yep, it's in the most obvious place. Like we suspected it's at Olympian, and where would you expect blood to be stored?"

"Somewhere cold."

"And where is the coldest place there? Remember, you even commented about how the basement felt like a fridge. That's where they have their stockpile. It is kept in the wine store."

I was frustrated that we hadn't given it enough thought. "Shit. We should have figured that."

"I kept my distance, but I know it's stored there. I saw Zeus leave the basement with a blue cool box like we used to take on picnics in England," he paused to check we recalled the image of our blue cool box. "After they'd left, I went to have a look. They hadn't even replaced the wine racks. I could see bags of blood. Here look. It's not red or gold like I expected." And he pulled a bag of dark amber coloured blood from inside his pants. The nearest I can describe the colour is the segments inside a blood orange. It certainly wasn't crimson like any other blood we'd ever seen.

"No one saw you, did they? We still need that element of surprise. If they know the location is no longer a secret, they'll move it." I was trying to process all the new information.

"No, I was in and out. If anyone had seen me, I wouldn't be here now."

"Did you see Alyss or Athena?"

"Nope, they could have been anywhere."

"Maybe she listened to my advice for a change." I was clinging to the hope that she'd persuaded Athena to take her to the taverna.

"We should go to visit Giannis ourselves. To make sure." Kam was panicking. But I thought we would be safer at the sanctuary anyway.

"Yeah, pack a change of clothes for all four of us. Lindon put that blood back in your pants. I want to try an experiment while we have a chance, and I need it at body temperature."

He did as I'd asked. I hoped his sister had done the same.

I grabbed one of the four syringes that Kam had got from the pharmacy, throwing the B12 into the bin. I loaded the syringe with the plating solution.

"Lindon, give me the blood bag."

The pair of them watched as I pierced the bag with the sharp point of the needle. I started to transfer the solution from the syringe to the bag. I'd barely begun to push the plunger into the syringe, and the blood changed like a set of traffic lights from amber to red."

Kam expressed her amazement first. "Wow."

"Flipping heck, that was fast," observed Lindon.

"It's perfect," I concluded.

"I thought you wanted the plating solution to make weapons. I expected you to start gold plating various objects. Or create more golden darts," bemused Lindon.

"At first, that was my plan. Then I figured the solution had to contain some form of gold. Why waste time extracting it and sticking it to objects."

I returned the leftover solution back to the bottle, before flushing the syringe out and carefully returning the needle cover. I didn't fancy getting pricked by it.

"We have to be careful handling the syringes and solution. One prick and our immortality will be gone. Lindon, you load the solution into the car with the syringes. We should also have a dart each. Keep the tip covered for safety."

I checked my pockets. The Apollo amulet was still there. We had everything we needed. It was time to regroup with Alyss at the taverna.

≈≈≈

"Yiasas Rod and Kam. Welcome, and how are you?" greeted Giannis. He gave us both a double cheek kiss. "Lindon. It is good to see you again." Another double cheek kiss for Lindon. "Where is Alyss? Is she not with you?"

Shit. Kam and I looked at each other. My worst nightmare was dancing on ice, all the way down my spine. "We'd hoped she was with you. We told her she would be safe being near you."

"I have not seen her."

"What about Athena has she been in touch? They were together," Kam asked in desperation.

"I haven't seen or heard from either of them. Is everything OK?"

"No. We saw an opportunity, and we took it. We mortalised Poseidon, and then Lindon followed him. He'd gone straight to Zeus. We've fucked up. Now he will be immortal again, already."

"He would have found out sooner or later. You have only speeded up the process. What are your plans now?" he queried, appearing to show real concern.

"I don't know. The plan was for the family to regroup and then set about destroying their stockpile of amber blood."

"Then that is what you must do. If you don't, then the enemy has control. You must follow your plan; otherwise, the war will follow their plan and not yours."

He was right. We hadn't factored in Zeus finding out so soon. But we always knew he would find out at some point. Our plan was working, and if we change direction now, all is lost. That one sentence was the most profound statement I'd heard from a god.

"But what about Alyss?" pleaded Kam.

Then Giannis surpassed his previous peak of wisdom with another top-drawer comment. "Your plan is to destroy the blood supply. If Alyss is with Zeus, you will still need to destroy the blood supply. Nothing in your plan needs to change. If she is with Zeus, she will also be near the blood. Go and destroy it. If she isn't there, you know she is safe with Athena."

"Giannis be honest with us. Can we trust Athena?" I asked.

"Out of all the Olympians, Artemis and Athena are the two I would trust. You ask, can you trust them too? That is up to you. It is your trust to give."

Kam exhaled noisily, exhibiting her relief. "I hope you are right."

"Yes, and if you trust Athena, I will too. I bet she's taken Alyss to safety."

"I will not ask what the details of your plan are. But I am certain you will have a confrontation with Zeus. You and I both know what you must do."

I looked at him needing to hear him say it. I needed his consent to go ahead. "You mean…"

"Yes, you must go and collect the amulet of Zeus. He will not be able to harm you while you have it."

"But—" I protested.

"Remember. I told you that if you needed to choose, you should choose your family. Well, now you must choose. Protect me or protect your family. Do the right thing and get Pandora's box. You know where it is. But please, do one last thing for me, leave my amulet in its place. You don't need protection from me. I will be here for you, anyway."

Swapping the amulets left a very sour taste in my mouth. Taking the Zeus amulet would put Giannis' at mortal risk. All because one of my family might be at risk further down the line. I couldn't look him in the eye as we bade him farewell.

"We will return the amulet once Alyss is safe," I muttered.

"Of course. I will wait for you." He managed to smile at

us.

Kam had tears in her eyes as we bade him farewell.

I hugged him tightly. "Thank you and goodbye, my brother."

≈≈≈

Of course, we couldn't drive to the car park at Olympian. We ditched the car about three hundred metres away and made up the difference on foot. We each had a golden tipped dart sheathed safely in our pockets. Lindon took all four syringes and a hip flask full of the gold plating solution. He was going to the wine store.

Kam and I headed straight for Zeus's office. Our presence, though a risk, would provide the distraction to allow Lindon to complete his work.

For the first time ever, we didn't knock, we walked straight in. A quick look around the room told me they'd been expecting us. Alyss was there, thank God. So were Athena and Helios.

Despite knowing the damage we could do to him, Zeus was still full of self-importance and arrogance. "Rod, Kam, don't do anything hasty. Alyss is my prisoner."

I looked at my wife as she screamed at Athena. "You were supposed to protect her Alyss."

"I'm sorry, but you gave me no choice. What you did to Poseidon showed me you could destroy my whole family. I cannot let you do that."

All the while, Alyss was sobbing, and that made it my turn to shout. "No. What we did was show loyalty to your father. He wanted Poseidon beaten. Check the contract. We can use any fucking means and powers at our disposal."

She stood there open-mouthed, and she knew that I was right. She knew she'd been deceived by her father. She looked at Zeus. "You told me they were a threat to our existence. All the time, they were just doing what you expected of them."

Zeus did that squinty thing because he wasn't sure of me. I stared back at him. "We have done what you wanted. You should reward us, but instead, you take Alyss as a hostage."

His squint turned to a glazed stare. For the first time, I'd rendered him speechless, as his photophobia kicked in.

My brain was searching for everything we'd learnt over the previous weeks. In full ad-lib mode, I computed: Apollo was famous for taking male and female lovers. I remember Lindon laughing about it as he told us. Apollo was estranged from his father. Also, the way Zeus asked me what I thought about Alyss and Athena.

"Unless of course, you have another agenda. Have you told Athena that you're homophobic?"

Athena gasped. "Dad. He's not right, is he?"

"Of course he is. You are as bad as Apollo. How can we propagate the family if you have same-sex relationships?"

I couldn't believe it. A wild stab in the dark. Jumbled memories. So many clues.

Kam screamed at Zeus. "Then you should release Alyss! Why would you want her kept near you? Athena would still have access to her. They love each other for fuck's sake."

He couldn't process the contradiction. He looked puzzled.

"Athena. Untie Alyss?" I commanded.

Zeus didn't divert his stare away from me. I stood my

ground and stared back. It was Kam that went to Alyss to help Athena. I checked my pocket for the dart. Two darts and three gods. Had enough time passed for Lindon to destroy the blood supply? Where was he? My heart was pounding, and I could feel it pulsing in my ears. He'd taken too long.

Athena gasped again. I broke my stare to glance across at them. I could see the point of the dart poking out from Kam's fist. I could also see a small trickle of red blood roll down the back of Athena's hand. I readied my dart in my pocket, flicking the protective cover from the tip. *This is it*, I thought to myself. Unexpectedly, Athena didn't say anything, she merely wiped the blood from her hand. She looked at me and smiled, then left the office. Now I was the one covered in confusion.

I looked at Zeus, and he was still staring at me. I detected a tear on his cheek. I thought to myself, *his photophobia is giving him real problems today*. At last, he spoke. "You have destroyed my family. Why shouldn't I destroy yours?"

"I haven't destroyed your family. You've managed that all by yourself. I have saved the hotel from ruin. And what of you Helios? With your all-seeing eyes. How do you feel about being used by Zeus?"

"He hasn't used me. The hotel is saved, the island is safe. I got what I wanted."

"Oh, yes, I forgot. You see Apollo as a threat. He wanted your job, your chariot. You are as bad as your phoney King."

I looked back at Zeus. "You won't kill us. You can't kill us." I pulled the amulet from my pocket. "You are sworn to protect the holder of this amulet from harm. It is now in possession of my family, and you can't harm us. You must protect us."

Zeus wiped the moisture from his face and laughed. "Thank you for pointing that out, Rod." He picked up his mobile and made a call. "They have the amulet. Go to the taverna. If Athena is with Apollo, then kill them both." He threw his phone down onto the desk.

Alyss screamed at him. "No. Not Athena."

This was enough of a distraction for Zeus. He looked straight at Alyss. "Stupid girl you can join her if you wish."

Kam ushered Alyss to a position of safety behind us.

I looked at Kam, and she looked at me. I nodded. She launched her dart at Helios while I threw my dart at Zeus. Helios had a dart sticking out of his neck, and Zeus had one firmly embedded in his forearm. While they were still in shock and trying to process what had happened. I retrieved the darts. The last thing I needed was for them to throw them back at us.

Showing complete disdain for the position we had put him in, Zeus roared with laughter. "What is this? Baby spears with gold tips. Is that the best you can do? By tomorrow I will be immortal again. Stupid Englishman."

Where the fuck are you, son? Then with almost perfect timing, Lindon walked into the office. I turned to look at him. He gave a single nod.

I looked at Zeus. "No. You are the stupid one. I don't think you will. Lindon do you have a sample?" I held out my hand without looking away from Zeus. I felt the weight of the bag as he placed it in my hand.

"Is this what's going to make you immortal?" And I held

up the bag revealing that it had a small leak from where the needle had pierced it. I must say that it was a beautiful shade of crimson. The colour drained from Zeus. Helios looked terrified. *Now I have your attention.*

"What do you want? Do you want more money? Tell me what it will take."

"It's simple. Call off your hitmen. Don't kill your own children."

"I can't, it will be a sign of weakness. I am the all-powerful god."

"Well, you won't be powerful for long. You are now a mortal. You can start the journey back to immortality by putting your family before any petty squabble. Think about how lonely you'll be when you're the last surviving god of Olympus. You're at your strongest with your family around you. Look at us. On my own, I could never have achieved what I have without Kam, Lindon and Alyss. If I was like you, they'd all be dead now and most likely so would I. On my own I am nothing. Look at yourself, what have you got? Fuck all. At least you won't have to live an eternity in that state? We don't wish to destroy you. But if that is what it takes, then so be it. Make the bloody call."

He picked up his phone and dialled. He put it on speaker, and it just rang out. He tried again. There was still no response.

"OK. Cards on the table. Tell me about the people you sent to kill your children. Are they mortals or immortals?"

"It's Hestia and Poseidon," he whimpered.

"For fuck's sake. Yesterday you would have had those two killed as your sworn enemies. Now you've sent them to do what they wanted to do anyway. Don't you have a fucking brain?"

He started to shed real tears. "I know you are right. But… But I am a proud man."

"Then find some courage. What do you want? Decide. Choose now. Your brother and sister who would see you dead? Or your children? Stop and think about your beloved Artemis. Do you think she will want to know you when she learns what you've done?"

He sighed like a man that had lost the will to fight. "Please go and save them."

"Are you sure? There can be no going back."

"Yes." And he started to sob.

Bloody hell. I never thought I'd see such a fearsome being buckle the way Zeus had. But I still had my doubts. Could we trust him? Were his tears genuine? Or maybe it was his photophobia.

Lindon shouted, "I'll get a bike. It'll be quicker."

"No, you won't. Haven't you been listening? We're at our strongest when we're together. We'll all go in the car."

I always said I wouldn't travel the mountain roads at night. It was frightening enough up there during the day, and we didn't have time to wait for the sun to rise.

≈≈≈

I started the car and turned the headlights on. *Fuck.* I could instantly tell the passenger side headlight wasn't working. That was the one I needed most to highlight the edge of the road. The side where the steepest drop was.

"Lindon, you sit in the front. Your job is to keep me away

274

from the right-hand edge of the road. When we get there if any of you see Poseidon or Hestia launch a dart at them. Don't stop to talk or ask questions; just do it. We all know who they are. I'll find Apollo and return the Zeus amulet to him."

After what seemed like hours, we arrived at the taverna. I didn't even close the car door before I dashed inside first. Giannis was flat on his back on the floor. I knelt beside him and squeezed his hand. "Giannis, my brother. Please reincarnate."

He blinked and looked up at me. Then he looked over my right shoulder. I sensed what was coming, and I felt a weight drop on me. My back buckled under the weight. I rolled to my left to ease the pain in my back. I came face to face with Poseidon. He'd jumped me from behind, and he was about to strangle me again.

Kam screamed the words, "Oh no you don't."

The next vision I had was a dart protruding from Poseidon's ear. He roared the way only a god can. He released his grip on my neck. I sensed what he was going to do. But I retrieved the dart first. I stuck it in his eye for good measure. The hole in his ear would have only mortalised him. He could still kill me as a mortal. I was glad that Kam liked to play with long-stemmed darts. I was rewarded as the golden point of the dart passed through the thin barrier at the back of his eye socket. The darts flight fell to the ground as he started to spasm. He wasn't coming back from that. But we'd lost a dart.

A loud banshee-like noise caught my attention, causing me to look in Lindon's direction. He had his hands full with Hestia. She was the source of the wailing, and she was scratching and biting him. He was on the ground, and she was on top of him. His dart was on the floor out of his reach.

Getting to his feet, Giannis shouted, "She's mine and he grabbed a scythe from the wall. He slashed hard at her, plunging the golden tip of the tool into her neck. As she mortalised, he swung the implement to his right and returned it to his left at speed. It didn't break any bones her head was still attached. But the scythe cut deep into her neck spilling more than enough red blood to finish her. Her deadweight slumped onto Lindon.

Kam went to his aid and dragged the now deceased goddess from our son. "Where's Athena?"

"She is with the keeper of the box. When she told me what had gone on with my father, I sent her there for safety. It is the one location no one would know."

I handed the amulet back to Giannis. "Thank God and thank you. There were other events once Athena left Olympian. Zeus and Helios are now mortal. From what I can figure, you and Athena are the only immortal gods left on the island."

"My step-mother Hera will still be about, but we have no concerns about her."

We retold what we'd seen at Olympian Dreams, and described how Zeus, King of the gods, sobbed and chose his children over his siblings.

"He is nothing to Athena and me. He must accept that I am bisexual, and Athena is a lesbian. Otherwise, he can rot in his mortality."

"The power is yours. Without the amber blood and no one

to donate it, he is certain to die at some point. Whether he gets a transfusion is in your power. Unless you, Athena and Hera can donate enough blood, he will remain mortal. The choice is yours but remember, his time is now finite. You should talk to him."

Kam suddenly remembered the events at Olympian. "Oh shit." Giannis looked at her, not having heard her swear before.

"What?" we all echoed in unison.

"When Athena untied Alyss. I stabbed my dart into the back of her hand." Her face betraying the panic she was feeling.

I looked at Lindon and raised my right eyebrow. He knew I was asking him a question. With a beaming smile, he looked at me. "Yes, I did, Dad."

"Well done, son," and I explained that we'd planned to keep twelve bags of the amber blood, for family emergencies. When we embarked on the destroying mission, we didn't know if Alyss or Athena were still immortal.

"I went better than that. I doubled it. In case we needed it. That's what took me so long to get to the boardroom."

"You have a very wise son. It must run in the family." He licked his lips and gave Lindon a massive hug and a kiss - on the mouth. Lindon blushed and wiped godly saliva from his lips.

I looked at Giannis, and like a brother mentoring his sibling, I gave him some advice. "You now have more reason than ever to make amends with your father. He has the fathers love that you crave and you have access to the immortal blood he needs. I'm sure he'll be pleased to see you both and want to put the long past behind him. But first, we must immortalise Athena."

FAMILIES – *Better Off Together*

Giannis knew exactly where Athena was. And he took the opportunity to introduce the family to the keeper of the box. "Petros, this is the Prince family. Rod, Kam, Alyss and Lindon. Family, this is my lifelong friend Petros." We each shook hands with Petros.

"Please, you can call me Pete."

It was also an appropriate time for Giannis to return the amulet of Zeus. Once more, it would protect him from Zeus's wrath. We all hoped he would never need it.

In return, Pete gave us the amulet of Apollo.

Giannis joked. "I don't know about you having my amulet. I need a Prince family amulet."

The door opened, and there stood Athena. "What's all the fuss about, I'm trying to... Apollo, Alyss!" She couldn't contain her excitement. I don't think she could decide who to hug first.

Kam, full of remorse for her actions, hugged Athena. "I'm so sorry for pricking your hand with the dart."

"Think nothing of it. It kept Alyss safe. You didn't have a

choice."

There was nothing more we could do until morning. We returned to the Taverna, and the drinking started with a celebratory shot of ouzo. "If this is going to get messy, I have to make a call first."

"Zeus, your children are safe. Rhodes is saved." There was no reply save for the sound of a grown man crying down the phone. I spoke into his sobs. "We will speak later, my friend." And I hung up. *Did I just call him a friend?*

Giannis and Athena had much to discuss, and they retired to the taverna living quarters. The family stayed in the bar area and talked. "Now this is what I call a lock-in," cheered Lindon as he leapt over the bar. "Mythos all round, or do we go straight for the ouzo?"

Kam set the tone. "I could sink a bottle of ouzo to myself. Especially if it's not tampered with." So much love and tears flowed that night. We made many pledges to each other. We all agreed that we were at our strongest when we were together.

I couldn't take my eyes off the bodies lying in the dimly lit corner of the room. At one point I'm was sure I saw movement. "Guys. Did you see that?"

The whole family chorused, "What?"

"I think I saw Poseidon move."

Everyone stopped and looked. I shit myself. It was like one of those late-night ghost story evenings me and my mates used to have when I was a kid.

"Go and check." Urged Kam as she always did when we heard a strange sound in the house back home.

Lindon had become protective of me. "Be careful, Dad."

With a dart in my hand, I staggered drunkenly across to where Poseidon lay face down on the floor. With as much accuracy as I could muster in my inebriated state, I stuck the pointed end of the dart into what appeared to be the nape of his neck. I recall I was trying to recreate the actions of a matador I'd seen in a film when I was a child. I missed, of course, and ended up catching his jugular. There was no movement except for a trickle of dark red blood. It was clear it hadn't been oxygenated for a while.

"He's dead," I announced in a whisper, still fearful of waking the dead. I shuddered as I realised that it was me that had killed him in the battle.

I think we all fell asleep in the bar. I woke last, so I can't be sure. My head hurt so much. The others had obviously been awake for a while. Giannis and Athena were busy clearing up the mess left by the two dead gods. The bodies had already been removed.

"They are going to an appropriate place. They will be buried at sea, on the Aegean side," announced Athena.

"Where are they now?" I asked.

"In the freezer." Then she giggled.

"Have you and Giannis decided what you are going to do about your father?"

"Yes, we will go back to Olympian with you and speak with him. Apollo may drop the Giannis alias. He is still wary of Dad."

"Zeus will have to know he has a lot of making up to do."

Giannis joined the conversation. "Yes, he won't even

know about the double supply of blood until we are sure. For now, all I want is for him to prove himself as a good father. He must immortalise Athena again." And he looked at her with a love that only a brother can give to his sister.

I looked out of the window at the mid-morning sun. "Helios is still working, even if he is a mere mortal. Apollo, play your cards right, and you might get the golden chariot." I felt really uncomfortable calling him Apollo. "Can I still call you Giannis? I can't get used to the whole Apollo name."

He laughed again. "Rod. You can call me whatever you like. You've earned that right."

Somehow, I wasn't convinced that our work was done. We still had a family of gods to fix.

≈≈≈

When we arrived at Olympian, I went alone to see Zeus. The atmosphere in the room was different. It was as if a light had been turned off somewhere. Zeus looked broken. He had a look that reminded me of the look Filipos had when the Argonists destroyed the hotel.

"Like I said on the phone, we reached the taverna in time. Your son and daughter are alive and well. Though Athena, like yourself and Helios, is mortal for the time being."

That bit of news perked him up a little. I could see he was relieved.

"What of your family?"

"We are all well and closer than ever."

"I want you to teach me how to be a family man. I want to be as close to my children as you are to yours."

"That is half the battle. You want to change, and maybe as

time goes on, you will learn. Now is the best time to start. Athena and Gian... I mean Apollo are here, at Olympian. They want to meet with you. But you must know that they will need a lot of reassuring."

"Tell them I want to see them."

"There you go. You still have so much to learn. What you meant to say is, *ask them if they would agree to meet, because I would really like to see them.*"

"That's what I said didn't I?"

"No, you didn't, you commanded. Athena and Apollo are adults with their own free will. You should ask them and not bark orders. If they ever say no, that is their right. Don't blow up and throw thunderbolts. Ask them if they can explain why they declined. It will allow you a much better understanding of them. They are people … er, gods in their own right. Consider that your first lesson."

Somehow, I think the battle to turn Zeus into a family man was going to be a greater challenge than saving the island.

I left him with time to think and re-joined the others. "Guys, we can't be with you when you meet your dad. What you discuss with him is between yourselves, make sure you meet him with your eyes open. You will have to remember he is old and rather set in his ways. He has been King of the gods for a long time, and he's used to commanding for the things he wants. He wants to be a father rather than a king. Don't be afraid to remind him of that."

We did the whole double kiss thing, and the family left for Kamiros. We had to give the amber blood a home somewhere. It was agreed it should remain close to us. It had already lived in far too many fridges.

≈≈≈

"Vangelis, dear friend. I'm so pleased to see you again." The kids looked at me. I don't think they'd ever heard me use Filipos' first name. I hugged him and double kissed him.

"Did you manage to make the right decisions?"

"Oh yes. It is a time for great celebration. I want to throw a party at Helios, for all the staff that have remained loyal to you. I want all the hotel's guests to be there. With luck, I will be bringing some special dignitaries myself, and I would love you to meet them."

"Of course, whatever you want. When?"

"I'll update you."

"I suppose you want a room."

"Yes, but not 208, keep that for the guests. I want your worst room. I've had enough of luxury and Olympian."

He became indignant. "We don't have poor rooms. You know that."

"I know. I was teasing you."

"How about my bungalow? But there's no maid service."

"That sounds perfect. You're a true friend, Vangelis."

He looked at me with wet eyes and firmly announced. "No. We are family."

The next day or so was spent relaxing and planning the celebration. The only contact we had with the gods was to give Zeus enough of the golden blood to immortalise Athena. We let him know we had enough for him and Helios, but they had to prove themselves first.

It was refreshing to be able to just lay on sunbeds on the

lawns at Helios and hold family discussions that didn't involve war planning. We had to stop Filipos from spoiling us with delivered drinks and snacks. The hotel still had guests that might have resented seeing us get his unique version of filoxenia.

Some of the discussion instigated by Lindon was about how we could become gods. Lindon and Alyss thought it was possible. They spoke about things called *blogs* and *memes*. How easy it should be to create an online persona. He remembered what Apollo had said about going to neighbouring villages and spreading a false witness statement.

"You mean, you create fake news."

"Kind of," he replied.

"Kind of nothing. We'd get locked up in prison or an asylum. It's called fraud."

"But you told us a god is a god if people believe and follow. That makes every *YouTuber* or celebrity a god."

"Exactly. You can't make yourself a god. It's your followers that do that by promoting and sharing. You need to find something that's worth your fans following. You need to be a solution to an unanswerable question. With science nowadays, there aren't many questions to be answered. Then they will make you a god. Anyway, enough philosophy, we have a party to organise."

He looked disappointed, but I knew he would find a way. His mind was already older than his mortal years.

≈≈≈

The party was something to behold. It was a themed party, centred around the Greek myths. Filipos had a golden trident made, and it took pride of place at the beach bar. It was my suggestion, but he wouldn't let me pay for it. This allowed him to tell everyone it was his idea. I didn't burst his bubble. The party started in the hotel and finished up as a beach party. At least the part of the beach that hadn't eroded.

Every guest of the hotel had special treatment. Many of them used the hotel's sheets as togas. We didn't complain or tell them that togas were more likely to be from Roman myths. We gained a host of five-star ratings on various travel sites. Filipos was happy indeed. I pointed out that if he did this every week of the season, he would never get a bad review again.

The special guests included the mortal Zeus. Immortals, Hera, Athena, Artemis and Apollo. Because it was night-time, mortal Helios also appeared. They had a fantastic time. It meant they got to dust down the clothes they hadn't been able to wear for hundreds of years.

They'd already managed to start building their own stock of blood for Helios and Zeus. Which meant we got to keep twelve bags for our personal use. Every few weeks we each donated a pint of our own blood to our stock. It turns out even immortal blood has a sell-by date.

The Olympian family were making good progress in rebuilding their relationships. Filipos was introduced to them by their real names. Though, we did omit to say they were Olympian gods. He thought they were an eccentric family, but he liked them. He liked them even more when he found out they were D80 Ltd, and they were stepping down and handing Helios back to him. They'd started a trust fund to pay for the refurbishment. The refurb was to take place throughout the winter, meaning Helios didn't need to close for the 2018 season. Filipos got to keep his part share of Olympian Dreams too.

Lindon almost had the last word. "Dad, I've checked, and there are three hundred and seventy Greek gods. That's one massive family. We still have a lot of work to do."

Kam shrugged his comment off. "They can wait. We have a party to enjoy."

Alyss just looked into Athena's eyes and kissed her.

Me? I continued to worry over the small details. We still didn't know if cronies were immortal. I gazed toward the sea that was hidden in the darkness. I listened to the waves break on the soft pebble beach. Each wave reminiscent of the sound made by a bag of marbles being tipped on the floor. The waves forming a slow, steady cardiac rhythm, while the pebbles were playing their own tune, a more sinister, erratic tune of confusion. *What will my legacy be? The human that took on the gods. But what will people remember me for? This was my destiny, and the world wasn't allowed to know about it.*

I snapped out of my thoughts and raised my glass. "We are better off together. Yamas." And we all downed un-spiked ouzo, as the DJ played *'There Are More Questions Than Answers' by Johnny Nash.*

THE END

Appendix 1

Places

Here you will find descriptions of locations on Rhodes. Some of them have played a role in the story. For more detailed reports and additional sites, I suggest going online and visiting:

<u>Rhodesguide.com for their village descriptions</u>

This website has been most helpful in generating supplementary information for the following places.

Afantou

This location is one of the oldest villages or towns on Rhodes. It gets its name from the Greek word for hidden – *Afantou*. It was a settlement that couldn't be viewed from the sea – hence its name. It was born in a time when boat-borne criminals or pirates used to raid the islands of the Mediterranean. The islanders would leave the coast to hide inland. Unfortunately for tourists, this also means the sea can't be seen from Afantou.

It's around five kilometres (three miles) from Faliraki. Surrounded by agricultural land consisting mostly of orchards and olive groves. Afantou is also famed for its carpet making. It is home to around seven thousand people. Because of its size, you can find all types of shopping there.

Crossing the Rhodes to Lindos main road takes you to the beach. Afantou beach is the longest beach on the island. The beach is around four kilometres (two and a half miles). Like all of the beaches on the south side of the island, the water is warm, calm and clear.

There is a nearby golf course. And at the time of writing it is the only golf course on the island. Provided, of course, that you don't include the *crazy-golf* courses in some resorts.

Like many of the towns and villages of Rhodes, Afantou has a church as a focal point. While at this location, you should visit it. You will find it next to the main square. Once inside, you will see icons and frescoes dating to the seventeenth century. The church is dedicated to the Holy Mary, and the town holds its celebration day in August, with a substantial religious and folklore festival. The square is a social centre for the friendly local community. Be sure to say hello.

Archangelos

The name Archangelos derives from Archangel Michael. On the surface, Archangelos gives the impression of being a contemporary town centre. In reality, some say that Archangelos is one part of Rhodes that is the most devoted to keeping village traditions. This is another village that developed when islanders moved away from the coast to hide from pirates. Visiting the narrow side streets brings out the real Archangelos. You will be able to witness village traditions such as bread baked in old wood-fired ovens. Skills and crafts which have been passed down from earlier generations. Archangelos has a population of around five and a half thousand.

Exploring the back streets will reveal the impressive church of the Archangel Michael, and it dominates the village. The narrow streets around the church bring a sense of their history. This lets you step back in time and imagine what life would have been like in bygone times.

On the rising ground about three kilometres (just under two miles) from the village as you journey towards Stegna beach, you will find the cave of Koumellos. The cave is known for its stalactites. And it is rumoured to communicate with the sea and maybe even Poseidon.

Damatria

Located towards the north coast of Rhodes, just slightly inland from Paradisi and the airport. With a population of little over six hundred, it is a relatively small village. Despite its size, it is steeped in history. It is believed to be the only village still in existence that dates back to the Dorian era of the eleventh century BC. This is confirmed by excavations in the surrounding area. The location has been continuously inhabited for over 3,000 years. It is believed believe this settlement got its name from the sanctuary of the goddess Dimitra. Dimitra is recognised as being Demeter. Maybe at some point, Demeter and Persephone visited together on her break from Hades. Damatria is an attractive village with a central square arranged. Most of this village continues to retain a traditional feel. Exploring the local area will let you discover natural springs and archaeological sites.

Embonas

Embonas (or Emponas) has always been one of the families favourite locations when we wish to purchase wine brewed on the island. It is famed for its wineries and vineyards. While it may not have any striking architectural features, it's one of the most popular suggestions for a trip inland on Rhodes. With a population of around one thousand, it combines folklore, a lively atmosphere, good food and excellent wine. It is a village which is full of life all year round with several tavernas serving people who come here from all over the island. It is the most important grape-producing village on Rhodes. It can be found on the wine roads, by following the signs.

It is popular throughout the holiday season, but visit at harvest time, and you will find the streets full of baskets of grapes. The villagers will welcome you and let you join in with the harvest celebrations. You will see courtyards spread with vine fruit to make sun-dried raisins. If you visit the wineries in the village, you will get a guided tour by one of the winery workers. If you visit at the right time, you will have ample opportunity to taste the local wines. Many shops will also offer you samples of many of their wines. If you visit by car, you may have arguments with the rest of your group over who will be the nominated driver.

The village offers an opportunity to discover the history of the area and its associated folklore.

Faliraki

Faliraki is the most popular and the most organised beach on Rhodes. The beach stretches to five kilometres (three miles). Because of its proximity to Rhodes Faliraki gained popularity and is considered as the party capital of the island. Since the departure of the Club 18-30 operator, It no longer lives up to the poor reputation it developed. Faliraki is all about fun and amusement. With water sports, cafeterias, night clubs and restaurants, there is something for everyone. The primary industry here is tourism. Faliraki Water Park is one of the largest in Europe and most certainly the largest in Greece.

Fanes

From the airport travel westwards, along the north coast for around fifteen minutes, and you will come to the village of Fanes. As you approach Fanes, a left turn takes you to the village itself. If instead, you make a right-hand turn you will find a sandy beach and the last of the big hotels as you travel west. It is this location that you will discover Paraskevi and To Kyma, both of which feature in the story. With a population of around eight hundred, here you will find a beautiful fishing harbour. Fanes is on the breezy side of the island. Windsurfing and kitesurfing are hugely popular in the area, given the broad flat sands and northern exposure. The cooling breeze and the shade of the tamarind trees accommodate those that don't want the searing heat of the Eastern side of the island. At the back of the beach, you will find welcoming tavernas. The village itself is set inland and is characterised by multi-coloured buildings. We are getting into the countryside by the time we reach Fanes. The primary income here is from agriculture and farming.

Ialyssos

Ialyssos is the second largest town on the island. This location was the inspiration for naming Alyss in the story, and it is the location of her resting place. Before 1976 it was called Trianda (Trianta – which is the Greek for thirty). Trianda is now considered to be a village within Ialyssos and is described later. Ixia is another tourist resort that also falls under the municipality of Ialyssos In the 2011 census, its population was returned at over eleven thousand.

On the seaward side of the main road – as in most resorts on the island – you will find the touristy area of the town. The landward side of the road usually presents you with the area where islanders live. The beaches are shingle and pebble. As get closer to Ixia, the beaches become more organised because of the large hotels. As this is the windward side of the island, there are many opportunities for water sports. There are kiosks, mini-markets, fast food outlets, cafes and restaurants just a short distance away.

Ialyssos was one of the three ancient cities dating back to 1500BC. (Along with Lindos and Kamiros). Travel up the hill of Filerimos which is described elsewhere, and you will find one of the most important archaeological sites of the island.

Kalavarda

Kalavarda is a charming village that is near the archaeological site of Ancient Kamiros. Its proximity to Kamiros is the reason for its inclusion here. Ancient Kamiros was the inspiration for naming the character 'Kam'. Kamiros is also where the characters resting-place is located. Kalavarda is considered an inland village as it is about a kilometre from the beach. It has a population of about five hundred residents. The surrounding area is mostly linked to agriculture. Its landscape is dominated by the peak of Profitis Ilias. Nearby woodland is one of the homes of the famous Rhodian Deer. Returning visitors choose Kalavarda as a location for their holiday because it is not a tourist resort.

Kalithea

Kalithea covers a wide area with a population close to ten thousand. When visitors refer to Kalithea, they often mean Kalithea springs. Its location is near to Faliraki, but with a completely opposite nature. Kalithea is relatively quiet. The beaches, bays, coves and caves in the area offer something for everyone. Kalithea Springs or Spa was built in 1920 by the Italians during their rule of the island. It is said that in 460 BC, Hippocrates, father of all physicians, drank and recommended the healing qualities of Kalithea waters. Recently the domed pavilions and archways have been renovated. The mathematician in me adores the symmetry visible when inside the larger domed structure. Many people visit the area for its crystal-clear sea waters and magical scenery. Kalithea Springs is often the first choice for those that wish to have their wedding on Rhodes.

Kremasti

Kremasti lies on the north coast and is the location that provided the inspiration for Olympian Dreams. It has a population of just over five thousand. As you head out of the airport, and head to Rhodes town it is the first town/village you pass through. It features a wide pebble beach with the usual sun-loungers, parasols and waters-sport facilities. This part of the island suffers from the coastal erosion that is highlighted in the story. Given its proximity to the airport, visitors need to be aware that aircraft are at around five-hundred feet as they pass overhead when landing at the airport.

The town is dominated by a large church. The church, Panagia Katholiki (Virgin Mary) is one of the largest and most beautiful on the island. The interior is decorated with beautiful murals and wood carvings.

The town is famous for its 'Panigiri' or Festival of the Virgin Mary, held on August 15th each year. Kremasti also hosts the Panhellenic Craft Fair, in the third week of August. These two events make August a perfect time to visit Kremasti. On the landward side of the town, there is a hill that has the ruins of a medieval castle.

Kritinia

Kritinia Castle is a medieval castle that looks out over the sea towards Chalki. Standing on a pine-grown hill on the north-western coast of Rhodes welcomes you to the region of Kritinia - what the 650 inhabitants of the village refer to it as the forgotten frontier land. Visitors rarely make it past the castle, but it is worth visiting the village itself. This is predominately a farming community. What makes it worth a visit is the rugged beauty of the landscape

Lindos

Lindos is the jewel in the crown of the island. The town is located in the shadow of the ancient city of Lindos. The hill towers over the town and is home to the acropolis. The community itself is made up of whitewashed buildings and narrow streets. This location is the resting-place of Lindon. You may recall that his tomb is located in one of the cafés of the town. Though it is one of the most popular tourist locations, its population counts to little over 1000 residents.

Monolithos

Like Kritinia, Monolithos is known for its medieval castle. The rocky highpoint has the medieval castle at its peak. Within the castle walls stands the church of Agios Panteleimon. Below the castle, you will find a stone building, which is home to a small and friendly café. The road leads on to Fourni, the beach at Monolithos, ideal for those who don't mind pebbles, waves. If you enjoy seclusion, it is a very peaceful setting for a beach. With a population of less than two hundred, the village itself is small and well-maintained with just a few small tavernas.

Paradisi

Paradisi is a village on the north coast of the island. As you exit the airport and turn right towards the bottom of the island, Paradisi is the first town you will enter. Its proximity to the airport is highlighted by the fact that it is adjacent to the runway. It is a traditional village where traditional houses coexist with more modern buildings. The village square is the main social focus for the local inhabitants, and it is here that you will find cafeterias, bars and restaurants. The village square is where I have stood many times to wave off family members and friends as their flight leaves the ground and heads skyward. The village with the beautiful name – Paradise – is home to just over two-thousand-five-hundred people.

The main road from Rhodes Town heading south goes straight through the village, and the road is narrow in places. Many times, I have come face to face with a coach or a lorry in Paradisi. As for the sunsets, these are certain to create memories to bring back home to. There are many Byzantine churches, both within the village and in the local surroundings. If you are near Paradisi at the end of July, visit the celebration of Saint Marina. The locals are incredibly hospitable, and one can enjoy the festivities outside the church.

Pefkos

Apart from summer homes belonging to people from Lindos, this relatively low profile 'resort' area is made up of small hotels and rooms to let, occupied chiefly by groups of Scandinavians, British, Germans and Austrians. The main streets of Pefkos (or Pefki), back from the shore, have everything: mini market, pharmacy, cafés, bars, restaurants. Pefkos is just a couple of kilometres away from Lindos. Pefkos was always a small fishing village, but modern developments have turned it into one of the key purpose-built holiday resorts on the island. Quiet by day but with a buzzing nightlife. I visit mostly to catch up with friends that work in the hotels of Pefkos. The name Pefkos derives from the Greek for a pine tree. I am using it as a location in book two of The Prince of Rhodes.

Theologos

Theologos also called Tholos, is a unique coming together of a colourful traditional village and a quiet resort. This location was the inspiration for the Prometheus Hotel in the story. Theologos has an assortment of shops, taverns, bars and restaurants. These can be found around the tourist hotels and apartments. Its exquisite beach can be breezy – an ideal place for windsurfers. The traditional way of life still thrives in the village itself. You can expect a warm welcome from the friendly people living there. The old centre of Theologos is built in traditional Rhodian style. With tall shuttered buildings and narrow streets.

Trianta

Trianta was the former name of Ialyssos (it was changed in 1976). I like to think that Ialyssos is on the seaward side. Where the tourists can find the sea and endless multi-cultural restaurants for the diverse guests that visit. To me, Trianta is on the landward side at the foot of Filerimos hill. Here is where you will eat among the locals. Even when the summer season is busy, Trianta manages to keep the character of a typical Rhodian village. When talking to people, you will find they interchange the names Trianta, Ixia and Ialyssos without any apparent logic.

Medieval Town of Rhodes (or Old Town)

In the Medieval Town of Rhodes, you will enjoy one of the most enchanting walks on the island. Do not be misled by the term 'medieval' into thinking that what you will see is ruined and deserted building. This location is alive and well. This location was the inspiration for naming 'Rod' in the story. The tale refers to the Old Town as one of the ancient cities of the island, which was a bit of poetic licence. The medieval town was in reality, formed when the three ancient cities came together to create a single centre of administration.

When you pass through one of the gates in the walls of the Old Town, you are entering the oldest inhabited medieval town in Europe. A busy tourist centre of around 6000 people. The inhabitants live and work in the same buildings in which the Knights of St. John lived six centuries before. It can get hectic, especially when cruise ships bring their guests to the island.

In Old Town, you will see a range of medieval buildings, mosques, churches and traditional fountains. Shops and cafeterias are scattered throughout the Old Town, all combining together to create a unique blend of tourism and history. Our fondest memories of Old Town have been made when we have moved away from the busy shopping streets. Exploring the back lanes, seeing Greek people go about their daily lives.

Rhodes New Town

Is the nearest you will get to city life on the island. It is the place to go if you want to eat and shop like a Greek, away from the touristic trappings of the Old Town. The town has a buzz of activity both day and night.

Other Tourist Attractions on the Island
Filerimos

Filerimos is located near the village of Trianta. It is at the peak of Filerimos hill looking down on the village. It stands on the site, which was the Ancient city of Ialyssos. Archaeologists have discovered the necropolis In Greek this means 'city of the dead'. What they had found was a designated cemetery of ancient Ialyssos. In 1876, excavations revealed a Hellenistic temple of Athena Polias. This was considered to be proof of the prosperity of Ialyssos, up until the city of Rhodes was founded. On the way to the acropolis, you will come across the foundations of the temple of Zeus and Athena. On the top of the hill stands a beautiful church that is dedicated to Holy Mary.

A path of Cypress trees provides shelter for shrines that depict the stations of the cross, as Jesus took his last journey to Calgary. This path leads to a seventy-metre-high cross. Inside the cross, there is a steep stairway leading to the top – the views from this vantage point are outstanding. It is an experience to look down and see planes flying below where you are stood. (You don't need to climb the cross to get this view). Feeding the peacocks here is an experience not to be missed.

Rodini Park

Rodini park was probably the first park in the world to be landscaped. It is believed to have preceded the roman occupation of the island in 42BC. It remained popular with the Romans who enhanced the features of the park with an aqueduct. The park encompasses a natural stream, which is a natural habitat for freshwater turtles. It's a pleasure to come here, to get a respite from the heat of the day. Enjoy the shaded walks following the banks of the stream. A walk of about ten minutes will bring you to a tomb carved into the rock. The tomb dates from the Hellenist period.

Seven Springs

One of the most delightful days out on Rhodes, Seven Springs offers a quiet and mystical landscape. Even under the heat of summer, it is a hidden gem of coolness. Water flows from the springs all year round, and contribute to forming a small lake. You can reach the lake by walking through a narrow tunnel. The tunnel is 186 metres long. Be sure to wear suitable footwear and be prepared for socks and shoes to get wet as you walk through ice-cold water. On a hot day, it is a relief to feel the coolness on your feet. The lake doesn't dry up in the summer due to a dam built during the Italian occupation. The area of Seven Springs and the nearby forest is suitable for walking. And the cover offered by the forest is further relief from the heat of the sun. Maybe get your hotel to pack a picnic lunch for you. We often visit a supermarket to buy the ingredients to make our own packed lunch.

Valley of the Butterflies

On the north-western side of the island between Fanes and Theologos, travel about 5 kilometres inland, and you will come across the Valley of the Butterflies. This tree laden valley is one of the most appealing sites on the island. During August, thousands of butterflies appear in the valley to breed. Although they are referred to as butterflies, they are actually Tiger Moths. During the rainy period, the moths, still in the caterpillar stage, remain in the nearby forest. Throughout this time they feed on the leaves, before constructing their cocoon. As June approaches, the final metamorphosis occurs. The moth in all its glory makes its appearance. They continuously move towards areas where the humidity is highest, following the stream in the valley. When they finally arrive at their chosen breeding area, they rest before breeding. And the life cycle starts all over again.

Please be aware: It is illegal to make loud or sudden noises that may frighten the moths into flight. Remember they are there to rest and they are nocturnal.

Tsambika Monastery

Tsambika monastery is located just off of the main Lindos to Rhodes road. Travelling from Lindos towards Rhodes, the turning for the monastery is before the turn to Tsambika beach. The track leads half of the way up the hill. From this point onwards, you will have to walk up the 350 steps. If your vehicle is heavy, you may have trouble getting up the very steep slope to the car park at the top. There is a small parking area just before the steep climb. On the top of the hill, you will find the tiny, Byzantine church, dedicated to the Virgin Mary. It's perched at an altitude of some 300m featuring some truly spectacular views of the coast. This makes all the effort worthwhile.

Legend has it that women that find it difficult to conceive should climb the hill barefoot to pray the Virgin for fertility. If the task is successful, a child born to the mother should be named Tsambika (female) or Tsambikos (Male).

Appendix 2

Language Learning

Choris skata. Literal translation 'without shit'. We might say 'I was scared *shitless*'.

Malaka. Commonly thought to mean wanker. Google translates it like an asshole. Can be used in a friendly manner between friends, but it can be an insult otherwise. Using it may get you into trouble.

Yiasas and ***Yiasou.*** The same meaning is attributed to both words – Hello. And just to confuse things it can also be used to say goodbye. Yiasas is formal. It is considered the polite version. Yiasou is informal, and you might use it with a friend or a child. The term is made up of two words yia (or Geia) and sas or sou.

Oxi. No.

Nai. Yes. I know it confuses the life out of me too. Why does a word that sounds like no mean yes?

Skata. Shit.

Efharisto. Thank you.

Pippa. Google translate won't tell you. But a lot of Greek people will know what it is. Just ask a friendly Greek. Just be careful not to use a questioning tone. Pippa??

Nero. Water.

Numbers include ***Hexa*** – six, ***Hepta*** – seven and ***Octo*** – eight.

Poly. is very or many, like in a polygon.

Filoxenia. Hospitality.

Signomi. Sorry.

Parakalo. Another confusing word. It can mean 'please', 'you're welcome' or 'can I help you?'

Synechise. 'Go ahead' or 'carry on'. In the story we hear **parakalo synechise** – please carry on.

Kalinychta. Good night.

Kalimera. Good morning.

Kalispera. Good afternoon or Good evening.

Pame. 'We go' or 'let's go'.

Eftychisméno néo étos. Happy New Year.

Se sas. To you.

Kai. And.

Pollá chrónia. Many Years.

To Kyma. The (To) Wave (Kyma).

Paraskevi. Friday

Diávrosi. Erosion.

Poly nostimo. Very (Poly) Delicious (Nostimo).

Hepta Piges. Seven (Hepta) Sources (Piges) or springs used in the context of the story.

Petaloudes. Butterflies.

Yamas. The Greek equivalent of *Cheers*. The correct spelling for yamas is *yiamas*. It consists of two words, *yia* and *mas*. The full phrase would be *stin iyia mas*, which can also be used. The exact translation is *to our health*.

Gamisou thnitos. Fuck you mortal

Gamisou. Fuck you

Thnitos. Mortal

Appendix 3

Here is the reward challenge to everyone that has read this book. Throughout the story, there are FIVE key locations identified. These have been revealed as the Princes find their way through the war with the gods. Four of them have been described quite openly, and these are the tombs of where the family's spirits are interred.

You may recall that (In alphabetical order):

1.   Alyss is at Ialyssos. Under a cylindrical shaped stone. On Filerimos hill, close to the entrance to Temples of Athena Polias and of Zeus.

2.   Kam is at Old Kamiros. As you approach the entrance to the city, you will see some rectangles of recently laid concrete adjacent to a series of rose beds (or are they bougainvillea? The one nearest the entrance is the one that covers Kams resting place.

3.   Lindon is at Lindos. His tomb is a little better hidden.

It is inside a taverna/café, but some clues in the story will help you figure out which one to look for. It really is an excellent café in the heart of Lindos. I would ask that if you locate it and go in, please be polite enough to buy a drink or something to eat.

4.   Rod is at the Acropolis of Rhodes. You may recall his memorial stone is a cuboid under a hawthorn tree.

5.   The fifth location hasn't been named (deliberately). Again, there are plenty of clues to where you will find it. The exact location was referred to as the little church by the graveyard where Rod's soul was happiest.

There are six reward amulets available, one for each location and one major reward.

To claim your reward for finding a location, you need to place your copy of this book on the 'tombstone' or hold it by the sign that names the church. Take a photograph of it and email the picture to *rau@sigmadeltabooks.com*. There is no need to put your address or contact details. If you are the first person to email the image for a location, you will be contacted via email. We will reply to the **email address of the sender. We can then make arrangements to get the amulet to you.

To claim the star reward, you simply have to send ONE email containing all five pictures (same as above). The amulet for this reward is larger and more stunning than the ones described in the book.

We ask that while you are touring the island looking for locations, please be mindful of the local population and any monuments you visit. The intention is to encourage people to visit more of the island, not do the work of the gods.

One last thing, be careful in case you come across any D80's.

Happy Hunting

Rod, Kam, Lindon and Alyss

**Your email will not be shared with any other organisation or used for any purpose other than to let you know if you have earned a reward or notify you of a second book.

Printed in Great Britain
by Amazon